THE MIRRORWOOD

Also by Deva Fagan

Nightingale
Rival Magic

THE MIRRORWOOD

DEVA FAGAN

atheneum

ATHENEUM BOOKS FOR YOUNG READERS

NEW YORK   LONDON   TORONTO   SYDNEY   NEW DELHI

ATHENEUM BOOKS FOR YOUNG READERS
An imprint of Simon & Schuster Children's Publishing Division
1230 Avenue of the Americas, New York, New York 10020

For information about special discounts for bulk purchases, please contact Simon & Schuster Special Sales at 1-866-506-1949 or business@simonandschuster.com.
The Simon & Schuster Speakers Bureau can bring authors to your live event. For more information or to book an event, contact the Simon & Schuster Speakers Bureau at 1-866-248-3049 or visit our website at www.simonspeakers.com.

Interior design by Jacquelynne Hudson
The text for this book was set in Adobe Caslon Pro.

Manufactured in the United States of America
0322 FFG
First Edition
2 4 6 8 10 9 7 5 3 1
Library of Congress Cataloging-in-Publication Data
Names: Fagan, Deva, author.
Title: The Mirrorwood / Deva Fagan. • Description: First edition. | New York : Atheneum Books for Young Readers, [2022] | Audience: Ages 10 to 12. | Audience: Grades 4–6. | Summary: Since birth Fable has been cursed by the Blight, a twisted magic that has left her without a face of her own, forced to "steal" the face of others; now the Blighthunters, who believe anything touched by the Blight must be destroyed, have found her, and pursued by apprentice Blighthunter Vycorax, she and her telepathic cat, Moth, flee into the Mirrorwood, a thorny forest trapped in time and filled with perils—determined to confront the source of the Blight and just maybe break the curse. • Identifiers: LCCN 2021019367 | ISBN 9781534497146 (hardcover) | ISBN 9781534497160 (ebook) • Subjects: LCSH: Magic—Juvenile fiction. | Blessing and cursing—Juvenile fiction. | Identity (Psychology)—Juvenile fiction. | Face—Juvenile fiction. | Quests (Expeditions)—Juvenile fiction. | Friendship—Juvenile fiction. | Adventure stories. | CYAC: Magic—Fiction. | Blessing and cursing—Fiction. | Identity—Fiction. | Face—Fiction. | Adventure and adventurers—Fiction. | Friendship—Fiction. | Fantasy. | • LCGFT: Action and adventure fiction. • Classification: LCC PZ7.F136 Mi 2022 | DDC 813.6 [Fic]—dc23 • LC record available at https://lccn.loc.gov/2021019367

To Melissa,
who helped me find my way through
the thorniest part of this forest

CHAPTER ONE

I *was wearing my sister Gavotte's face* on the night the blighthunters came to our cottage. All eight of us were crowded around the table, waging a fierce poetry battle to decide who would get the last slice of Da's gooseberry pie. Indigo was arguing passionately that "savage" really did rhyme with "cabbage," which was probably why none of us noticed the threat except Sonnet, who didn't care for gooseberries.

"There's someone coming down the lane." Sonnet rose from the table and went to peer through the diamond-pane window beside the door.

A spark of worry nibbled at me. Hardly anyone came all the way out to our farm. We were too close to the Mirrorwood. Our cozy cottage—a bit ramshackle with the extra rooms tacked on over the years to handle three sets of twins—lay on the farthest edge of town. If you stood in just the right spot, you could see the enormous wall of thorns bristling along the northern hills. A prickly promise, meant to bind away the magic of the blighted realm and keep it from tainting the rest of the world.

But it hadn't worked. Magic still escaped. Dribs and drabs, like the spatters of madder and saffron that flecked Mum's apron after a day working her dye pots. Fragments of raw blight that warped whatever—whomever—they touched. Twists, we called them. You might suddenly sprout wings or claws. Your skin might turn to flames or ice.

No wonder folks were scared of it. I would be too. That is, if I weren't already blighted.

For me, the greatest danger wasn't the thorns or the corrupting magic. It was being discovered by those who thought anything touched by the twists had to be destroyed: blighthunters. The crimson-coated warriors trained to fight and kill people like me. But surely there was no reason for hunters to visit our farm.

"Is it Aunt Nesta?" I asked hopefully. She was family. She knew my secret. She was safe.

"No," said Sonnet. Her shoulders were stiff, and there was a note of wary tension in her voice. "There's two of them. Riding horses."

Da and Mum exchanged a look. Mum's lips had gone tight. "Allegra," Mum said to my twin sister. "Best be ready, just in case."

Allegra groaned. "It's not my turn. Can't Fable go upstairs? It's probably just another peddler."

I started to push away from the table. "It's okay. I'll go. But if they're selling charms against the blight, buy me one," I added, trying to make a joke of it.

No one laughed. Indigo was glowering at Allegra. "Ease up, Leg. It's not Fable's fault. One extra day won't do you harm."

"Oh, I know exactly how much harm it does."

She didn't look at me, but I flinched anyway. Allegra was my twin sister, and I knew she loved me. But you can love someone and still be angry at them. Not that I blamed her, after what I'd done to her for the first five years of our lives.

Sonnet, still at the window, drew in a sharp breath. "They're wearing red coats."

No one spoke. No one moved. Hunters wore red.

"Everyone stay calm," said Mum, her voice brisk and businesslike, as if she were negotiating the price of her wool. "We'll handle it like we always do."

A chilly pit had opened in my belly. We'd had close calls with hunters before. Last summer my brother Thespian had to truss me up in a burlap sack and carry me over his shoulder, pretending I was a lumpy bag of turnips, in order to pass a hunter on the road to Aunt Nesta's. But they'd never come to our house. And I hardly ever left our family farm. The last time I'd seen anyone other than family was . . . oh. Oh no.

Last week. I'd been out gathering wild strawberries at the edge of the northern woods. The miller's son had passed by along the old hunters' trail. I'd run as soon as I saw him. But had he seen me?

More importantly, had he seen the face I was wearing?

I couldn't answer those questions. All I could do was try to be what I'd always been: Allegra's identical twin. I gulped, looking at my sister.

"Go on, then, take it." She slid closer along the bench, wearing a look of grim resignation that stabbed me in the gut. It wasn't fair. I didn't want this either. I'd give anything not to be like this.

"Sorry," I whispered, cringing at just how useless the word was, after everything I'd already done to her. Everything my blight had taken. "Sorry" would never be enough.

She only closed her eyes, bracing herself. I reached out to brush my fingers against her cheek.

That was all it took. My curse, my blight, woke hungrily. Buzzing warmth rippled up my arm, my neck, tingling across my face as skin shimmered, bone shifted, and my face reshaped itself. The wavy brown hair I'd borrowed from Gavotte lightened to Allegra's honey blond. My nose shrank, turning snub. A heartbeat later, and no one would have guessed that I was anything other than Allegra's identical twin.

Only my family knew the truth: that I was a blighted face stealer.

Allegra whimpered, gripping the edge of the table as if someone had just torn away a bit of her soul. That was how she'd described it, the one time I dared ask her how it felt. Thespian had tried to tell me it wasn't bad, like standing up too fast and getting a head rush, but I think he was just trying to make me feel better. Allegra always told the truth, even when it hurt.

I scooted back along the bench, giving her space. No one else said anything. Mum and Da had never made a fuss over my face stealing. I think they wanted to pretend it was an everyday thing, like feeding the chickens or washing the dishes. Not a curse that could have me and my entire family imprisoned, or worse.

I ran a hand over my hair. Allegra's hair. It would be fine. Hunters had never visited our house before, but we'd practiced how to handle it. Just act normal. Absolutely normal.

"They've hitched their horses at the post," said Sonnet. Mum went to wait with her by the door, while Da cleared away the dishes and Gavotte covered the last slice of pie with a napkin. Thespian sat at the end of the table, watching me out of the corner of his eye, the way our sheepdogs watched the flock.

I knotted my hands together, feeling utterly miserable. Moth sprang up onto my lap, butting his head against my fingers and purring. I cuddled him closer, his warm weight steadying me, as usual. Making it easier to breathe, to think.

Do not worry, his voice whispered in my mind. *If the hunters try to take you, I will slash out their eyes.*

"My sweet, bloodthirsty fluff." I skritched him between the ears until his purr became a deep drone.

"Oh, yes, talk to your cat," said Indigo dryly. "That'll convince the hunters there's nothing to investigate."

"Lots of people talk to their cats."

Indigo arched a brow. "But how many of the cats *talk back?*"

I ignored them. No one could hear Moth except me, in any case. And right now he was the only thing keeping me from falling into a complete panic.

Sonnet returned to the table, sliding onto the bench

beside me, her shoulder bumping mine. "Remember what I taught you, Fey? If they grab you, go for the eyes. Or the throat. Or the instep." Her hands, resting on her thighs, were clenched into tight fists. It made something sharp claw at my throat. I didn't want my family to have to do this. To risk themselves for me.

Sonnet's eyes fixed on the door. A moment later, a thump rattled the heavy oak.

Mum squared her shoulders, then reached for the handle, swinging it open. "Good evening," she said, her voice cool and calm. "How can we help you?"

"Good evening, madam," said the man on the doorstep. I couldn't see much of him, only the way his tall shadow fell over my mother. His voice was as cool and chilly as deep-buried stone. "Might my apprentice and I come in? I don't wish to trouble your family, but it would help us greatly if we could ask a few questions."

Dread shivered through me. The miller's son. He *had* seen me last week, out by the strawberry meadow.

If I'd been wearing Allegra's face—or any of my siblings', really—I'd have waved and called a hullo. There wasn't such a great difference in size between us, though Sonnet and Thespian had both shot up since they'd turned sixteen over the winter. Even so, I could still pass myself off as them, from a distance.

But that day I had been wearing my father's face. Including his long, luxurious brown beard. I was a good two feet shorter than him, so on me, it fell to my belly button. Indigo said it made me look like an overgrown gnome. So instead of waving and hulloing, I'd run, sprinting off into the woods like a startled rabbit.

I hadn't told anyone about it. The boy hadn't chased after me, so no harm done. Besides, if I told my parents, they might decide not to let me wander the wilds anymore, and I couldn't bear the thought of losing my last bit of freedom. It was too dangerous for me to go to town: I couldn't always control my blight, and the last thing I needed was to bump into someone at the market and accidentally steal their face. The farm, the fields, the woods, they were all I had. The only place that I could walk freely, breathe deep, feel like a normal twelve-year-old girl.

Clearly, I was mistaken.

If only I could sprint away now and lose myself in the green woods. But it was too late: Mum had already ushered the hunters inside. It would look suspicious to deny them. I sat stiffly, frozen in fear, as the two crimson-coated figures stepped into the large main room of our cottage. There were several empty chairs, but the hunters ignored them, choosing to stand before the hearth.

All the better to chase after anyone who tried to bolt.

"My name is Telmarque," said the man. He was tall and bony, with white skin and sunken black eyes that made his hollow-cheeked face look disturbingly skeletal. "And this is my apprentice, Vycorax." He nodded to the girl beside him.

She looked about my age, but the firm set of her jaw and

her intent brown eyes made her seem older. So did the sword hanging from her belt. Even the scattering of freckles across her brown cheeks didn't soften her.

Her eyes narrowed. She'd noticed me staring. I jerked my gaze away, desperately hoping she'd think I was just a curious farm girl who'd never seen a hunter up close.

"May we offer you some tea?" asked my father. "And we have walnut cakes." Da probably would have offered tea to the demon prince of the Mirrorwood if he showed up on our doorstep, he was so unfailingly polite.

But Telmarque waved aside the offer. "No. We must attend our work. The evils of the blight do not rest."

Moth settled himself more comfortably into my lap, and I fought a wild, desperate laugh at the irony of it. But there was a sting, too. I didn't think I was evil. But I hurt people. Hurt my own family, every day of every week. So maybe he was right.

Mum cleared her throat. "Then, please, let us know how we can help you be on your way."

"We've had word of a strange creature spotted in the woods near here. A young man from the village encountered it last week. A foul, hairy beast."

I stifled a huff. Da's face might be a bit hairy, but he wasn't *foul*.

The hunter continued. "Small but vicious, he said. He managed to chase it off, but it's still out there." Telmarque's lip curled, and he set one hand on the hilt of his sword as he spoke. "Have any of you seen something like this?"

He fixed each of us in turn with a skeletal stare. The air in the room seemed to have thickened, grown dim and chilly as a winter fog. We all shook our heads.

"Be very certain. We must find this beast and destroy it. We cannot afford to risk the taint spreading."

"Is that how it works?" asked Indigo, innocently arching their eyebrows. "I thought the twists from the woods caused the blight."

"Indeed," said Telmarque. "But anything blighted is tainted with the evil of the Mirrorwood and must be destroyed."

Mum shot Indigo a warning look, but they continued on, irrepressible. "Wouldn't it be better to go after the source? You seem to have plenty of sharp, pointy things. Can't you go inside the Mirrorwood and use them on the demon prince to stop all this for good?"

Silence. A weight like storm clouds settled over the room. Telmarque narrowed his eyes at Indigo. "Hunters have tried. Tried and died. The thorns refuse entry to all, as you well know. This isn't some bard's fantasy."

"Very true," said Indigo. "You're *clearly* not the princess with a heart as pure as snow."

Telmarque's jaw clenched dangerously. Indigo never could resist a sly comment. And worse, they were doing it for me. Defending me. And risking the attention of the hunters in the process.

"I saw something," I blurted out. "Yesterday."

It worked. Telmarque fixed his gaze on me, like a knife

stabbing a choice but slippery bit of meat. "What?" he demanded. "What did you see?"

"I thought it was a bear. It was over to the east, on Hay Hill." I held my breath. Please. Please let them think the foul, hairy beast was only a bear.

The apprentice Vycorax cleared her throat, straightening her shoulders before she spoke for the first time. Her voice had edges, carving out her words, claiming them. "I already searched Hay Hill, sir. There wasn't anything there."

"We'll search again," snapped Telmarque. He gave a curt nod. "Thank you for your time. If we have other questions, we will return."

The words felt like a threat, whether or not he meant them that way. Telmarque strode toward the door. "Come, Vycorax. Let us see what you missed."

The girl stiffened. She glanced at me, the furrow between her brows deepening, before hastening after the elder hunter.

Slowly, Mum closed the door behind them. We sat, not speaking, not moving, as if even a small sound might draw the hunters back. Finally Mum let out a soft sigh. "They're gone. Riding east."

Gavotte punched her twin in their shoulder. "Indigo! What were you thinking?"

Indigo crossed their arms, looking unrepentant. "I was thinking that craven ham-wit ought to stop bullying innocent people and go fight some actual evil if he's so slobbery over it."

Mum sighed. "It would've been better to say nothing at all." She flicked me a worried look.

My heart pinched. "I just wanted them to go," I said. "It'll be okay, won't it? They'll go to Hay Hill and won't find anything. Or they'll just think the boy in the woods saw the bear too."

"Ah, yes, the *bear*," said Da. "You know, I hear that bears are great fans of gooseberry pie." He nudged the last piece toward me, smiling.

But I could see the worry in his eyes. I could feel it all around me, a sticky, sickening heaviness in the air. It matched the fog of fear in my chest. This was my fault. All I'd wanted was to pick strawberries, and instead I'd brought blighthunters to the farm.

"Thanks, Da, but I'm not hungry." I scooped Moth into my arms as I stood. "Besides, Indigo had the best limerick. I'm going to bed."

"It's a clear night," Gavotte offered, watching me in that way of hers, like she could see the color of my thoughts. "You were going to show us the new constellation you found in that book of star charts you're always poring over. The Nose Picker?"

"The Rose Picker," I said, though I was pretty sure she knew the real name. She was trying to make a joke of it, to cheer me up. And I loved her for it. Loved *all* of them.

"Thanks, Gav, but I'm not in the mood for stargazing," I said, retreating up the stairs. "Good night."

My family had always bound tight, protecting me, even

letting me borrow their faces to hide my secret. To keep the red wolves away.

But they couldn't keep me safe forever. Eventually, the wolves would catch me. And if I didn't do something, they would catch my family, too.

Chapter Two

*I*t *was late the next afternoon* before I convinced Mum to let me out of the house. I was still wearing Allegra's face when I stepped outside. The skin had faded a bit, going gray around the edges, the eyes sagging slightly, but still good enough to pass me off as her twin. Not that I expected to meet anyone where I was going.

I told Mum I'd check on the sheep out in the far pasture. And I did. They were fine, fat and happy and fluffy as meringues. But I didn't stop there. I climbed the fence, Moth leaping lightly beside me, then pushed through the thickets and out into the birch grove. It was one of my favorite spots: the slim white trunks, the rustle of the leaves, the scattering of speckled red toadstools in the fern-fringed grass. It was a place I could think. Could try to find some space inside me that was Fable, no matter what face I wore.

As far as I knew, I'd never had one of my own.

When my sister Allegra and I were born, everyone thought we were identical twins. We had the same honey-gold hair, the same blue eyes and tip-tilted nose. But there was a difference: I was the hale and hearty child, always climbing a tree or singing a song. Allegra was the sickly one, kept in bed more days than not by a strange illness no healer could cure.

Until the first day I went to the village school and came

home with the face of the miller's daughter, green-eyed and curly-haired. Until Allegra climbed out of her sickbed, suddenly full of energy, smiling and laughing and chasing the chickens.

That was when my parents realized it wasn't a sickness that made Allegra weak. It was *me*. For five years I'd been borrowing her face, borrowing her strength. Maybe even her soul.

Somehow, one of those twisted bits of magic from the Mirrorwood had found me. Slipped into the cradle where I lay swaddled, or caught me crawling in the grass on my pudgy baby hands. I was too young to remember how it happened. All I knew was what it had turned me into. A girl with no face of her own. I could only steal the faces and energy of others. Nowadays I could control it better, but back then I didn't even realize what I was doing. All it took was a touch and I could be anyone.

At first we thought maybe I could just stop. Maybe if I didn't touch anyone, I'd go back to my true self. To a face that was mine, only mine. So we waited.

Within a day my skin started fading to a colorless gray. Two days and my lips and nose began to blur like fog in the morning sun. Three days and I could barely speak, barely breathe. There was no true Fable. Only emptiness. Nothingness.

Without a borrowed face, I would die.

Some parents might have turned me over to the hunters then and there. But my family loved me. Loved me enough to keep my blight a secret. Loved me enough to lend me their faces. Between my five siblings and my parents, I could get through a week. Borrowing a face for a day didn't seem to do much harm.

Except.

Except I *hated* it. Hated hurting them. Hated being a burden. Hated that we all lived in fear of discovery. Last night had been close. Too close.

My family did everything they could to protect me, but it wasn't enough. If something was going to change, I had to make it change. I was the blighted one. This was my responsibility.

I drew a bracing breath. My feet felt heavy, sunk deep into the familiar soil. Into the land that had been my only home for more than twelve years. This birch grove was along the far northern edge of the farm. I'd never dared go farther.

I forced myself to take one step. Then another.

The birches gave way to a thicker, darker forest of oaks and beeches. I trudged through them, climbing over the vast tangled roots that wove across my path like serpents. I should turn back. Run home, to my family. To safety.

But home wasn't safe. Especially not if I was there. I didn't know what I could do. I just knew I had to do *something*.

The tangle of trees opened, releasing me into a clearing at the top of the rise. And finally I could see them.

Thorns. A towering wall of briar and bramble that stretched even taller than the highest oaks. They spread along the horizon, curving away to the east and west. According to the stories, there was an entire realm inside. Villages, lakes, farms. The sleeping prince and his castle. The land must have had some other name, centuries ago, but we knew it only as the Mirrorwood. The source of the blight.

The wind whispered along my neck, raising goose bumps under the coil of Allegra's honey-blond braids. "How far away do you think it is?" I asked Moth, who had settled himself comfortably atop a large stump so overgrown with moss it looked more like a fat green pillow.

Why does it matter? Moth's tail lashed as he followed my stare.

It was a good question. It shouldn't matter to me. I wasn't a princess, and I certainly didn't have a heart as pure as snow, not after everything I'd put my family through.

Once, that story had given me hope. I'd begged Indigo to tell me the prophetic tale, over and over again, sitting breathless as they described the princess fighting her way through the terrors of the Mirrorwood to the castle at its center, where she faced the most terrible enemy of all: the demon prince who had first cursed the land with the blight over a century ago, casting the true prince into an endless slumber and taking his place.

Maybe it was just a story, but stories had power. And I had to believe this one was going to come true someday. That it was more than a fairy tale. But my hopes had worn thin lately. When would the princess decide to show up? How old would I be when she defeated the demon and restored the true prince? When the blight lifted and I finally had my true face?

Maybe I was wrong. Maybe it was just a child's tale invented to pass a chilly night around a dull tavern hearth. My chest ached with the thought. I needed it to be true. I needed to believe that the curse could be broken. If not by the pure-hearted princess, if not by the hunters, then by *someone*!

I let out a long sigh that was perilously close to a sob. "Ugh," I said, because if I was talking then maybe I wouldn't be crying. "Why did I even come here? I'm just some girl from a sheep farm."

You are not just some girl, said Moth. *You are Fable.*

"Yeah, well, I don't think that's . . ." I trailed off, squinting at the velvety green stump he was sitting on. There was something strange about the shape.

I marched over to kneel beside the thing. It wasn't a stump. There was stone beneath the moss. Not rough boulders but smooth blocks bound with mortar. And . . . were those letters carved along the top? I waved for Moth to move. "I need to get a closer look at this."

He stretched out even more luxuriantly across his mossy cushion. *It is better as a bed.*

"Really, Moth, I need to see it." I tried to scoop him up, but he evaded my grasp, springing down to the ground on his own. He sat there, regarding me balefully.

But I didn't have time to feel guilty. Now that I could see what was inscribed along the top of the not-stump, all I could feel was a bone-deep, heart-thrumming awe.

"'The Well of Mirachne, Lady of Dawn, Guardian of Dreams,'" I read. "'Offer, and let thy wish be granted.'"

A wishing well! I'd heard of such things, of course. They could be found scattered across the lands. But I'd never seen one.

I could barely bring myself to touch the old gray stone. I half expected it to spark back, to set me ablaze. Lady Mirachne was one of the Subtle Powers. Immortal. Inscrutable. Beings with vast and unknowable power. Dangerous, too. One of Indigo's favorite stories involved a pair of desperate young lovers who went to one of the Subtle Powers for help, only to end up tricked into a bargain that left one of them a fox by night, the other a crow by day, so that they could never be truly together.

But it wasn't Mirachne in that story. It was the Bannon, and everyone knew he was the Power who caused nothing but trouble. Mirachne was the lady of dreams. It was she who set the wall of thorns in place, centuries ago, to keep the blight from corrupting all the world.

A spark kindled in my chest. This was it. This was how I could fix things. Lady Mirachne granted wishes. Maybe she could make mine come true. I set my hands against the edge of the stone that lay across her well. It didn't budge.

Fable. This is not wise. The Powers are not to be trusted.

"I have to do something." I gave the stone another shove, harder this time. Finally it scraped open, revealing a slice of damp-smelling darkness.

There was definitely water below. It flashed and glimmered, reflecting back a patch of the afternoon sky above. A creamy oval stared back at me, and I flinched. I'd never cared much for mirrors. But that could change. Everything could change if Lady Mirachne granted my wish.

I patted my pockets for a suitable offering. I had no coins. No jewels. Only a plum turnover, slightly squashed, which I'd brought in case I got hungry. Well, it would have to do.

With trembling fingers, I pulled it out, holding it over the dark, damp well. Cool air rippled up, chilling my skin. I closed my eyes so that I didn't have to see Moth glowering. This was going to work.

"Please, Lady Mirachne. Please send a hero to break the curse of the Mirrorwood."

I waited another heartbeat, then released my plummy offering. There was a distant sploosh. Then silence.

I opened my eyes warily. I surveyed the wall of thorns in the distance. My heart sank. It was as dark and impenetrable as ever.

Of course it was. What was one wish going to change? I didn't even know if Lady Mirachne was listening. There were plenty of fairy tales about the Subtle Powers, but it wasn't like I knew anyone who'd actually encountered one. Well, Indigo did claim they once played a game of dice with a strange, red-eyed man out on the north road and won a pair of socks that never needed darning. But Indigo had a tendency to . . . embellish . . . their stories.

Still, the Subtle Powers must be real. The thorns were real. The blight was real. And maybe my wish had been heard. Maybe it would just take time for the hero to get here. Time, I quickly realized, I might not have. Not with the blighthunters prowling so close.

I squinted at the distant thorns again, a nameless yearning in my chest. "What do you think is on the other side?"

I do not wish to know. It is an unnatural place.

"Says the talking cat." I skritched his head, and he leaned into my fingers, purring deeply. I tried to take comfort in the warm rumble.

Says the girl who can hear me.

He had a point. I had never figured out whether my ability to hear Moth was his blight, or part of mine. No one else could hear him, but that might just be because he didn't deign to speak to anyone else. Who knew, with cats?

Either way, I couldn't hate his talking the way I hated my face stealing. Because Moth was the one being in the world who always knew me, no matter what face I wore. And the fact that I could hear him, that was something that belonged to me. That didn't change. Moth was a fixed star in my shifting, dizzying sky.

I pressed my face into Moth's silky neck, letting his low purr drive away all my fears and unanswered wishes. "I'm glad I can hear you," I told him. "I don't care if it's unnatural."

Then why do you wish to change what you are?

I let out a long sigh. "Oh, I don't know. Take your pick. The fact that I'm a face-stealing lamprey sucking the life out of my family? That I almost got caught by hunters last night? The fact that everyone else is going to grow up and leave and live their lives and I might never find out who I could be if I wasn't blighted?"

I hadn't meant to say that last bit, but it surged up from my chest, the fiercest and most sharp-toothed of all my fears. I drew in a ragged breath, fighting to keep from falling even farther into the bleak pit yawning open inside me.

"I appreciate the confession," said a girl's voice from somewhere behind me. "That's going to make this so much easier."

I spun around just in time to see the hunter's apprentice Vycorax step from behind a stand of oaks. In one smooth motion she drew her sword, brandishing it between us. "Now," she said, "I suggest you surrender."

Moth growled. *Are we fighting or running?*

But my mouth couldn't move. My feet were stones, sinking into the loam. All I could do was stare at the tip of Vycorax's sword, my insides quaking. My parents had warned me, time and again, what would happen if the hunters discovered me. My mother had even once taken me to see the poor, mangled remains of a man cursed with ears like a bat. The hunters had killed him and set him at the busiest crossroads as a warning.

No doubt they would do the same to me.

"And don't bother running," she drawled. "I tracked you here easily enough."

She'd tracked me. Like a beast. Like a rabid wolf. That was all I was to her.

It was unfair. I wasn't *evil*. Dangerous, yes, but I'd be no trouble if they would only leave me alone.

"Why surrender?" I said, abruptly furious. "You're just going to kill me."

Something shifted in the apprentice's eyes. A flicker of doubt? Then she shook her short black hair. "Anything blighted must be destroyed. It's the only way to keep the curse from spreading."

Of course that was how she'd see it. But I wasn't giving up that easily. "Or maybe you're just lazy," I snarled. "You'd rather murder people you're afraid of than try to break the curse."

"We've tried!" she snapped back, as if my words stung her. "You heard what my father said."

"Telmarque is your father?"

She lifted her chin defiantly. "Yes. And he's one of the best hunters in the order."

"Not good enough to break the curse, though."

"You think you could do better?" scoffed Vycorax. "You're just a blighted little farm girl."

Her words kicked me in the chest. She wasn't wrong. I'd spent most of my life no more than a mile from the same cozy house, surrounded by fields and dells I knew better than my own heartbeat, trusting my parents to keep me safe. They hadn't coddled me—no room for that on a farm—but my knowledge extended only to things like how to wrangle a truculent ewe and what flowers made the best yellow dye. I *was* just a blighted little farm girl.

A soft warmth curled around my leg. Moth pressed close, his fur fluffed in fury. If only I could be so brave. So fierce.

Was it so impossible? There were plenty of stories about everyday people like me doing grand things. Assistant pig-keepers who saved the realm. Hatmakers who undid wicked spells. If they could do great things, why couldn't I? I'd spent the last twelve years letting other people protect me. I'd even sacrificed my plum tart to summon a hero to save me.

But maybe it was time to try saving myself.

The Mirrorwood wasn't that far away. Maybe a farm girl *could* break a centuries-old curse. I bounced on my toes, quivering with the possibility. Then everything would change. I wouldn't be a danger to my family. I could finally start living my own, *real* life.

I stood straighter, summoning my fury and fear and despair and braiding them tight into something like hope. "Yes. I think I can. And you can't stop me."

She has a claw, Fable, said Moth. *She is dangerous.*

He was right. The girl might only be a hunter-in-training, but that blade looked painfully sharp, and she seemed to know how to use it. She was dangerous. But so was I. Or at least, that was what she thought.

Just as Vycorax was about to take another step, I called out, "You'd better not come any closer, or you might get blighted too."

She froze.

My threat had worked. I'd turned the girl's fears against

her. It was rubbish, of course: my family was around me day in and day out, and none of them had shown any sign of blight. But if the girl thought my touch could curse her, maybe I had a chance of escaping.

I backed away, coaxing Moth after me. "Come on, Moth. We have work to do."

Vycorax watched me, her eyes wide. Then she gulped, stiffening her shoulders. "No," she growled. "I can't let the blight spread! It's my duty to stop you!" Jaw set, she started toward me.

Curse it! I had one last trick, though the thought of using it turned my stomach. Maybe I was just proving that Vycorax was right. I was dangerous. But she'd left me no choice.

I lunged at the girl, reaching for her face.

My fingers brushed her cheek, and that was all it took for my blight to do its work. A familiar tickle fluttered over my skin, not quite painful. The weight of Allegra's honey-gold braids lifted. I blinked, my eyes suddenly slightly farther apart. My lips felt thinner, my chin sharper. My skin warmed from rosy cream to freckled brown.

Vycorax staggered woozily, then fell to her knees. Blearily, she blinked up at me and gave a small gasp. "You . . . you took . . . my face!"

There was no time to waste. I pelted away, Moth a gray streak beside me, heading for the deeper woods. But I'd gone only a few paces when something flickered crimson at the corner of my vision. I shrieked, trying to duck, but I was too slow.

An arm wrapped around my waist, pinning one arm to my side. Another clamped across my shoulder, pressing something cold and sharp to my throat. A man's voice rasped harsh and triumphant in my ear. "That's far enough."

Telmarque! Blight it. I should have known Vycorax wasn't alone.

CHAPTER THREE

I tried to breathe lightly, to hold myself still and tamp down the panic rolling through me. At least Moth was free. I could see him crouched under a clump of ferns nearby.

"Careful, Father," croaked Vycorax. "She only needs to touch your face to steal it."

"I am more than capable of dealing with a blightborn. The real question is, are you?"

I turned my head a fraction, surprised by his harsh tone. Da never spoke to me like that. Even when I'd forgotten to pen the ram and he ate an entire patch of Da's prize turnips.

But Vycorax didn't flinch. Only clambered to her feet, brown eyes bright with fury and vengeance. "Of course," she said stiffly.

"You had the girl at your mercy and yet she lives. If not for me, she would have escaped."

The girl's lips wobbled for a heartbeat; then she lifted her chin. "I . . . I wasn't ready. But I am now, Father. I swear. I won't let you down."

I couldn't see Telmarque, but I felt his huff, felt the shift of the blade against my throat. "We shall see."

What was he going to do? Terror ran icy fingers along my arms, my legs.

Suddenly I was stumbling forward toward Vycorax. Her

eyes went wide briefly, but she rallied, lifting the tip of her sword to press against my collarbone.

Telmarque stalked to her side, dagger sheathed, arms clasped behind his back, his attitude almost scholarly. Like a teacher advising a wayward student. "Very well. Go on, then. Show me what you've learned. What is the best way to dispatch a blightborn like this?"

"I—I need to stab her through the heart." Vycorax looked faintly ill as she spoke, but that might've been only the weakness from having her face stolen. The cool touch of her blade still hovered at my throat, terrifyingly close.

"Indeed," said Telmarque. "What are you waiting for?"

"Nothing, Father."

But still, she did not strike me down. Her eyes seemed caught by my face. *Her* face.

I wanted to close my eyes, to look away, to bury myself in some useless dream that Da would come crashing out of the woods to save me. That Lady Mirachne herself would appear in all her golden glory to whisk me away. But they weren't here. It was only me, in my stolen face, and all I could do was stare back at the girl, desperately hoping her hesitation might become mercy.

"I did not raise you to be weak, Vycorax," said Telmarque.

"I'm not weak. It's only that . . . she looks like *me.*"

"Because she's blighted," he spat. "Even now she steals your strength. Strike her down and be done."

The girl drew in a bracing breath and clamped her lips tight. She drew back her sword, preparing to take the blow.

Please, thundered my heart. *Please*. I didn't care if it was true mercy. I just wanted to live.

The girl's eyes locked on mine. Her grip trembled. She did not strike.

Telmarque gave a growl of frustration. "Very well. I thought you had your sister's strength, but it seems I was mistaken. I will finish this, since you cannot." He drew his sword and advanced toward me.

"No, Father. Wait—"

The girl's protest was lost as a yowling gray fury leaped at Telmarque from beneath the nearby ferns. The hunter staggered back, ducking. His free hand lashed out. A feline scream turned my heart to ice. Even Vycorax froze, her dagger lowered now, watching her father with wide eyes.

Telmarque held Moth by the scruff of his neck. The cat writhed and spat, clawing at the air.

"Moth!" I screamed. "Please don't hurt him! He's just a cat!"

Do not fear, Fable, said Moth. *I am not the one about to have his eyes torn out.*

With a growl, he suddenly coiled his gray body, kicking out his rear paws to slash at Telmarque's face. Telmarque screamed, dropping his sword. He pressed his other arm to his eyes. But still, he held Moth.

I will finish him! Run, Fable! Flee!

"Not without you!" I lunged forward, slamming my heel into Telmarque's instep, just the way Sonnet had taught me.

He staggered back, hand spasming. Moth fell free, landing lightly upon the mossy earth.

Telmarque snarled, trying to snatch at me, but the movement was sloppy. Blood streamed down his face, pouring from the four slices that cut across his left eye. Vycorax dashed to his side.

This was my chance. My chance to flee.

Instinct tugged me south, toward the cottage. My family would rally around me. They'd fight for me, no matter the cost.

But I couldn't do that to them. They'd already given too much. No, there was only one option for me now. One place I had any hope of making things right. Of ridding myself of the blight and setting myself free.

So I ran north, toward the Mirrorwood.

Branches whipped my stolen face, tore at my stolen hair. Moth raced beside me, a ripple of gray in the green shadows. North, we had to go north. If I could just reach the Mirrorwood and somehow slip inside, I would be safe!

Well, as safe as I could be inside a cursed realm ruled by a legendary demon prince. Still, it was better than being pursued through the woods by angry hunters who I was quite certain wanted to kill me.

I could hear Telmarque shouting, "After her, you fool! Catch that blightborn and finish her if you want to remain my apprentice!"

I caught a glimpse of scarlet between the trees to my left.

Vycorax was trying to cut us off. I veered right, each breath rasping my tight chest, legs on fire with fear and desperation. The woods ahead were darker, thicker. Everywhere I looked was a jumble of branches and clinging vines. I drove myself toward the shadows, into the tangles. It was my only chance.

"This way, Moth!" There was no sign of Vycorax, but I couldn't risk slowing. I shoved aside the branches blocking my way.

Pain lanced my palm. Pricks of fire scraped along my cheek and across my arms. Thorns! There were thorns on the branches. Were these the magical briars of the Mirrorwood? Or just a bit of wild blackberry? Shadows clung to me. The bramble wove a dark veil above, blocking out the late-afternoon sun. I had to fumble my way forward, but every movement sent jabs of pain along my skin. There were barbs everywhere.

Then I felt something smooth, a bit of branch. A feathery brush of leaves. A shifting, a murmur. Wood creaked, vines slithered, and abruptly my way was clear. Was my vision playing tricks? A tunnel had formed among the branches, leading deeper into the greenery. I spotted Moth at my feet and bent to scoop him into my arms. I didn't dare lose him. We had to stay together, especially now.

Deeper, darker, the tunnel carried us onward. Shivers raced over my skin. The way was clear, and yet it felt as if I were running through cobwebs, my entire body sticky and slow. The next moment the ground spun faster, taking my stomach with it. I gritted my teeth, fighting a swell of dizziness. One step, another. Another. And then . . .

I stumbled out into a dusk-tinged meadow. No more clinging vines. No more stabbing thorns. I'd made it through.

My melting legs collapsed. I fell to my knees in the soft grass, staring into a clump of tiny blue flowers trembling on thin, arching stalks. And they stared back.

Each bright blue bloom held a pale, goggling eye.

I yelped, scrambling away as the blooms tilted, following my movements. I'd never seen such uncanny things. Not in any wood or meadow I knew.

Moth coiled himself in my lap as he spat at the flowers. They seemed more curious than menacing, but even so, their unblinking floral stare made my skin crawl. I wrapped an arm around Moth, cuddling him closer. His tail lashed as I held him, his head craning over my shoulder to peer behind us. I felt his body tense. *Fable. Look.*

I turned, looking back the way we'd come.

The tunnel behind us was now an enormous, unbroken wall of thorns. Not just a hedge along the lane, not just a bit of briar that dared you to prick yourself snatching the ripest berries from its heart. This was like the wall of a fortress. In the deepening dusk, I could barely make out the top of the hedge, flung high against a sky starting to sparkle with stars. How had it gotten so dark so quickly? It wasn't even dinnertime.

"We did it," I said shakily. We had made it inside the Mirrorwood.

The tunnel is gone, said Moth, his tail lashing. *We are trapped.*

I breathed in. Out. Panic still fluttered in my chest, but I had to be sensible now. Be like Da and find the honey, not the sting. I'd come here for a reason, even though I'd been rather forced into it.

"Only until I break the curse," I said. "And look on the bright side. At least this way we're safe. There's no way the hunters can find us now."

Moth's green eyes glimmered. *I do not think you understand the meaning of that word.*

"Hunter?"

Safe. He swiped a paw at one of the eye-flowers as it bent toward him. *We are inside the cursed realm now. We are not safe.*

I scanned the meadow. The blue eye-flowers were faintly luminous, dotting the darkening grass with a shimmer of light. "It doesn't look that dangerous. It's kind of pretty, actually." I leaned forward to get a closer look at a spotted toadstool I'd noticed among the flowers. Probably not edible, but—

"Aaaa!" I snatched my hand away as the mushroom tilted back, revealing a fang-fringed mouth hidden under the cap. It snapped and snarled viciously. I scooted back, then stood.

I told you, said Moth. *Nothing here will be as it seems.*

"Don't you have anything more reassuring to say?"

Moth twined against my legs, warm and soft. *We are together,* he said. *And you are strong and clever.*

I crouched down to scoop him into my arms, burying my face in his soft neck for a long moment, until he grew tired of my embrace and struggled to be released.

I could do this. The thorns had let me through. Me, the blighted little farm girl. I had gotten farther than all those mighty hunters and countless other heroes. I managed a shaky grin, wishing Vycorax could see me. Let her see what this blighted little farm girl was really capable of.

Of course, she'd probably just try to kill me again. Whatever had made her hesitate at first, she'd been eager enough to chase me, especially after her father's ultimatum. I wondered how angry he'd be with her now that she'd lost me a second time. Not that I felt a single jot of sympathy for the girl. She surely had none for me.

What now? Moth stared at me expectantly.

Good question. Indigo had told me a dozen different versions of the story of the Mirrorwood, scrounged from whatever passing bard they could find. There was an entire realm in here. Villages, farms, lakes, forests. Some stories said the land within the thorns was sleeping. Some said it was caught in an endless long night. Some said it was strange and twisted, everything blighted into nightmare versions of itself.

But they all agreed on one thing: to end the curse, a princess had to make her way to the castle at the heart of the blighted land and wake the true prince who slept there, trapped by the curse of the wicked demon who had taken his place.

Maybe I was foolish to look for truth in wisps of legend. But I knew by my own shifting face that the curse was real. And this realm within the thorns was real too. So there must be some truth to the rest of it.

A chill breeze shivered over me. I wrapped my arms around my midsection. Did I really have any hope of setting things right? I was no princess. No hero.

But I'd gotten this far. I was inside the Mirrorwood. According to Telmarque, not even the blighthunters had managed that before.

It was like when Gavotte taught me to dance. It was so complicated, so many different movements, that I thought it would be impossible. But she told me not to think about it like that. *It's all just steps. Take one, then another. Go slow if you need to.*

And all those stories made it clear what my next step should be.

"All right, no sense wasting time," I said, gathering my gumption. "We need to find the castle." I set the great curve of the thorn wall behind me. Ahead, on the far side of the meadow, lay a dark smudge of forest. "Looks like we're going through those woods."

Moth twitched his whiskers, a gesture I took to be his version of a shrug, and followed as I picked my way gingerly through the field of eye-blooms. I wasn't normally squeamish about stepping on things—you couldn't be, living on a sheep farm—but somehow it was much harder when the thing you were stepping on stared back at you. "Sorry!" I hissed, accidentally smooshing one of the blooms. At least the snap-jawed mushrooms were easy to avoid. Maybe this wouldn't be as bad as I thought.

Finally we reached the edge of the wood. It was lower and denser than the forest outside the thorns. The trees twisted and curled in a distressingly human fashion, thrusting out arms to warn us away and turning their bulging bodies aside, as if ashamed to be seen. Roots rippled across the earth, even bowing up in arches high enough for me to pass beneath. We scrambled over them, under them, by the ghostly light of tiny, pale-green mushrooms that gleamed like foxfire. It was almost charming, until I caught a shiver of movement from the corner of my eye. I snapped around to find a line of bulbous caps perched up along a fallen log beside me. Had they been there before? Had I missed them? Or were they following me? Given my first experience with a mushroom in these woods, it seemed wise to be cautious.

"What do you want?" I demanded.

Nothing. Because they were only mushrooms.

Moth, ahead of me, turned back, fixing me with his green eyes. *Fable, who are you talking to?*

"No one." I was letting my fears get the better of me. Just because I was inside the cursed realm didn't mean every rock and leaf was trying to murder me.

A terrified shriek split the night.

It had come from the woods to my left. My body knotted tight with uncertainty. Maybe it was just a bird. A blighted

owl with a hoot like a scream. The cry came again, wrench-
ingly near. It wasn't an owl. It was a human. A girl.

Fable, do not—

I missed whatever else Moth was saying, because I had
already taken off, dashing toward the scream. I knew it was
foolish. I might well be running straight into something far
worse than vicious fungi. But if there was someone else here,
someone else just as lost and terrified as I was, I had to help
them.

Foxfire mushrooms edged my path, as if leading me
toward the sound. I hurtled over roots and ducked under
grasping branches until I burst out into another open
meadow, even larger than the first.

In the middle of the field hunched a dozen enormous
beasts, hulking monsters with shaggy dark fur and heavy
heads bent under great curling horns. They formed a loose
ring, clustered around a single smaller figure at their center.
A girl, the one who must have screamed. A girl with a face I
knew all too well, because I was wearing it.

Vycorax!

The beasts towered over her menacingly. I froze, not
wanting to startle them. Those horns looked perilously
sharp. And if they didn't feel like stabbing us, the creatures
could probably trample us to death. Moth, being sensible,
had chosen to remain in the woods. But I didn't have that
option.

"What are you doing here?" I did my best to keep my
voice calm, quiet.

"What does it look like?" she spat back. "Trying not to get eaten by these blighted monsters!" One of the beasts swung its massive head at her as she spoke. She shrieked, dodging the snap of enormous sharp teeth.

"No, what are you doing *inside* the Mirrorwood? Why are you here?"

"Because I was chasing after you, you blighter! I almost had you, but then there were all these briars to cut through and then there was a tunnel and then I was here!" Her voice was ragged with fury and panic. "Getting eaten by blighted demon bears."

I inched a few steps forward, eyeing the nearest beast. It didn't really look like a bear. In fact, it reminded me a little of our sheep back home. Now that I was closer, I even saw that it had cloven hooves, not claws. But whatever they were, the monsters were definitely interested in Vycorax. Another of them snapped at her, giving a furious rumble as the girl dodged this way and that.

"Don't just stand there," she called. "Throw me my sword! I dropped it somewhere over that way!"

I scanned the grass around me until I spotted a long gleam of steel near a clump of red chicory. But I didn't pick it up. "Why?" I called back. "So you can murder me to prove you're a proper hunter?"

"No, so I can save us both from these monsters!"

"They aren't attacking *me*," I pointed out. In fact, I wasn't even sure they were attacking *Vycorax*. They kept snapping at her, to be sure, but there was something strange about the movements. They weren't actually biting her. It was as if they were aiming for something else entirely.

I squinted at the ground near Vycorax's feet. In the evening gloom it was hard to be sure what I was seeing, but I had a pretty good guess what was going on.

"Of course," Vycorax snarled. "Why should I expect a wicked blightborn to help me?"

"Good question," I said, crossing my arms. "You're the one who tried to kill me. Why *should* I help you?"

CHAPTER FOUR

*T*he great beasts rumbled, pushing inward, closer to Vycorax. She gulped, fear cracking through her fierceness.

"I promise I won't try to kill you," she said, her voice spiraling high. "Please help me!"

"Fine," I said. I stalked over to her sword, but instead of picking up the weapon, I tore free a handful of the red chicory sprouting beside it. Advancing on the circle of shaggy monsters, I held out the ruddy leaves, shaking them enticingly. "Here, big fellow. Is this what you're after?"

The nearest shaggy beast turned toward me with an eager snuffle. A shiver of triumph flickered through me. I was right! They acted like sheep because they *were* sheep. Just . . . enormous monster-sheep with giant horns.

"Don't worry," I called to Vycorax. "They're not trying to eat you. They're after the red chicory. You're standing right in the middle of a patch of it. I'll get this one to move, and you should be able to slip out." I backed away as I spoke. Rumbling hungrily, the shaggy sheep trundled after me.

Up close, the beast was rather terrifying, even though I was pretty sure it only wanted the leaves in my hands. It was about five times as big as our largest ram back home, with horns that curled and split and curled again, each point gleaming as sharp as a thorn. The sheep opened its mouth to reveal a fearsome hedge of teeth. I threw down the handful of chicory, backing away as the beast snapped at it hungrily.

"Come on!" I called to Vycorax, who was still standing frozen in the center of the rest of the flock. "Get out of there!"

She gulped, then leaped out from the circle of shaggy sheep-monsters. She skidded to a stop a few yards away from me to retrieve her sword. Hefting it, she turned back toward the foraging beasts. "All right, you blighters, time for payback."

"Don't!" I cried. "They're not hurting us!"

But Vycorax paid me no heed, advancing on the nearest shaggy monster as it peacefully chomped down on a mouthful of red chicory. Before I could stop her, she'd slashed out, aiming for the creature's flank. Horror clogged my throat. I braced myself for blood, terror, death.

But there was no bellow of rage from the beast. It didn't startle or even give more than a faint rumble of annoyance. The blade had struck true, but it hadn't cut. Instead, it hung, trapped in the thick black wool that covered the beast.

Vycorax shrieked in frustration, tugging at the hilt of her sword. It didn't budge. "It's stuck!" She pulled harder. Now the beast took notice, lifting its massive head and glancing back at her like I might glance at a fly buzzing around my ears. It gave an ominous rumble.

"Leave it!" I shouted, running toward her. "Come on! Do you want to make it mad?"

The shaggy beast lowered its sharp horns, pawing at the ground and giving a long, low grumble. Then it charged, each heavy step sending a shiver through the earth.

I grabbed Vycorax's elbow, jerking her toward the trees. "That way! It won't be able to chase us in those woods!"

Thankfully, she listened to me this time. We ran, panting, as a horrible thunder of angry sheep-monster hooves chased after us.

I dove into the thick woods with Vycorax a hair behind me. The pounding pursuit rumbled to a halt. The monster gave a menacing groan. Its deep breath shuddered in the air. We crouched silent in the dim wood. Waiting.

Finally the thump, thud, thump of heavy cloven feet retreated into the distance.

I let out a long, ragged breath. "I think we're safe."

A pair of green eyes blinked at me from the shadows nearby. *There's that word again,* said Moth. Of course he would wait until now to deign to reappear.

"Shush, you," I told him. "You're the one who hid in the forest."

His whiskers pricked. *I was not hiding. I simply do not care for enormous sheep.*

"Well, the sheep are gone," I told him. "Like I said. It's safe. Relatively."

He blinked. *You are sitting next to a blighthunter, Fable.*

"Yes, but she promised not to kill me."

"Are you talking to a *cat?*" asked Vycorax. Her eyes were wide, looking between Moth and me.

"Yes," I admitted. Then, more fiercely, "But if you try to hurt Moth, I swear I'll rip out every hair from your head and use them to weave a rope to throttle you."

Vycorax blinked. "What? No, I'd never hurt a cat. Look at him. He's adorable." Moth gave a satisfied purr. I huffed. Traitor.

"You can really hear what he's saying?" asked Vycorax wonderingly.

"Yes. Inside my head."

"Oh." She sounded almost wistful. "That must be . . . nice."

"I thought you hated anything touched by the blight?"

Her face scrunched up. She glanced at Moth, then back at me. I wondered if she was remembering what she'd said to me. How not that long ago she'd had a sword in her hand, the point ready to slice me open.

Finally she coughed. "Well. I mean, yes, but there's no harm in a talking cat, is there?"

I shot Moth a wry glance. "That depends on how much you want to learn about mouse anatomy." Even that didn't sway the charmed look on the girl's face. She knelt down, starting to skritch the spot between Moth's ears. He purred even louder.

I probably should have been happy she didn't want to murder my talking cat, but instead, it just made me angry. She could accept Moth but not me. A flash of heat burned up my throat.

I marched over and scooped Moth into my arms. "You'd better go now," I said. "If you travel any deeper into the forest, you might not find your way back to the thorns."

"Why would I be looking for the thorns?"

"Oh, I don't know," I drawled sarcastically. "Maybe so you can escape this cursed realm before it turns you into an evil blightspawn too?"

Vycorax stood, her lips pressed to a thin, determined line. "I can't run. I'm going to break the curse. That's why I'm here."

"What?" I shook my head. "No, that's why *I'm* here. You didn't even think it was *possible*! You just chased after me and got in accidentally." I must have been holding Moth too tightly, because he yowled, leaping from my arms to the forest floor.

"You don't know that." Vycorax crossed her arms.

Maybe you're both here to break the curse, said Moth.

"Ha. That's a joke," I said. "She's a hunter and I'm blighted."

Vycorax looked at Moth. "What did he say?"

"He said that we could work together. Which is *clearly* ridiculous."

I waited for Vycorax to agree. To snarl or growl or laugh. But she only stood, looking at me thoughtfully. "I keep my promises," she said. "I won't try to kill you."

"I heard your father. He said you couldn't be his apprentice if you didn't get rid of me." I backed away. There was a bit of a trail leading into the woods, edged with more glimmering mushrooms. I meant to follow it. Alone.

"Because you're blighted," she said. "But if we broke the curse and you were cured, then there wouldn't be any reason to kill you."

"There's never been a reason," I said sharply. "Except that you're scared of me. And because your father told you to."

She looked away, digging the toe of one black boot into the soft earth. "Well, my father's not here. So what he thinks doesn't matter."

"And what do *you* think?" I demanded. "Aren't you afraid I'm going to attack you and . . ." I waved my hands in the air.

"Summon butterflies?" asked Vycorax, frowning curiously at the gesture.

"No! Steal your soul. Taint you with the blight."

Vycorax sniffed. "I can take care of myself. You might have my face, but you're not me."

"So you *do* think that." I ground my teeth. This was a waste of time. It was ridiculous to think that I could actually work with a blighthunter. With someone who thought I was evil.

I spun around, heading for the mushroom-lined trail. Moth followed, weaving through the ferns beside me. He was the only companion I needed.

Unfortunately, he wasn't the only one I had. Vycorax jogged after me, her quick steps scuffing the fallen leaves.

"Where are you even going?" she called.

"To the castle," I said. "To find the prince."

"Like in the bard's stories? You really think they're true?"

"Oh," said a melodious voice. "They most assuredly are."

The words fell over us like the glimmer of a falling star, like the breath you let out after making a wish. But when I searched for the speaker, I could see no one. Only Vycorax and Moth and a dense circle of trees. Then I realized that the grove where we stood had gotten brighter. A golden glow shimmered down from above. It wasn't the stars. It wasn't the moon.

It was a woman. She perched gracefully on one of the mossy branches, her long pale gold skirts trailing down, small bare feet hanging some ten feet above us. I had never seen anyone so lovely, and I paid a lot of attention to faces. Hers was perfect. The sort that a painter could try to capture for years and never master. Sunshine-bright hair flowed over her shoulders, some of it worked in small braids gemmed with jewels. Her eyes were a gray so pale they might have been shards of mirror or the work of a silversmith. All of her was glittering, gorgeous, impossible.

I felt like I should bow. Or beg for her favor. Or compose an epic poem in her honor. Like it might shatter me utterly, just to know her name.

"Greetings," she said, in that same voice, the one that could call mermaids from the sea and stars from the sky. "I am Mirachne."

"M-Mirachne?" Vycorax sounded as wonderstruck and bewildered as I was. "Lady Mirachne, as in one of the Subtle Powers?"

A thrill rippled through me. Of course such otherworldly, impossible grace and loveliness couldn't be mortal. It made me squirm, remembering the foolish offering I'd made earlier at her well. How had I ever thought a plum turnover would be enough to entreat such a being?

Moth, on the other hand, spat, his tail fluffing. He retreated behind my legs. What had gotten into him? Well, maybe he didn't care to be in the presence of a being more impressive than himself.

Thankfully, the gleaming, golden woman didn't seem to have noticed. She merely inclined her head to Vycorax's question. "Indeed. I am Mirachne of the Dawn, Mistress of Dreams and Delight. And I am here to aid you, daughters of the earth, if you wish."

Giddy joy swept through me, melting me like sugar over a blazing flame, filling the air with a sweet caramel scent that drove every other thought from me except the need to make this beautiful, gold-gleaming woman happy. To earn her smile.

Something sharp stabbed me in the leg, breaking me from my daze. I snapped my mouth closed, then looked down to find Moth's green eyes staring back at me. *Take care, Fable. The Subtle Powers work to their own ends, always. Be wary.*

Worrywart. Still, best to be cautious. "Aid us how?" I managed to ask.

"You seek to break the curse, do you not?"

Had she heard us arguing? Or had she been listening back at the well? I supposed it didn't really matter. She knew our plight. She truly felt it. Her silver eyes practically glowed, radiating pure and perfect sympathy.

"Yes," said Vycorax. "That's why I'm here." She shot me a look, as if daring me to contradict her in front of the lady.

"Yes," I added belatedly. "I want to break the curse."

Mirachne swung one delicate heel. Shimmers fell from her, a rain of light that sparkled over the moss below. "I, too, desire that the curse be broken. For this realm to be free and the true prince restored to his place."

"Why?" I asked, aware of Moth's green eyes on me, his warning in my mind. "Why do you care what becomes of the mortal realm?"

For a brief moment Mirachne's eyes narrowed. Something flashed there, lightning-quick, thorn-sharp, and a stab of fear shook me. Who was I to question one of the Powers? I gulped and braced myself to be turned into a toad or a snail. Vycorax gave me a scornful look, sliding a step away, as if to distance herself from my unforgivable ignorance.

But Mirachne only gave a silvery laugh, tilting her head. "Let me tell you a story, and perhaps you will understand. You have heard versions of it already, sung and rhymed by your mortal bards. But this will be the true tale."

I reached down, stroking Moth's hackles, trying to soothe him—and myself. Lady Mirachne was an immortal, unknowable being. She had no obligation to explain her motives. What mattered was that she wanted to help.

A bubble of hope lifted me. Maybe I really could break my curse.

She slid from her perch then, light as a cloud, floating down to hover just above the glimmering moss. Mirachne swept her hand, and the glimmers shifted, spinning, gathering. They formed a pool of silver. A mirror, set into the mossy ground.

"There were once a brave queen and a wise king who ruled their land in peace and prosperity. Yet they lacked the one thing they truly wished for, their heart's desire: a child."

A flick of her fingers, and the pool gleamed with color. I saw figures within: a handsome couple in rich purple, each wearing a bright golden crown. They looked to each other, desolate in their riches.

"There is nothing that moves me so greatly as a wish of the heart," said Mirachne, sighing sweetly, pressing a delicate hand to her chest. "A wish of the most secret soul. Nothing in this world has greater power."

Her eyes glittered as she spoke, spilling a hungry brightness. "I gave them the child of their dreams. A beautiful boy who would never know pain or sorrow. And they loved him dearly, from the first moment they held him."

Light kindled in the king's arms, transforming into a tiny baby. The child was lovely, with the rich brown skin of the queen, the copper-gold hair of the king, and a grace and beauty that surpassed them both.

"Alas, no perfection can exist in the world that the Bannon does not try to thwart," said Mirachne, her beautiful features turning as sharp and cold as winter frost. "Of all the Subtle Powers, he is the most deceptive. With his clever words, he tricked the queen into allowing him to grant the prince a blessing of his own."

In the pool, a shadowy figure advanced upon the doting parents and newborn prince, cloak swirling with menace. His face was cast in a deep darkness that hid all but the glint of his bloodred eyes. I shuddered, wanting to back away, but I had to know the end of the tale.

"But the Bannon's blessing was in truth a curse: if the prince were to ever see his true reflection before his thirteenth birthday, he would perish, and a prince of nightmares would take his place. The queen paid the price for her foolish bargain with her own life, leaving only the king to guard his beloved child."

The red-eyed shadow spread arms like dark wings, looming over the king and the child bundled to his breast.

"Couldn't you stop him?" demanded Vycorax, looking as if she wanted to leap into the vision pool and join the fight.

Mirachne shook her head sadly. "Would that it were possible. But the Old Law forbids the Powers from acting directly against one another. It fell to the king to keep his son safe. And he did try. He decreed that every mirror in all the realm be destroyed. With vigilance and bravery, he fended off the curse until the eve of the prince's thirteenth birthday."

The prince within the pool grew older. A tumbling toddler. A laughing lad. Finally a youth, starting to sprout up lithe and tall. A boy about my own age.

"And then . . ."

The image within the pool went dark.

"What happened?" asked Vycorax, leaning closer.

Mirachne gave a delicate shrug. "I do not know, though I have no doubt it was the Bannon's work. Somehow, the prince saw his true reflection."

"But he didn't die," I said. "He's only asleep, right?"

Mirachne nodded. "I could not stop the Bannon's curse, but I could at least slow it. The prince sleeps, and all the realm sleeps with him."

"And the demon prince?" asked Vycorax, one hand on her hip, where the hilt of her sword would have been.

Mirachne's lip curled. "Yes, that foul imposter was spawned at the moment the curse struck. He has stolen the true prince's life. His castle. His realm. But he is a wicked pretender, a monster so twisted by nightmare that he corrupts everything he touches."

The darkness shifted. Shrank, revealing a solitary figure swathed in shadows. He had the same brown skin, the same coppery hair as the prince. There was even a sort of horrible beauty in his sharp features, the cut of his pointed ears, the curve of golden horns at his temples.

I peered closer, caught by dismay and wonder, then yelped as the nightmare prince abruptly turned, staring straight out from the pool. Was this . . . real? Could he somehow see us?

Those eyes. Bleak. Black. Endless. They were eyes that would pin you and wither you to ash. I shuddered, stepping back.

Mirachne swept her hand in a quick arc, and the pool vanished, leaving only moss.

"It was he who unleashed the blight," said Mirachne.

"Those terrible magics would have corrupted all the world had I not cast up my wall of thorns to bind them away. And even that barrier is imperfect." Her silver eyes lanced into me until I couldn't bear it and looked away. She must know I was blighted. Did she think I was like the demon prince? Corrupted?

I knelt. Breathed deep. Ran a hand along Moth's soft back, steadying myself. "But if we can find the true prince and wake him, then everything will be better? That's what all the songs say." Then the prince would set everything to rights. Banish the demon. Purge the blight. Give me my true face.

Mirachne's silence loomed ominously.

"It's something more," said Vycorax. "Isn't it?"

"Yes," said Mirachne. "In order to wake the true prince, you must destroy the false prince who holds him captive."

"Destroy?" I asked, my voice quavering slightly.

"Kill," said Mirachne.

CHAPTER FIVE

Vycorax rallied first. "How?" she asked Mirachne. "How do we kill a demon?"

I wished I could feel so brave. How had I ever thought I could do this? I didn't even know the true color of my own eyes. Wrangling a herd of monster-sheep was one thing, but this? I'd spent practically my entire life on one patch of farmland. I didn't know how to use a sword. Even now, the demon prince's black eyes haunted me, making me feel like the tiniest, most insignificant worm.

"I want nothing more than to help you," said Mirachne, gorgeous regret in every line of her perfect features. "But alas, even the Subtle Powers must follow the ancient law. I am bound not to interfere in the mortal world unless a mortal invokes my aid."

"Haven't you already helped us?" I said. "You let us in through the thorns, didn't you?"

"Indeed. That was what you wished, was it not, daughter of earth, when you stood at my well? For someone to enter the Mirrorwood and break the curse? And so they did. Two heroes, to set things to rights." She gestured to Vycorax. And to me.

I gaped. It had worked! Well, sort of. When I'd made the wish, I'd been thinking of the princess with the pure heart, or some dashing knight maybe. Not *myself.*

But at the same time, the revelation filled me with a new strength. Mirachne had *chosen* me. Well, us. If she believed I could do this, maybe I had a chance. Except . . .

"I'm sorry," I said miserably, "but I don't have any more plum turnovers. Or anything else that's fit to offer you, my lady."

Mirachne laughed, a musical trill like gentle raindrops. "Dear girl, it wasn't sweets that invoked my aid. It was something far more precious."

"What?" I asked.

"Your *wish*," said Mirachne. "That is the power you hold. I may help you, but only if you trust me with the deepest wish of your heart."

"That's easy, then," said Vycorax. "I wish to kill the demon prince and break the curse."

Of course she would barge in first. Still, there was nothing that said two people couldn't wish for the same thing, was there?

Mirachne breathed in deeply, as if inhaling the perfume of some rare rose. "Yes. That will do." She tilted her head, sunshine hair shimmering, as her gaze drifted to me. "And you, Fable? What is your wish?"

Moth, still coiled at my feet, grumbled. *Beware, Fable. A wish is power.*

Mirachne only smiled at him indulgently, taking the grumble as a sign of interest. "Ah, Sir Cat, do you have a wish as well?"

Moth hissed, his entire body arching. *I wish nothing. Nor*

should you, Fable. He spat, then leaped away into the woods. *I will return when* she *is gone.*

"I'm sorry," I said hastily, seeing a faint frown dive between Mirachne's golden brows. "He . . . he's not usually so rude. But it's been a long day."

"Indeed," said Mirachne, her voice chilly as she stared into the shadows where Moth had disappeared. "Cats. Tricksy creatures. Unreliable, for in the end they care only for themselves."

I started to protest, only to blink, dazzled, as she turned her full smile upon me. "Well, daughter of earth? Have you a wish to share?"

My tongue turned dry. I gulped. How could I deny Lady Mirachne? Or the deep, desperate thrum of my own heart? I'd come here to save myself. And here was one of the most powerful entities in all the world, offering to help me. It would be utter foolishness not to accept. I loved Moth, but he was a cat. He didn't understand the ways of humans. And I wanted to be free of my blight more than anything.

"I wish I had my true face," I said in a rush.

Mirachne's gaze transfixed me. I felt like one of the butterflies I saw once in a traveling cabinet of curiosities, pinned to a velvet box. Helpless. Then she smiled, releasing me. "Poor girl. You carry a heavy burden. But not forever."

My heart bumped up into my throat. "Really? So you can do it? You can get rid of my blight? Give me my real face?"

"Indeed. Once the Bannon's curse is broken, the prince will be able to cure you of your blight. But it will not be easy.

The demon prince is dangerous and very, very powerful. No mortal weapon will wound him. In order to destroy him and cleanse this realm of the blight, you will need a blade that can cut through even dreams."

Vycorax nodded briskly, as if magical weapons were an everyday topic of discussion for her. "Where can we find a blade like that?"

Maybe it was somewhere pleasant. Being guarded by a secret clan of talking badgers who would feed us tea and buttered toast. Hidden behind a beautiful crystal-blue waterfall.

"You must seek out the Withering," said Mirachne, her silky brow furrowing. "A most fearsome beast. Its claws are so sharp, they can tear the world itself to shreds. When it hunts, it does not devour. It obliterates."

All right, then. Not pleasant. I glanced toward Vycorax to see how she was taking this. Much better than me, judging by the way she bounced up on the balls of her feet. "And this Withering, is it guarding the blade?" she asked.

"In a sense," said Mirachne. "You must track the Withering to its lair. You must enter while it slumbers and claim its sharpest tooth. That is the weapon that can slay the demon."

Vycorax nodded, looking brave and determined, not at all like someone who'd just been told they needed to hunt down a reality-destroying beast to steal one of its teeth to slay a demon prince. If only I could have borrowed a bit of her fierceness along with her face. These plans to break the curse were getting more and more perilous by the hour.

"And that is only the first of the challenges you will face," Mirachne continued. "The demon pretender will not go quietly. He is a cruel and terrible monster, unwilling to lose his hold on this land."

"But you can help us," I said. "With our wishes."

"Only within certain bounds." Mirachne's lips crimped as if she were tasting something unpleasant. "The Bannon has involved himself, and the ancient laws forbid us from acting directly against one another. Until his curse is broken, I can only guide and advise. I must trust in you, daughters of earth, to have the courage and determination to set this right."

"We do," said Vycorax quickly. "We will."

I wasn't so sure about courage, but I had the determination. It had gotten me this far. I wasn't going to back down now. "We'll break the curse, my lady," I said. "You can count on us."

Mirachne's smile was a promise, a poem, a falling shimmer of perfumed petals. "I am glad. Farewell, for now. I will return to you when the demon has been banished, to see that your wishes are granted."

"Wait!" called Vycorax. "Which way should we go? How can we find the Withering?"

Sparks of light had begun to dance over the Power's hair, her gown, her skin. She gave a sad smile. "I fear the Withering is beyond even my sight. But if you travel north, you will find signs of its passage. Just be wary that it does not find you first."

The sparks brightened to a blaze that haloed her against the gloom of the wood. Then it winked out, leaving a scattering of glitter drifting in the night.

Vycorax let out a long, slow breath. "I wasn't even sure the Subtle Powers were real. And now we're working for one of them." She shook her head, as if dazed.

Honestly, it was kind of reassuring. If even Vycorax—brave and fierce blighthunter—was overwhelmed by this, maybe it was all right that I felt like someone had just put me on the back of a dragon and told me to fly.

I took a breath. Vycorax had said *we*. And Mirachne had accepted both our wishes. "So you're all right with this? Working with me?"

Vycorax crossed her arms. "We both want to break the curse."

Well, she had given her word she wasn't going to kill me. And honestly, I really didn't want to do this all on my own.

"Right," I said. "I guess we're working together, then."

Vycorax gave a small huff. "I guess that means I need to call you something other than *blighter*."

"Fable," I said.

"Vycorax."

We stood there awkwardly. It seemed like we ought to shake hands, but I was afraid she'd flinch away from me if I offered. In the end, she shrugged and I crossed my arms, and then both of us looked away at the dark trees surrounding us.

"So," I asked, "now what? I don't suppose you have any supplies?" I looked Vycorax up and down hopefully.

She patted the pockets of her crimson coat. "No. Only a bit of coin. Not that there's anywhere to spend it."

There is a village. Moth stalked out from the darkness. His eyes gleamed like small moons. *If you are done making foolish wishes.*

I ignored the second part. I'd made my choice and I didn't regret it. Right now I cared more about the first thing he'd said. What sort of village could we hope to find, here in the Mirrorwood? Of course there had been people here once. A whole realm full of villages, taverns, mills. Farms. My throat closed with homesickness, but I swallowed hard, banishing it.

"He says there's a village," I told Vycorax.

She looked dubious. "Lady Mirachne said the realm was asleep. What use is a village?"

"They might have food. If they're sleeping, they won't care if we borrow some." I turned back to Moth. "Did you see any of the villagers?"

Yes, said Moth. *They are doing strange things.*

"What sort of strange things?" You had to be careful making assumptions about cats. Moth found outhouses inexplicable, whereas casual murder was a part of his everyday life.

They are hopping around like the floor is burning their feet while other humans make strange noises with reeds and drums. And eating sausages, but that is not strange. Sausages are delicious.

"It doesn't sound like they're asleep," I said, looking to Vycorax. "It sounds like they're . . . dancing? And eating sausages. Maybe it's some sort of festival?"

She crossed her arms. "We're not here to dance."

"No, but we're going to need food and a place to sleep. And someone there might know something about how to find the Withering."

Vycorax tapped one foot, her jaw tight. Then she gave a reluctant nod. "All right. But I'm going in prepared."

"What exactly are you prepared *for*?" I asked Vycorax as we made our way toward the glitter of lamps. Whiffs of smoke and roasted garlic and caramel drifted on the night air, along with a distant whistle of pipes and the thrum of drumming.

She hefted her makeshift quarterstaff, spinning it from hand to hand. I had to admit, it was rather impressive, especially for something she'd just fashioned from a sturdy branch. "Anything. A hunter has to be ready to confront evil at all times. Especially here."

"It looks like a normal village to me," I said as we pushed out from the trees into an open meadow. At least, it looked like my home village, Wychwode, which was the only basis for comparison I had. Whitewashed cottages with thatched roofs clumped along the outskirts, while larger buildings of stone lined the cobbled main street like books on a shelf. A river curved through the center, spanned by a sturdy bridge.

Of course, I'd never seen Wychwode done up like this,

with streamers hanging from every door and bunting along every fence. Booths and tents filled the street, spilling out into the village green, where lamps hung from ropes stretched between the trees, turning it into a fairyland of light and color.

Vycorax glowered at the scene. "This doesn't make any sense. Mirachne said the realm was sleeping. Like the true prince." She waved for me to follow her as she crept cautiously toward the green, hidden behind a line of empty carts. We crouched at the end of the last wagon, scanning the scene before us.

"They're definitely *not* sleeping," I said.

Even so, it all felt like a dream to me. Villagers strolled between the tents, laughing. They gathered in smaller clusters to chatter and share paper cones full of candied nuts and popcorn. I stared and stared until my eyes ached and my chest swelled with a yearning so sharp it felt like it might slice me open.

How many nights had I waited up for my siblings to return from the fall festival or the village jubilee? How many times had I begged Indigo for stories or nibbled slightly stale doughnuts, trying to imagine what it would be like to taste them fresh and crisp? How often had I dreamed of dancing under strings of colorful lanterns, caught in a river of music?

But it had always been impossible. Even if I wore Allegra's face, there was a risk of attracting attention. Questions. Hunters. The one time my parents had tried to take us all to the spring market fair, I ruined it by accidentally stealing the face of a sweetseller when she pinched my cheek to tell me how Allegra and I were such an adorable matched set.

"Have you ever been to a festival?" I asked Vycorax, hoping she wouldn't hear the painful ache in my voice.

She pursed her lips thoughtfully. "I once helped Father chase down a blighted pig that tried to escape into a harvest hay maze."

"No. I mean for fun. You know, to eat candied apples and watch the tumblers and tease your sister about her crush on the strong man." Telmarque had mentioned Vycorax having a sister, hadn't he?

"No," said Vycorax. "We didn't have time for that sort of thing. My training was more important." She spoke sharply, but I saw how she glanced wistfully back toward the tents.

"We should just go," I said. "Look, there's the sausage-seller right there." Moth, coiled near my feet, gave a loud purr of approval.

"No." Vycorax shook her head. "What if they're all blighted?"

"*I'm* blighted," I reminded her.

Vycorax sat back on her heels. Her eyes gleamed in the shadows, watching me. "But you don't want to be. That was your wish. To be rid of your blight. Because you know it's evil."

I bit the inside of my cheek as her words tangled in my chest, growing thorns. I did hate what my blight made me. That it had robbed me of being myself. That it forced me to rely on the charity of my family and put them in danger.

But in spite of everything, I tried to be a good person. I did my chores without complaining (well, mostly). I told Thespian jokes and sat with him out in the barn when he was in one of his black moods. I always let Allegra take the last piece of cheese toast even when she'd had more than her share, because I knew it was her favorite. I wove my father crowns of gildweed for the spring festival so that he would sing his silly song about being the king of sheep. I *loved* my family. I wasn't an evil person.

"Look," I said finally. "Would you rather go eat sausages and play games at the festival or wander around the dark forest and run into more giant murder-sheep?"

Vycorax frowned furiously at the woods behind us, then at the sparkling lights and tents. "Fine," she said. "We'll go to the festival. But hunters *don't* play games."

CHAPTER SIX

Thweet!

The third dart smacked right into the tiny black circle at the center of the target. I gave a loud whoop. "You did it!"

I almost slapped Vycorax on the shoulder, remembering at the last moment that she might well take it as some sort of attack. Instead, I vented my excitement by bobbing up on my toes and jabbing the last of my sausage-on-a-stick toward the sky.

Even Vycorax looked pleased with herself, judging by the bright sparkle in her eyes. "Ha! I sure did!"

She turned her attention to the man running the booth, who looked completely befuddled. Which was understandable, given that Vycorax had just won her tenth straight round.

It had been a magical night so far. The fair was everything I'd hoped for, and more. The only sting was that my family wasn't there with me. That I couldn't watch Sonnet smash the hammer on the bell-ringing game or tear off with Allegra and Gavotte to join the circle dance. But Vycorax was better company than I'd expected. Which was good, since Moth had abandoned me long ago, no doubt to steal leftovers from innocent festivalgoers.

"I'll take the biggest one," she said, pointing above him to the line of velvet animals hanging from the ceiling.

The man cleared his throat. "Of course, miss. Just a moment."

Vycorax gave a scornful snort as he turned away. "I bet he didn't think I could do it. Ha. He's lucky I'm stopping at ten. I could clear out his entire booth."

I gave her a wry look. "I thought hunters didn't play games."

"This isn't a game," she said archly as the man held out her prize, a plush gray rabbit as big as her head.

"What is it, then?"

She tossed back her hair. "Training."

"Do you normally get stuffies as rewards for your training?"

She shoved the velvet bunny at me. "No. That's for you."

My humor melted into astonishment. "Me?"

She shrugged. "I don't need it. And besides, I saw how you were looking at it."

I clutched the rabbit to my chest as heat flooded my cheeks. It was true. I'd been remembering how Allegra came home from last year's fall festival with a stuffed velvet pig with the most adorable curly tail. Sonnet had won it for her. She'd promised to win one for me this year, but that wasn't likely, now that she'd been offered an apprenticeship at the smithy in Little Puckling. Sonnet would be gone by the end of the summer, boarding with the smith's family for at least a year.

My chest squeezed. Would I be back in time to say good-bye? Or maybe the better question was whether I'd be back at all. I gripped the velvet more tightly. No, I was going to do this. And when I saw Sonnet again, I'd be wearing my own, true face.

"Thank you," I said when I found my tongue.

Vycorax looked down at her feet, shrugging. "It's nothing." She turned back to the booth. "Hey, one more thing," she called to the man.

He stiffened. "I'm sorry, miss, but I really should let some other folks—"

"No, I'm done play—er, training," she said. "But we wondered if you could tell us what this is all about. What exactly are you celebrating?"

The man boggled at her. "What are we *celebrating*? The prince's birthday, of course!"

"Er. Which prince?" I asked warily.

The man chuckled, as if it were a joke. "Prince Rylain, of course! Our beloved boy! Graced by Lady Mirachne herself, with beauty and honor, strength and daring, and all good things." He shook his head, tsking. "Where are you from, girl, that you don't know of our bonny lad?"

Something was very, very strange. The prince he was talking about must be the true prince. The one who lay in an enchanted sleep. Why were these people celebrating his birthday? Hadn't that already happened? More than a hundred years ago? Was this what Mirachne meant by sleeping?

I gulped, glancing at Vycorax, who spoke up smoothly. "We're from the south. Thessequa," she said, naming our realm.

"Ah," said the man, nodding. "Foreigners. Well, may the blessing of this day be upon you."

"And this Prince Rylain," Vycorax asked, "how old is he?"

"His Highness will turn thirteen at midnight. Even now the worthies gather at Glimmerdark Castle for a grand masquerade in his honor," said the man proudly. "While we honor him here in Fenhollow, in our own humble way."

"Good, good, well, he has our best wishes too, of course," said Vycorax, backing away from the booth into the shadows of a nearby oak. She thumped the butt of her quarterstaff against the grass as I joined her.

"That doesn't make sense," said Vycorax. "Mirachne told us that the prince was cursed on the eve of his thirteenth birthday. But that was over a century ago! These people act like it hasn't even happened yet. And I haven't seen anyone who looks like they might be blighted."

"Maybe that's what Mirachne meant about the entire realm being asleep?" I suggested. "They're caught in a sort of dream or something?"

"Ugh. *Magic.*" Vycorax grimaced. "Well, at least they have good sausage. And maybe one of them knows something about the Withering."

I glanced around at the happy, chattering crowds. "You'd think if they knew there was a terrible reality-eating doom-beast out there, they wouldn't be so cheerful."

"Well, maybe we can figure out more in the morning. Once it's light, I should be able to scout for signs so we can track it down. I'm going to go check out that inn over there and see if they have room. You coming?"

"I'll find Moth," I said. "We'll meet you there."

She hesitated, glancing around. "Will you . . . that is, are you going to be okay? By yourself?"

I stared. Was she—a blighthunter—actually *worried* about me? Was that why she was frowning like that, the corners of her eyes crinkling with concern?

Vycorax coughed, gripping her quarterstaff. "I mean, try not to steal anyone's face. We don't want to get run out of town."

No, of course she wasn't worried about me. Only about the harm I might cause. Because I was corrupt. Touched by evil magic. "I'll be fine," I said stiffly, then marched off toward the tents.

Frustration carried me nearly to the end of the row, each step thumping the ground. I shouldn't have expected anything more. Vycorax wasn't my friend. At best, she was a reluctant ally. She didn't care what I thought, how I felt. She only cared about cleansing me of the blight. Once that was done, she'd have no reason to bother with some girl from a sheep farm.

A small child was passing by, following her fathers. I thrust the plush rabbit Vycorax had won at her. "Here, do you want this?" She squealed and clutched the stuffed toy as her parents thanked me.

There. Good. No sense getting confused about things. Better the sting of it now than the brutal crush of disappointment later. I folded my arms across my chest, feeling the chill of the night creeping through my thin homespun shirt.

Lights sparkled, music drummed, and delicious scents swirled around me. But I didn't feel like a part of it anymore. If only Indigo were there to make a silly joke or tell me a story. Or Thespian, who always understood my moods and didn't try to make me explain them, just sat silently, his steady presence a promise that it would pass.

A large crowd was coming along the path. A family. I counted seven kids. There was plenty of room. It wasn't as if there were any real danger of me touching one of them, but Vycorax's warning buzzed at me, a hornet I couldn't slap away. Hastily, I ducked into the nearest tent, sheltering behind the heavy purple cloth. Laughter drifted past. My heartbeat slowed as the family passed, but the hollow ache remained. Then I turned, and what I saw drove every other thought away.

Purple velvet draped the inside of the tent. Ribbons ran from side to side, and along them hung dozens of masks, gleaming in the lamplight. Some were brightly painted. Others exploded with curving feathers and ruffles of lace. Many were gemmed or dangled loops of beads or fringed tassels. There were masks meant to disguise your entire face and others that covered only the eyes.

My mouth hung open, wonder shivering out of me in a long, slow sigh. I'd never seen such lovely things. Well, some of them were lovely. Others had hooked green noses, bat wings, or wriggling crowns of serpents. I shuddered, catching sight of a bone-white skull decorated with crimson spiders. Why would anyone choose one of those horrors? I turned away from the grotesque array, drawn by a shimmer of pearls and lace on the far wall. My breath caught, frozen in my throat.

It was surely the most beautiful mask of them all. A full feminine face, her creamy skin decorated with swirls of gold and edged in scallops of lace. More gold glinted on her brow: a crown, beaded with pearls.

I glanced around. There didn't seem to be a proprietor. But surely it wouldn't do any harm just to touch it. To try it on. With trembling fingers, I plucked the princess mask from the ribbon, holding it up, staring into the empty eyes. I turned it around, lifting it to my face.

Normally, I hated seeing myself. I was always wearing someone else's face. It was never *really* me. I didn't need any more reminders of what I was—or what I was not. But this was different. This was a face that belonged to no one else. I wasn't a fool. I knew it was only a mask. But still. I could imagine, just for a few moments, what it would be like to have a face of my own.

I searched the nearby walls for the silver sparkle of a mirror. Nothing. No, wait, there was a wooden frame—it must be one of those enormous freestanding mirrors that you could angle to see yourself from tip to toe. But when I moved to stand in front of it, only bare wood stared back.

Of course. There weren't any mirrors in this realm. They'd

all been destroyed on the orders of the king, to protect his son from the Bannon's curse.

Maybe it was just as well. My true face was unlikely to be dripping in pearls and wearing a crown. I'd be happy just to have my own nose. Maybe a dimple. No one else in my family had dimples.

I was about to replace the princess mask when someone stepped from the shadows. A face I'd seen before, reflected in Mirachne's pool. Pointed ears swept back from his sharp-cut features. Two horns curled from his brow. And he was staring right at me.

I shrieked, leaping back and dropping the mask.

The demon lunged. But not at me. He scooped the mask out of the air, catching it before it could come to harm. He took a pace back. "I'm sorry," he said. "I didn't mean to scare you."

I stared at him, my panic turning into hot embarrassment. The sharp cheeks, the dangerously furrowed brow, the ears, the horns—they weren't real. Only papier-mâché. It wasn't a demon. Just a boy wearing a mask.

"It's okay," I said quickly. "I should have realized. I mean, we're in a mask shop. Is this your family's tent?"

He sounded about my age, though I couldn't be sure as the gruesome mask hid nearly all his face. He had a spindly look, as if his bones had grown faster than the rest of him. A dark cloak hid most of his clothing, but the glimpses I caught were clearly high-quality material. Dark velvet and creamy silk. He was certainly no farm boy.

My question seemed to take him aback. Then he nodded, moving to replace the princess mask on the wall. "Yes, you could say that. And you're a stranger."

I nodded. "From Thessequa."

"Here to celebrate our darling prince's birthday?"

I hesitated. There was a strange, bitter twist in the boy's words. He seemed considerably less enthusiastic about the holiday than the dart-booth man had been.

"Of course," I said. "I wish Prince Rylain all the best. We've all heard stories of how generous and brave and kind he is."

"Oh yes. He's as kind as a rose."

What did he mean by that? Roses were a strange choice. Indigo always used them in their poems about love. *Because of the ironic contrast, Fable. The sweetness of the scent and the sting of the thorn. Just like love.*

A prickle of unease twitched through me. I shouldn't be here, talking to this boy. I could just imagine Vycorax shaking her head at my foolishness. "I really should—"

"Can you help me with something?" the boy asked.

Me? Just because I happened to wander in from the street? I cleared my throat, not wanting to be rude. Especially when I'd already acted so oddly about his mask. "What?"

"I need to choose a mask to wear to the ball."

"Isn't that happening now?"

He shrugged. "There's still plenty of time. It's not midnight yet. So. What do you think of this one?" He gestured to the demon mask he was currently wearing.

Why did the question feel like a test? I had no idea what answer he was looking for, so I gave him all I could: the truth.

"It's frightening," I said. "But also sort of . . . pretty. Once you get past the horns and the eyebrows. I suppose the real question is, do you *want* to scare people?"

He didn't answer. Only stared at me. "What would you pick for me?"

I felt a buzz of pressure on my skin. He was watching me so very closely. I wasn't used to talking with strangers, with people I hadn't known for my entire life. None of the clues were there, none of the familiar little gestures and smiles.

And now here was this boy, asking my opinion. His piercing dark eyes demanding I define him. That grotesque mask taunting me with the face of my enemy. The sooner I was out of there, the better. I scanned the displays, searching for anything I could reasonably suggest.

"There you are," said a voice behind me.

I spun around, nearly jumping out of my skin. Vycorax stood at the entrance to the tent. Moth crouched beside her.

"I got us a room," said Vycorax. "Are you done here?"

"I was just—" The words froze as I turned back. There was no boy. Only dozens of empty masks staring at me.

Thankfully, the Green Oak seemed to be a perfectly normal inn. No mysterious mask-wearing boys, no hint of blight. Just a warm hearth, a cozy room, a bed big enough that Vycorax and I could share, with Moth curling between us. The kind-eyed woman who ran the place seemed entirely convinced by Vycorax's story that we were sisters and that our parents had sent us to take a room while they stayed up late for the dancing.

Vycorax flopped onto the mattress so heartily it nearly bounced me off the edge, where I was sitting to take off my boots. She gave a long sigh, sinking her head onto the pillow.

"Is something wrong?" I asked.

"No. Just . . . that was fun. Although my stomach feels a little strange."

"Probably because you ate two entire caramel apples," I said.

She made a noise that I would have called a giggle had it come from anyone who wasn't a blighthunter. "I have no regrets," she said. "They were amazing."

I curled myself under the blanket. Beside me, the lantern spilled a golden light. Not so dazzling as Mirachne's glow, but still a dream come true. Tonight I'd wandered around a lantern-lit festival, feasting and laughing and feeling like a normal girl for the first time in years. I slid a sideways glance toward Vycorax. Maybe we both had.

"Hey." She propped herself up on one elbow. "Where's your rabbit?"

I bit the inside of my cheek, not wanting to shatter this warm golden glow. "Oh. Er. Moth was jealous. I didn't want to hurt his feelings, so I gave the rabbit to a little girl."

Moth, curled between us, lifted his head at that and gave a growling protest. *I am in no way threatened by some velveteen interloper.*

"See?" I said. "He's still touchy. Best not to talk about it."

Vycorax made a tsking noise, skritching between Moth's ears. "Poor thing. Don't worry. We know you're one of a kind."

Moth, apparently mollified, began to purr. Then snore. Soon Vycorax joined him. A hazy, lazy peace filled the room.

But sleep wouldn't come. I kept thinking about that masked boy. Who was he?

His dark eyes had watched me so carefully. Almost like he knew who I was. Why I was there. Could he be some sort of spy for the demon prince? Maybe that was why he was wearing that particular mask. But why would a spy for the demon prince want my opinion on what mask to wear to a ball?

I shoved my thoughts away. This was a cursed realm, full of oddness, and the boy was just one small part of it. I needed sleep, especially if we were going to be hunting the Withering tomorrow. I had to focus on our mission, not some strange boy. And most definitely not the homesickness swelling in my chest. What did my family think had happened to me? Had Telmarque gone back to the farm? Was he threatening them?

The terrible thoughts chased one another around and around in my mind as I struggled to silence them. Moth rumbled, snuggling closer to me, and I tried to let the drone of his purr fill my mind.

I must have managed it eventually. Because I was sound asleep the next morning when a piercing shriek tore me awake.

CHAPTER SEVEN

*T*hieves! Scalawags! Intruders!"

I bolted upright, blinking in the bright morning sunlight that was streaming through the nearby window. It lit the entire room: the hearth, the armoire, the washstand. And the woman standing at the foot of the bed, brandishing a broom like a spear. "Out! Out, you vagrants!"

The handle poked my shoulder. I yelped, scrambling back to press myself against the headboard. Moth had leaped up as well. He crouched beside me, hissing, his tail puffed with anger. Vycorax had already rolled away, landing neatly on the floor beside the bed and seizing her quarterstaff. She swept it out, catching the next poke of the woman's broom. With a sharp twist, she sent the broom flying away, then spun her staff around to jab at our enemy.

Who really shouldn't *be* our enemy, given she was the same kind-eyed innkeeper who had ushered us into this very room last night.

"What's the meaning of this?" demanded Vycorax. "We paid for a full night's stay. And breakfast! Not a beating!"

"I've never seen you before in my life," sputtered the woman, her cheeks flushed. She started to slide sideways, clearly bent on recovering her broom.

"You saw my silver well enough last night." Vycorax frowned at the woman. "Maybe you spent too much time at the festival wine-stalls."

"Last night?" The woman made a graceful dodge, grabbing up her broom again. "The prince's festival is today. Which is why I've no time to deal with you hooligans dirtying one of my rooms when I'm expecting a full house tonight!"

She made as if to sweep me—quite literally—out of the bed, but just as she drew back her broom, someone darted through the door behind her. "Elfara, stop!"

The innkeeper, Elfara, whirled round. "Trudibeth?"

Then she gasped. So did I. Even Vycorax drew in a sharp breath.

The woman who'd just entered, Trudibeth, was clearly blighted. Her skin was purplish, mottled like a bruise. Her ears were long and tufted, like those of a goat, and she had two tusk-like teeth curling over her bottom lip. But her eyes were soft and blue and fixed on the innkeeper with an intense desperation.

Then she gave herself a small shake. She held up her hands, palms out. "It's me, Elf. Trudibeth. Ha, I got you, didn't I? These festival masks are something, aren't they? You didn't even recognize your own wife!" She laughed, but there was a bitterness beneath it.

Elfara trembled, staring at the monstrous woman, her brows knit together. As if she were trying to unravel a knot with her mind, to see something through the shadows. The confusion in her eyes made me feel hollow, like I was watching someone teetering at the edge of a cliff, and there was nothing I could do to stop them from falling. But after a moment, her expression slowly cleared.

"Trudi?" Her voice trembled, but it grew stronger as she spoke. "Stars, it *is* you! Why are you wearing that ridiculous mask?"

The tusked woman brushed a hand over her long ears. "Oh, this," she said lightly. "I got it at one of the shops setting up out on the green. I'm just trying it out. I thought I'd wear it later, for the dancing."

Elfara stalked over to slap Trudibeth lightly on the shoulder. If I hadn't been watching Trudibeth so closely, I wouldn't have noticed how she cringed. How she was still standing tense, like someone braced against a door they didn't want opened.

"So that's where you've been?" demanded Elfara, though her voice was softer now, teasing. "Off having fun, leaving me to deal with these interlopers, hmm?" She pointed to the three of us, still cowering. Well, *I* was cowering; Moth and Vycorax were crouching in readiness.

Trudibeth gave us a sharp look. One tufted ear twitched. It was most definitely not a mask. But Elfara had accepted the explanation, almost as if she didn't want to understand the truth. Or couldn't see it.

The tusked woman made a tsking sound. "These young

ladies are paying customers, Elf!" She shook her head. "This is my fault. I must have forgotten to tell you. They arrived late, after you were already asleep."

Elfara still looked puzzled. Like someone trying to remember a dream. Or trying to wake from one. "I—maybe I forgot. My mind is like a sieve these days. I'm sorry, Trudi. Oh dear. I'm so sorry," she added, dipping her head to Vycorax and me, blinking several times, as if trying to clear a dazzle from her eyes.

"No harm done," said Trudibeth, squeezing Elfara's shoulder. "Why don't you go get started on breakfast for our guests? I'll make sure they have what they need for washing up."

She led Elfara gently but firmly to the door. As soon as her back was turned, Vycorax leaned close, whispering urgently. "That's not a mask. She's blighted. We need to get out of here."

"No. We need answers," I whispered back. "And she just helped us avoid a walloping."

Vycorax sniffed. "Speak for yourself. I had no intention of getting walloped by a *broom*."

The door clicked closed. Elfara was gone. Trudibeth regarded us, her arms crossed over her broad chest. "So. You're not timespun. Are you blighted?"

"No," snapped Vycorax before I could respond.

Trudibeth gave a small shake of her head, eyes wide with wonder. "But then how . . . ? Are you from *outside*?"

I stood, brushing out the hem of my shirt. One of my

fingers caught in a tear. The mark of my passage through the thorns. It seemed foolish to pretend. Trudibeth clearly knew more than the others in Fenhollow. But how?

"Yes," I said. "My name is Fable. This is Vycorax. And Moth," I added, as he sprang back up onto the bed beside me. "We came through the thorns yesterday. Lady Mirachne brought us."

I should probably have admitted that I was blighted too. But I'd kept the secret so close, so tight, it was hard to break. And what would Trudi think? She might *look* monstrous, but I was the one who stole people's faces.

Trudibeth uncrossed her arms. They hung stiff along her sides. "Then you're here to break the curse." A note of desperate longing edged her voice. Like someone who had almost given up on a long-held dream.

"You know about the curse?" I asked. "Everyone at the festival last night acted like it hadn't happened yet."

"Because they're timespun," said Trudibeth, sighing heavily.

"What does that mean?"

"It means, as far as they're concerned, the festival wasn't last night. It's tonight."

Vycorax and I shared a look. "That doesn't make sense," I said. "We were there. We ate sausages. We played games."

"You expect a blighted realm to make sense?" asked Trudibeth, her purple lips curving around her tusks. "I'll explain as best I understand. It was the eve of Prince Rylain's birthday, and all the realm was in a tizzy. Elf and I were beside ourselves with the preparations, the village festival, all of it. It was"—she sighed, looking out the window for a moment—"a wonderful day. Until just before midnight. I'd gone out to the barn to check on the horses, and I saw something, out in the woods. Sparks of light, but they were twisting and shimmering. I went closer, and one of them touched me, and then . . . I was this." She gestured to her purple skin, her ears, her tusks. "Blighted."

"It must have been a twist!" Vycorax frowned fiercely. "So *that* was when the curse struck. Rylain saw his reflection, fell asleep, and the demon took his place and released the blight."

Trudibeth shrugged. "I don't know. I've heard stories from other folks like me, folks who can still move freely, telling of the demon in Glimmerdark Castle. But I've not dared to go see for myself. Elfara needs me. My village needs me."

"What's wrong with them?" I asked. "You said something about being timespun?"

"It's part of the curse, as best I can tell," said Trudibeth. "All the Mirrorwood is stuck, trapped in that last day, the eve of Prince Rylain's birthday. Elfara, our daughters, the other folks here in Fenhollow, they don't know anything's amiss. Every day they wake just as they did the day the curse fell. The only folks who aren't affected are those of us with blights. We're the only ones who can travel freely. The only ones who can see what's really going on. Much good that it does us," she added bitterly.

"That must be what Mirachne meant," I said, "about the

entire realm being asleep." It had sounded peaceful enough when she'd told us. A kindness. But this wasn't kind. At least not for Trudibeth and the others like her.

"They just keep reliving the same day?" Vycorax looked boggled. "Can't you explain what's really going on?"

Trudibeth's shoulders sagged. She leaned heavily against the wall. "There's no point. And . . . I don't want them to look at me and see a monster."

Sympathy stabbed me. Even Vycorax looked uncomfortable. But Trudibeth shook herself, stood straight, and fixed us both with a stern look. "I knew the Subtle Powers wouldn't abandon us. I knew someday someone would come to break the curse. So. Here you are. Tell me how I can help you."

We left the village a few hours later. Elfara made up for our rude awakening with an enormous breakfast of pancakes with raspberries and honey, while Trudibeth scrounged up some extra supplies and clothing. I traded my torn home-spun clothes for a soft rose-colored shirt and nut-brown breeches. The innkeepers' two adorable daughters plied Moth with treats and asked Vycorax endless questions about her quarterstaff.

And then it was time to hunt the Withering.

"Have you ever actually seen it?" asked Vycorax as we followed Trudibeth over the stone bridge, away from the village of Fenhollow. Back in the green, folks were busy setting up the tents for the festival. I shook my head at the strangeness of it all. What happened at midnight? Did they collapse back into piles of canvas and rope and secretly roll themselves away?

"Only once," said Trudibeth, shuddering as she turned aside from the main road, taking us along a narrower track that cut across a meadow toward a distant forest. As best I could judge, we were heading deeper into the heart of the cursed land. Closer to the prince's castle.

"I didn't get a good look. It was too far away—thank the Powers—and edging on twilight. All I could see of it was a sort of smudge of gray. It moved like a hunting beast, crouched low along the earth. I was lucky it was on someone else's trail. Not so lucky for them, though, poor soul." She shook her head.

"Lady Mirachne told us it completely obliterates its prey," Vycorax said. She wore new breeches and a clean snowy-white shirt but had kept her blighthunter's vest in spite of the several thorn-torn rents that slashed the crimson wool. We both carried heavy packs now, full of travel provisions and warm bedrolls. Moth, unburdened, pranced beside me, occasionally slinking off into the grasses to investigate an enticing rustle.

"From what I've seen, that's true," said Trudibeth darkly. "See there, to the left."

She pointed to a small cottage near the edge of the woods. It looked abandoned. As we drew closer, I could see why.

Two of the walls were normal, whitewashed stone and mud. But the other two . . . they weren't *anything* at all. A hollow gray, like a morning mist that eats up the world. A formless *nothing* so empty and bare, it made my stomach flip just to see it.

Vycorax glowered at the grayness, gripping her quarter-staff as if she were considering giving it a good thwack. "The Withering did this?"

"Yes," said Trudibeth.

I took a step closer, then knelt near a bit of the grayness that pooled around the base of the cottage. Though "pool" wasn't really the right word. The shape of it was jaggedy. More like the holes I used to tear in the knees of my trousers. Fragments of moss and earth fringed the edges.

Vycorax stepped up beside me, gingerly tapping the tip of her staff against the grayness. The weapon sank into it. A finger length, a hand span, a foot. It was as if there was nothing there. No hidden cottage wall, no earth. *Nothing*. The staff itself appeared unharmed, but I scuttled back a few paces just to be safe.

"I wonder what would happen if you fell in," mused Vycorax. "What?" she added, at my look of horror. "It could turn out useful. You know. If we were being chased by another murder-sheep."

Only a hunter would see a pit of all-consuming emptiness and think of it as "useful." My stomach was already churning just looking at the stuff. Was that what I'd look like if I had no stolen face? Gray oblivion?

"This is the closest it's come to Fenhollow, thank the Powers." Trudibeth glanced away, scanning the nearby

meadows uneasily. "Elfara, our girls, the other timespun—
they wouldn't be able to run. They'd be trapped. Just like the
folks who lived here."

A new wave of horror surged through me as I stared at
the cottage. "People lived here?"

Trudibeth nodded grimly. She pointed to something
along the half-eaten wall. I squinted. It was the corner of
a window. And there, along the sill, something pinkish. A
hand. Disembodied, it hung there, gripping what was left of
the sill, frozen in the act of shoving it open. Probably trying
to escape as their home vanished around them.

"We have to stop this," I said fiercely. No one should have
to suffer that. No one.

Vycorax stared at the terrible scene, her knuckles pale as
she gripped her quarterstaff tightly. "We will."

I frowned. "You think the Withering is part of the curse?"
I turned to Trudibeth. "When did it first appear? Was it
when everything else changed?"

She scratched one tufted ear. "I'd never heard of it
appearing before that, except in fairy tales. I met another
blighted fleeing from the north a while back. He said it was
even worse up there. Entire forests blotted out. Farms gone.
Whole villages . . ." She trailed off, glancing back south, the
direction we'd come from, and swallowed hard.

Vycorax thumped her quarterstaff into the earth. "What
matters right now is finding the Withering's lair and getting
that tooth. Once we slay the demon and break the curse, it
should set everything to right."

I chewed the inside of my cheek, wishing I'd thought to ask Mirachne more about the Withering. But surely she would have told us, if it was important. She wanted us to break the curse.

"Is this where you saw it?" I asked Trudibeth.

She shook her head. "No. I found the cottage this way. I was farther north when I saw the Withering itself."

"Can you show us?"

Trudibeth hesitated. One of her long ears flicked. Then she squared her shoulders. "Yes. Of course. This way."

She set off across the meadow. Vycorax, Moth, and I followed, the soft grass billowy under our feet. It was all so lovely. And yet I could feel the hollow ache of that ravaged cottage behind me like a missing tooth. Like the empty chair at our kitchen table after my nana died.

And we were hunting the creature that had done that. It was enough to make my teeth chatter. I quickened my steps as the grasses grew taller, holding my eyes on the crimson flash of Vycorax's vest, marching relentlessly onward.

"It's not that much farther," said Trudibeth, pointing to a clump of willows ahead. "You can see the trail from those trees."

"Do you need to rest?" I asked when she made no move to continue.

She tugged at one of her ears. "No. I just don't usually go this far from home, in case the Withering comes. I might be the only one who could save them."

"How?" I asked.

She gave a wry smile. "I'm no warrior. Just an innkeeper. But I figure I could at least lead it away."

A chill danced over my skin, even though I was standing in the warm sun. Nearby, Moth pounced on a stray leaf. Everything seemed so utterly peaceful here, and yet it could all be shattered in an instant.

"You should go back," I said abruptly. "You've done enough. You shouldn't take any more risks. You've got Elfara and your daughters to think about."

Trudibeth grinned at me around her tusks. "You're the chosen of Mirachne. It's the least I can do. It's worth the risk if it helps you break the curse. If you can free the timespun and let us live our lives again."

The way she looked at me set a strange tingling up my spine. I'd come here to free myself. I hadn't considered that there might be other folks as trapped as I was. Or worse. I might not have a real face, but I had my family. They loved me. I had twelve years of memories, of moments of joy and sorrow strung like beads along the thread of my life.

Trudibeth had only a single bead. Over and over again, it slipped onto the thread, then off again. And if the Withering found her, if it found Elfara and their daughters, she'd lose even that.

We needed the Withering's Tooth. We needed to destroy the demon prince and wake this cursed land.

"I promise we'll set things right," I told her. "But this is enough. We can take it from here."

Vycorax, who had continued on toward the willows, gave

a shout. "I think I see the trail." She lifted her hand, shielding her eyes from the sun as she squinted at something I couldn't see.

Then she yelped, ducking low as she scrambled back to join us. "Get down!"

We crouched behind a clump of marsh grass. I scooped Moth into my arms, curling him against my chest protectively as I peered past the feathery fronds, trying to spot whatever had spooked Vycorax.

"What is it?" I whispered. "What did you see?"

"Nothing," she answered, her voice hollow. "It's *nothing*."

And finally I saw it.

There was *something*. Something my eyes couldn't quite latch on to. Something that slipped through the distant marsh, a shadow half-seen. A quiver of hot air above a fire.

And behind it: a trail of ragged gray blotches, ripped into the earth. As if each footfall tore away a bit of the world, leaving only oblivion behind.

The Withering!

CHAPTER EIGHT

Dread flooded me, my heart beating *run, run, run*. But the Withering had halted. I could almost make out the shape now. There was something wolfish about it. Four legs. Powerful shoulders.

I held my breath as its blunt muzzle blurred, lifting against the blue sky. Like a hound casting for a scent on the breeze.

"Is it hunting us?" I whispered. "Does it know we're here? Do you think if we just stay quiet it won't notice?"

Across the grassy meadow, the Withering gave a long, low growl. The deep rumble filled my ears, rattling my bones. Slowly, terribly, it turned that massive wolfish head straight toward us.

Trudibeth's long ears flattened. "I think it already noticed."

"Then we have to run," said Vycorax. "Try to lose it and double back onto its trail."

"No," said Trudibeth. Her jaw tightened, tusks jutting defiantly. "Once I distract it, you need to slip past and follow its tracks. Find its lair and finish your mission."

"Distract it?" I sputtered. "No. Trudi, you can't do that!"

"Yes," she said grimly, "I can. I'm fast. Hopefully fast enough to get it a good distance away. Keep it away from you. And Fenhollow."

The Withering had begun to stalk forward, each footfall rending the earth with slashes of gray. The air tasted like winter, freezing my lungs, shriveling my hope.

"There's got to be another way," said Vycorax.

"End this," said Trudibeth, her blue eyes fixed on us. "Set my family free. Do that. Please." Then she was gone, racing away back along the track. She cut sideways, out into the meadow, and started shouting and waving her hands.

The Withering's head swung abruptly toward her. Its growl intensified, becoming a bellow. One paw scraped the ground, tearing a swath of grayness.

"That's right, you fiend," snarled Trudibeth. "Catch me if you can." Then she dashed away into the forest. The Withering gave another bellow before leaping in pursuit.

"We need to help her!" I started to run after them, but Vycorax grabbed my arm.

"We can't! She's doing this to give us a chance!"

"She's going to die!" I wrenched against her grasp. "You're just going to let her sacrifice herself?"

Her expression crumpled, her entire body hunched as if my words had been a blow, a punch to her gut. "Yes," she said. "Because we have a mission, Fable. She knows what she's doing. We have to honor that."

I shook my head. All of me was shaking, trembling with frustration. There had to be *something* we could do!

Moth spoke, urgent in my mind. *Fable. We need to go. You do not wish for it to catch us, do you?*

I growled through gritted teeth and forced myself to turn

away. To settle my pack on my shoulders and follow Vycorax along the trail of the Withering.

But inside thundered a single thought: I was going to stop this. I was going to break the curse. No matter what.

We traveled in silence for most of the day. Vycorax followed the trail, and I followed Vycorax. But my thoughts kept drifting back to the meadow, to that last memory of Trudibeth racing away with the Withering behind her.

I kept spinning the memory around and around, looking at it from every angle, searching for something I'd missed. A way to change it. To fix it. Which was silly, of course. It was done. Even the timeless magic couldn't undo it, any more than it could fix that half-obliterated cottage we'd seen. If the Withering had gotten Trudibeth, she was already gone.

It didn't help that by midafternoon, the trail had led us into a sodden, squelching bog. Ramshackle wooden walkways and bridges spanned the scummy water in places, but more often than not we had to scrabble our way between the islands of turf, occasionally clambering over ridges of rough granite that poked from the mire like the rotting teeth of a sunken giant.

No, Moth said, hissing when I tried to carry him across a bit of soggy turf. *It is wet, Fable. There is mud.* He leaped away, bounding onto one of the ramshackle wooden walkways. His tail lashed. *This way is much better.*

I gave the rotten planks a wary look. When I'd tested it,

the wood had creaked ominously. "We're too heavy to go that way," I said.

He spat, as if disgusted with humans in general. *I will find you when it is dry again.* Turning tail, he pranced off along the walkway.

If only I could follow. My boots were caked with sticky black mud. Slogging through the mire was exhausting work, and I was beginning to falter. Sweat dribbled down my back. Spotting a nearby boulder, I sank down, my pulse pounding in my ears.

"We need to keep moving," said Vycorax, peering up at the dusky sky. "It'll be dark soon."

"I just need to catch my breath." My entire body felt as limp as an overcooked noodle.

"We're not going to be able to follow the trail if it gets dark," said Vycorax. She swept her staff toward a distant patch of wither, narrowly missing a crow that had been perched on a nearby stump. The bird flapped into the air, cawing in protest. "Trudibeth gave us this chance. We can't waste it."

My fingers gripped the rough stone under me. "Do you think she got away?"

Vycorax was quiet for a long moment. "I don't know. But you can't let yourself think about it."

I gave a hollow laugh. "How? I keep seeing it, over and over. Seeing her running away. Seeing that thing chasing after her. Blight, and that cottage. That *hand*."

"So you put it in the box."

"What box?" I glanced around, half expecting to find an abandoned trunk nearby.

"You imagine it," she said. "A big, strong box tucked away in the back of your mind. Anything you don't want to think about, anything sad or scary that will distract you, you stuff it in that box, and you lock it tight."

"And that works?" I tilted my head, eyeing Vycorax, wondering what she had to lock away.

Her lips tightened briefly. "Most of the time. My father taught me. It's part of our training. So you can focus on the mission."

Right. And I knew all too well what her missions were like. I narrowed my eyes. "So when he ordered you to kill me, what happened? Did you forget to close the lid?"

Now she looked uncomfortable, eyes shifting away, watching the crow spiral over us. "Maybe."

"Because I looked like you."

"No. It wasn't just that."

I was about to ask what it was, then, but my own words suddenly rang back to me, driving away other thoughts. *Because I looked like you.*

And I still did. I had been wearing her face for well over a day now. The crow, which had settled onto a large boulder, gave a chuckling croak, as if laughing at me for not realizing it sooner.

"Blight!" No wonder I was feeling tired. And no wonder Vycorax was so spry. The stolen face must be starting to fade, whatever energy I'd taken returning to its proper place. I pressed my hands to my cheeks and ran my fingertips lightly over the bones, the nose, the brows of Vycorax's face, trying to compare it to the original that was currently frowning at me.

"What's wrong?" she asked.

"My face is fading. It only lasts for a day or two after I borrow it."

She snorted. "Good. Because you didn't *borrow* it. You *stole* it."

"It's not good," I said. "That's why I feel so wretched. I'm fading!"

"What do you mean? Aren't you just going to"—she waved her hands at me—"go back to your real face?"

"I don't *have* a real face!" The words tore out of me, harsh and jagged. Even the crow was silent, tilting his head one way, then the next, watching me with his scarlet eyes.

Vycorax shook her head. "You must. Otherwise . . ."

I drew in a long breath, trying to regain control of my quivering chest. "Exactly. Otherwise I fade away and die."

For a moment, I thought I saw pity in her eyes. Then she took a step back, setting her quarterstaff between us. Of course she'd see that as a threat.

"I'm not asking to take your face again," I told her.

"You didn't ask last time, either."

"Last time you were trying to kill me!" Outrage gave me a burst of energy. I stood, facing her, hands tightened to fists.

"If you hunters would leave people like me alone, I wouldn't have had to do any of it! I could've stayed at home. With my family. I never would've had to come to this cursed place."

I knew I sounded angry. I *was* angry. Trudibeth had sacrificed herself, but we still hadn't found the den of the Withering and it was nearly dark. I was hot, stinky, and tired. And in another day, I wouldn't even be that. Only an empty husk.

Unless I took a face. My fingernails dug into my palms as I stared at Vycorax. Her own knuckles paled as she gripped her staff tighter.

It wouldn't stop me, though. All it took was one touch. Then I'd be strong again. I'd have another day in her face to try to break this curse and be free. It would be so easy.

The thoughts curled and squirmed in my mind like maggots. It wasn't as if we were friends. Sure, she'd given me a plush rabbit, but she'd also tried to kill me! She was sharp and quick and dangerous. It was foolish to think we could work together.

"I don't need you or your face," I snarled. "Why would I want to look like a stinking hunter any longer than I have to? I'll find another way."

"How?" Vycorax demanded. "There's no one else out here."

The crow gave a caw as if in protest.

"I know that! You don't need to rub it in!"

"I'm not." She puffed out a frustrated breath. "I'm just trying to—"

"Girl need face?"

The words had come from the direction of the crow, still perched nearby on a toothy rock. We both stared at it. It looked like a perfectly normal crow, aside from its red eyes.

I cleared my throat. "Sorry, but did you just say something?"

"Nah. Not say 'something.' Say 'girl need face?'"

"You can talk!"

The crow fluffed his wings. "So can you."

I supposed I shouldn't be so surprised. This was the Mirrorwood after all. Where villages could get stuck in time and an invisible monster could eat away half a cottage.

"We make deal," croaked the crow. "You need face?"

"Yes," I said. "But . . . what do you mean 'deal'?"

"I have face. Trade to girl."

"Trade for what?" I asked warily.

The crow tilted his head, one red eye glittering as it roamed over me. He made a soft creaking noise. "Pretty buttons. Shiny."

I glanced down to the front of my borrowed shirt. The buttons were indeed quite shiny, sparkling with shifting colors even in the failing light of the day. A lump clogged my throat. Elfara had said they were shells from some distant shifting sea. But I'd gladly give them all up if it saved me from fading away.

Still, there was one slight problem with this plan.

"You have a lovely beak and feathers," I said, "but I can't take animal faces." It would have made my life considerably easier, though I'm sure Indigo would've teased me mercilessly.

The crow gave a cackle that sounded like a laugh. "Not *crow* face. Other face. Good face."

"Wait, what does that mean?" I asked. "If it's not your face, whose is it?"

"I go get. Stay there. Don't move. Trade button for face." He cocked his head, scarlet eye fixing me with an oddly demanding stare. "We have deal, yes?"

"Yes," I said, hastily tugging free one of the buttons.

"Fable," began Vycorax, "maybe you shouldn't—"

"Any face is better than fading away," I said. Not that she would understand. Besides, if I didn't like it, I wouldn't use it. No harm done. I'd just keep looking. I held out the button to the crow. "We have a deal."

The crow gave a loud croak. "Good, good. I get face. Back soon." He hopped lightly onto my hand, seizing the button in his beak. Then he launched himself into the air, flapping away.

I stood, arms crossed, feeling Vycorax's eyes burning into me as the minutes slipped past.

"Don't look at me like that," I told her. "It's not like you gave me any other choice."

"That's not fair." She actually looked wounded. Like I'd hurt her feelings.

"Fair?" I snapped. "Fair? Was it fair that I got blighted when I was a baby? Never even knowing who I really am? That I had to live my life afraid someone like your father was going to find out what I was and murder me? Is that fair?"

Vycorax looked away. "No. It's not." She breathed in. Held it. Then let it out. "I'm sorry, Fable."

I huffed. My insides still felt trembly from my outburst. I'd been expecting . . . something else. Not an apology. Now I didn't know what to think.

"It just seems strange, doesn't it?" she asked. "Where could he possibly be getting a face? We haven't seen anyone out here. What if he comes back with a swamp monster? This is *too* easy to be good."

"So long as it has a mouth and eyes, it could be a gorgon for all I care."

Vycorax looked past me, her brows pulling together. "It looks a bit small to be a gorgon."

"What?" I glanced over my shoulder to see the crow flapping toward us. Something dangled from his feet. Something that was *not* a face. He swooped over me, letting it fall into my hands.

It was a pocket watch. The sort that fancy folk wore on a chain across their coats. This one had been fine, once. But the polished golden case was clotted with mud. The glass was cracked, part of it missing. And beneath, the stern black hands stood frozen at eleven.

Meanwhile, the crow had settled himself back onto the boulder. His unnerving red eyes watched me.

"What's this supposed to be?" I demanded, holding up the watch. "You promised you'd bring me a face for that shiny."

"Is face," said the crow. "Clock face."

Vycorax snickered.

I ignored her. "But I need a real face!"

"Is real," said the crow.

"A real *person* face," I said. "With eyes and a mouth and a nose! Ugh." I waved my hands, scrubbing the useless conversation from the air. I'd wasted enough time on this. Time we could have been searching for the den of the Withering. "Never mind," I said, turning away, prepared to march deeper into the mire. "I'll just keep loo—oop!"

My foot had caught on something, nearly tripping me. I tugged it, but it wouldn't move. Had I sunk into the mud? I wrenched again, but my boot didn't budge.

"What's going on?" A raw edge of panic ran through my words. Vycorax ran to help, holding the boot while I tried to tug my foot free, but even that didn't work. This was more than mud and mire. Something else was pinning me here. Something invisible. Something *magical.*

I blinked at the crow. "What did you do?"

"I? I?" he croaked, sounding amused. "I did nothing. You were the one who agreed to the terms of our bargain. I merely fulfilled them."

I stared at the black bird. His voice sounded different now. Less harsh, more clear and human.

"Who . . . who are you?" I managed to ask.

The crow cocked his head. His crimson eyes glinted with dangerous mischief. Then he spread his wings. Beat them once, twice.

On the third sweep, he rose, black feathers stretching, reaching out, shimmering into the sweep of a long cloak. His beak melted away, revealing a man's face, long and lean and paper-white, thin lips quirked. Only the crimson eyes remained the same, watching me with wicked merriment.

"Haven't you figured that out already?" He made a tsking noise. "I really had hoped for a more worthy adversary this time."

Vycorax gasped, pressing closer beside me. "You're the Bannon!"

The crow man's smile widened fearsomely. He bowed low, his cloak of black feathers whispering like a thousand secrets as it swirled around him. "At your service."

"No. Not at our service. We don't want anything to do with you," snapped Vycorax. "This is all your fault!"

His grin only sharpened. "I take credit for many terrible things. Which exactly are you referring to?"

"The part where you cursed Prince Rylain and sent a demon to take his place and unleash the blight," I said, crossing my arms.

"Ah. You've been talking with my lady Mirachne."

"Yes," said Vycorax. "And we're under her protection. So you'd better let Fable go. Now."

The Bannon crossed his arms. "You really need to pay closer attention. We had a bargain, Fable and I. The terms were met."

"I never agreed to getting stuck here!" Heat flared in my

chest. He was lying. "All I said was that I'd give you that button if you brought me a face."

"I go get," croaked the Bannon, his voice gravelly and crow-like again. "Stay there. *Don't move.* Trade button for face. We have deal, yes?"

I stared at him, my hot anger shivering into cold dread. Blight me. I hadn't paid attention. He'd been just a crow. Silly and foolish, after a shiny button, nothing more. A faint, hopeless sigh slipped out of me.

I was the fool. A fool who was now trapped.

Chapter Nine

*T*he Bannon chuckled, his voice returning to smooth sweetness. "You agreed. And so you are bound."

"You're one of the Subtle Powers," I said. "If you wanted to stop me from trying to break the curse, you could have just magicked us into a pit or something. Why play games? Tell me what you really want."

"Oh, but I *like* games," said the Bannon. "And I never said I wanted to stop you from breaking the curse."

Talking with him was like trying to catch a bit of dandelion fluff. No matter how you jumped and snatched, it twisted away from your grasp. Sometimes the best thing was just to stop trying. To stand still and let it float down onto your hand.

The Bannon regarded me. He looked amused. I pressed my lips tighter, staring back. Waiting. Vycorax, meanwhile, had shifted her grip on her quarterstaff, as if she were preparing to beat the answers out of the Bannon if necessary.

"Oh, very well," he said, giving a dramatic sigh. "I promise to release you now if you swear not to seek the Withering's Tooth."

Invisible wings seemed to hum over my skin. The air

felt thick, heavy enough to press me down with expectation. The Bannon's eyes were hungry rubies, awaiting an answer.

"No," I said. "We need that tooth to break the curse. Lady Mirachne told us everything."

He gave a sharp laugh. "Mirachne can't be trusted. The tooth will only make things worse."

"Oh, right," said Vycorax. "But I suppose we can trust *you*. The lord of schemes and trickery?"

His crimson eyes glinted. "At least I always keep my word. I swear, if you promise to abandon the tooth, I will release you."

I glared back at him. "I'm not making any more bargains."

He sighed. "How disappointing. I had such high hopes for you. Ah, well. I do apologize for trapping you in such a dismal place. But, well, a bargain is a bargain. And I really can't have you waking the prince."

Vycorax had gone strangely tense beside me. She gave me a sidelong glance. Had she come up with a plan? Seen some way to escape this mess?

"Fable," she said, her voice strange and flat. "He's right. A bargain is a bargain. I'm sorry."

"Sorry?" I shook my head. "Sorry for what?"

"It was *your* bargain," she said. "Not mine."

For a long moment her dark eyes held mine. Then she spun around and tore off into the mire, leaping from rock to rock.

I gasped. Even the Bannon looked startled, his black

brows arching as he watched Vycorax vanish over one of the rocky ridges. Only her voice echoed back.

"I need to break the curse, Fable. With or without you."

I stood utterly still. My legs, my belly, my chest, all of me seemed to have turned to stone. Everything except my eyes, still fixed on the ridge.

But Vycorax was gone. She'd abandoned me to my fate.

"Honestly, I'm surprised," said the Bannon. "I thought you two were friends."

"Obviously not," I growled. "Obviously we were just . . . just . . ." My throat squeezed. It made perfect sense. Vycorax wanted to break the curse. That was what really mattered. She didn't need me. She was probably glad to be rid of me. I drew in a long, shuddering breath. It was fine. I'd be fine. I'd figure my way out of this. I didn't need her either.

The Bannon sighed. "Then I'll have to stop her the old-fashioned way." He gave me a cheeky grin. "Stay right there."

He swirled his cloak, spinning smaller, shifting back into a croaking crow that flapped up and away.

Leaving me alone.

My chest ached. If I breathed too deeply, I was afraid I might break something rare and fragile. Something that already felt cracked.

"Moth?" I said, curling my arms around my chest. "Moth? Please come back. I need you."

Nothing.

I sank into a crouch, huddling against the mud. So this

was it. And maybe it was a fitting end. I'd drift down under the slimy water. Easy enough to sink away, just another faded, forgotten thing.

For a long moment I bowed my head. Listened to the creak of insects, the hum of the tiny flies crowding around my head. A faint drip of water somewhere. The thrum of my own defiant heart.

I was still here. I was still me. And I hadn't faded yet. There must be some way to escape. Some loophole in the bargain. I'd promised not to move. And to trade the shiny button for the face.

I gripped the pocket watch, staring down at the cracked glass, the frozen hands. Could it be that simple? I couldn't give it back. But if I rejected it, would it reset the bargain?

There was only one way to find out. Hefting the watch, I took aim at a twisted tree growing from a large split boulder. Then I threw as hard as I could.

Just as Vycorax stepped out from behind the tree.

The watch smacked her square in the middle of her forehead. "Ouch!" She rubbed her brow, then glared at me. "Was that really necessary?"

I stared at her blankly. "You came back! But you said you needed to go break the curse!"

"Of course I did! It wasn't going to work unless the Bannon thought I was really abandoning you. I'd have been back sooner, but I needed to be sure he'd followed my false trail." She crouched, plucking the pocket watch from the earth. "There's no need to throw things at me."

"I wasn't," I said. "I was trying to break the bargain."

"Well? Did it work?"

I gulped. Bracing myself, I tried to lift my foot. The mire released it with a sucking squelch.

"Yes!" I did a little jig of victory, twirling and laughing. When I spun to a stop, I saw Vycorax was grinning back at me. For a brief moment our smiles met. I felt something flash between us. Something like the silent jokes I shared with Allegra. Something like the way I always knew when Indigo wanted me to pass them the pickles at the supper table. Something unspoken and unseen but as warm as the sun.

I coughed. "Thanks for coming back."

She gave a small shrug. "I'm a hunter. I don't leave my partner behind."

"Partner" didn't sound like the right word for what we were. But then, I didn't have anything better. We weren't friends, or even really allies. Was there a word for "person-ordered-to-kill-you-who-also-wants-to-break-your-curse-and-likes-your-cat"? Maybe if I survived this and made it home with my true face, I could ask Indigo to invent one.

The silence had turned awkward. Probably a sign that I should be focusing on our actual mission.

"Where now?" I asked. "The Bannon's going to be looking for you. For both of us, once he realizes I escaped. And it's getting dark."

It was dusk by then. A veil of mist had settled over the grim landscape, turning the sagging willows into long-fingered ghouls. "We need to find somewhere safe to rest," I said. "Like you said, it's too dangerous to keep searching in the dark."

"I saw a place we can hide while I was leading the Bannon away," said Vycorax. "Come on, I'll show you."

"Well? What do you think?" Vycorax asked. We stood— crouched, really—inside a low cave with a damp earth floor and clammy walls. The narrow mouth opened onto a wide stretch of open mire, now lost in the gloom of night.

Something in the distance gave an eerie wail. My heart twinged, thinking of Moth. He'd spent plenty of nights away back home, though. I had to believe he was okay. Probably having the time of his lives, chasing down swamp rats or something. He'd be back soon. He wouldn't leave me. Not here.

I backed deeper into the cave. "I think it's a good thing you spotted this place."

Vycorax looked pleased. "It's one of my father's rules. Always be aware of your surroundings. You never know when you might need a defensible position."

She busied herself setting out her bedroll along one side of the cavern. I did the same, laying mine against the opposite wall. It was dim, but not fully dark, thanks to a handful of fireflies that bobbled and sparked through the air, their colors shifting from gold to green to blue to violet to crimson to orange and back again, each one a tiny humming rainbow.

We shared some of the supplies Elfara had packed for us. "Why do you suppose the Bannon said that?" I asked between nibbles of apple cake. "About the tooth making things worse?"

Vycorax rolled her eyes. "Because he's a trickster who enjoys tormenting mortals. He doesn't need any other reason."

I picked a bit of walnut from the cake, rolling it between my fingers. "I guess so. I just feel like there's something we're missing."

"We don't need to understand it. We need to *stop* it." Having finished her mushroom pie, Vycorax shrugged off her crimson vest. She dug through her pack, producing a small sewing kit. She squinted as she threaded the needle. "That means finding the Withering's Tooth and using it to get rid of the demon prince so the real prince can come back and fix everything."

"Get rid of." Not "kill." Maybe she didn't like that word any more than I did.

I brushed the crumbs from my lap, pulling my knees to my chest. My bones felt heavy as lead. Gingerly, I ran a hand over my face. Two eyes, a nose, a mouth. All still there. I'd survive another day, but I needed a new face soon.

I felt the prickle of Vycorax watching me and hastily turned the gesture into a casual brushing back of my hair. "So, say we do it. We get rid of the blight. Set the timespun free. What will you do then?"

"What do you mean?"

"Well. You're a hunter. If there's no more blight, what will you do?"

I might as well have asked what she'd do with a pet elephant. She blinked. "I . . . I hadn't thought about that." She bent back over her work, the needle slipping neatly through the red cloth. "There's always more evil in the world that needs to be put down. I suppose Father and I will go hunting it."

"Oh."

"What? Why do you sound disappointed?"

"I'm not. It's just . . . Do you really enjoy it? Do you really *want* to spend your whole life fighting monsters?"

"It doesn't matter what I want." She lifted the vest, biting off the thread. "Someone needs to stand up to the bad things in the world."

I curled my arms more tightly around my chest. Just a few days ago, I was one of those bad things. Maybe I still was, in her mind.

Vycorax wasn't looking at me, though. She stared at the crimson cloth bundled in her lap. "I won't let the blight hurt anyone else. It's my duty."

Anyone *else*? But before I could ask what she meant, Vycorax flung the question back at me. "What about you? If you're not blighted anymore, what will you do?"

That was easy. I'd dreamed it so often it was almost a memory. What did you call a memory of something that hadn't happened yet? I'd have to ask Indigo.

"I'll go back home. I'll be with my family again, for real this time."

"For real?" asked Vycorax. "What, were they making you live in the barn or something?"

"No! They love me. They're the reason I'm still alive."

"You mean they let you take their faces."

I cringed, though she hadn't said it like an accusation. "That's why I need to break this curse. Why I need my real face. So I can stop stealing their lives and be myself." I sighed. "Whoever that is."

"Don't you know?" Vycorax asked. "Getting your true face is one thing, but it's not like you don't know who you are. I mean, you must know whether you prefer butter or jam on toast and what your favorite color is. That sort of thing."

I shifted uncomfortably against the lumpy wall of the cave. "I don't know. I always choose orange because that's the color no one else picks. Allegra loves yellow, and Indigo loves, well, indigo, on principle, they say. Thespian is pink and Gavotte is red and Sonnet is black, and my mum and dad always pick blue and green."

"Well, good thing we're going to end the blight, then," drawled Vycorax. "How could you possibly survive without knowing your favorite color?"

"I know it sounds silly," I said. "But it's more than that. I just . . . I want to be *Fable*. I want to be sure I'm really me. Not just some sort of pretend person reflecting whatever face I steal."

"Well, I can answer that," Vycorax said dryly. "You're wearing my face, and I can tell you for a *fact* that I'm not the sort of person who makes deals with random crows in the middle of cursed swamps for broken pocket watches."

She pulled the watch from her pocket, dangling it from her fingers. The cracked glass of the face glinted, catching sparks of color from the handful of fireflies zooming lazily around our cave. I knew she was making fun of me, but not in a mean way. More like how my siblings might tease and poke and prod.

She flipped the watch in her fingers. "Seriously, though. Does anybody really know for sure who they are? I mean, I always thought I could destroy any evil. That I wasn't afraid to do whatever it took to be a hunter." She scrubbed at the back of the watch with her thumb, scraping away a bit of dirt as if it were the most important thing in the world. "But I couldn't kill you. Not even when Father ordered me to."

The cave felt suddenly colder. The warmth of our conversation, of teasing and rainbow fireflies, all of it winking out. Why was she telling me this?

"Oh," I said stiffly. "Well. Sorry you didn't get to murder me."

Vycorax looked up sharply. "What? No, that's not what I meant. I meant that I didn't know who I really was, either. I'm not someone who murders people just because they're blighted. I'm the kind of person who would rather slog through a blighted bog after a magic tooth to fix things properly."

"Oh. Well. Thanks, Vyx."

She stared at me. "Vyx?"

"Sorry," I said. "Vycorax. I just . . . Back home my siblings and I sometimes call each other by nicknames. Allegra is Leg and Sonnet is Sonny. It's silly, I know."

"And what are you?"

"Fey."

She arched a brow. "Not Bull? Because you're pretty stubborn sometimes." She shrugged. "Call me what you like."

My cheeks felt hot. Like I'd gone too far, but at the same time, I didn't regret it. It felt good. Having someone I could tease. Vyx wasn't my sister, but she was more than just my ally now. I liked her. I was glad she was here. Somehow, it made the ache of homesickness less. Especially with Moth off on his nocturnal adventures.

Our cave was silent again, but not so cold. Vycorax squinted at the watch. She held it up, peering more intently at the back side. "You said you wanted to learn more about the true prince? Here." She tossed it to me.

I didn't have time to dodge, and it landed square in my lap. Gingerly, I twitched one of my feet, sighing in relief as my heel lifted cleanly off the earth. Whatever magic the Bannon's bargain had held, it was apparently broken for good now.

"How is a pocket watch going to tell me anything about the prince?" I asked.

"Look at the back."

I did. And gasped. There were thin, curving letters engraved into the watch case. I angled them to catch the firefly light, reading aloud. "'To Prince Rylain of the Mirrorwood, on his thirteenth birthday.'"

Wonder bubbled in my chest. "This belonged to the true prince! Or, at least, someone was going to give it to him. But why did the Bannon have it? And why did he give it to me?"

"Just to cause trouble, no doubt."

I couldn't help staring at the thing. It had been quite fine, once. A worthy gift for a prince. But who had given it to him? Was it the Bannon himself? For all I knew, the watch might be what caused the blight in the first place. Maybe that was why the thing was cracked and dented.

I opened it, squinting at the inside of the case. It looked as if there could have been something set into it. A mirror? If so, it was gone now.

"You're probably right," I said as I tucked it away. "Let's hope we can get the Withering's Tooth before he causes any more."

Chapter Ten

I *woke to a warm weight* purring against my chest. Not the last blur of a dream. Not a wishful fancy. A solid, real, feline body.

"Moth!" I flung my arms around him, burying my face in his side even as he gave a yowl of protest.

You are squeezing me. I do not like to be squeezed.

I let him go, propping myself up on my elbows as he regarded me balefully. It was morning, bleak gray outside, but nothing could dull the golden sparks of joy leaping through me. Moth. He was back. He'd found me!

Vycorax was curled in her blanket, still asleep, so I tried to keep my voice low, even though I wanted to shout and sing. "Moth! Where have you been?"

A cat has secrets, Fable.

It was what he always said. Back home, Moth would sometimes vanish, returning days later with a self-satisfied smirk. Sometimes with a new notch in one ear. Sometimes ravenous, sometimes full and fat. He never told me where he went. I always assumed he was indulging in romantic escapades. Or hunting. Or setting down rivals in whatever mysterious feline hierarchy ruled the farm. It didn't really matter, because he always found me. Always knew me, no matter what face I was wearing.

I fought the tremendous urge to squash him to me. To keep him from ever leaving again. Instead, I contented myself with skritching the spot between his ears, luring him back close, coaxing out a purr that droned deep into my bones.

"I missed you," I told him shamelessly. Not that he'd feel one jot of guilt. He was a cat, after all. But still, it was the truth.

I know. He preened.

"If your head gets any bigger, your ears won't fit," I told him. "And meanwhile I almost got trapped forever by the Bannon. I needed you."

His whiskers quivered. *But you were not trapped. You escaped. So you did not need me.*

I blew out a breath. "That's not—oh, never mind. I'm just glad you're back."

He purred louder, rubbing his head against my chin, my cheek. I cuddled him for as long as he let me, but soon he leaped away to investigate my travel pack.

Fable, he said. *I am starving.*

I strongly doubted that. I knew how capable he was of finding his own meals. More likely, he was taking advantage of my happiness in seeing him again. And it was working.

"Hold on." I rolled over to reach for the buckle. "I was saving the last of the sausage for breakfast, but I suppose—*ooof.*"

My head spun as a wave of weakness ran through me. I braced myself against the floor.

You are gray, said Moth. *You are not supposed to be gray.*

No kidding. "I need a new face."

Moth looked across the cave to Vycorax. His tail lashed. *Then take one.*

"Not hers," I said. "I promised her I wouldn't."

That was foolish. I would never promise the mice not to hunt them.

"It's not the same thing, Moth. She's . . . my partner. If she wants to let me take her face, fine, but I'm not going to steal it."

Moth blinked. *So instead you will fade to nothing?*

"No, I'll find someone else."

Ah. And you will steal their *face instead.*

I gritted my teeth. He was right. My blight left me no option. If I wanted to live, I was going to have to steal someone's face. Not taking Vycorax's wasn't some sort of noble choice. It was purely practical. I needed her as an ally. Neither of us could've made it this far without the other.

Right, well, that was the whole point of coming here. To break my curse. So I'd never have to steal another face again.

"That must be it," said Vycorax as we crouched behind a fallen willow, peering at the hulking hill in the distance. It rose at the edge of the misty mire, strangely symmetrical, like one of the old barrows where folk from the age of the first queens had buried their dead.

Vycorax had picked up the trail of wither earlier that mist-tangled morning, not far from our cave. A slash of gray that was deeper than fog, torn into the dark mire. From there, more ragged patches of emptiness led us out of the depths of the bog. There was one only a few feet from my hiding spot. Even when I tried not to look at the thing, it seemed to cling to my vision. It was almost like when you looked at the sun too long and it left spots you couldn't blink away.

Did the Withering leave them deliberately? Maybe it just obliterated everything it touched. How could we possibly steal a tooth right out of the mouth of a monster like that?

I shook off the thoughts before they could creep inside my chest and chew away my courage. What mattered was that the trail led straight to a dark arch in the side of the barrow.

I gulped. This was it. "Do you think the Withering is in there now?"

"We'll have to get closer to be sure," said Vycorax.

I tried to imagine a box, a nice sturdy chest of oak, bound in brass, like the one Da kept Gran's old armor in. I took the visions of the Withering tearing its claws into me, shredding me to nothing, and shoved them into that chest.

But they kept escaping. Or re-forming. My breakfast twisted and sloshed, and for a moment I thought it was going to escape too.

"You all right?" asked Vycorax.

"No," I admitted. "I'm trying to use the box, but the bad thoughts keep getting out."

She frowned, brushing one hand over the front of her crimson vest, tracing one of the repairs she'd made last night. "I swear, Fable, I'll do whatever I have to do to keep you safe. Moth, too," she added.

Moth preened again. *I do not require protection.*

"He says thank you," I said, shooting him a look. His ears swiveled, his version of a shrug.

"I mean it," said Vycorax, her brown eyes fixed on me. "That's who I am. I'm a person who protects people. Especially my friends."

I flushed, staring at the tips of my boots. "I don't think your father would be happy to hear you calling a blighter your friend."

"He's not here," she said. "It's you and me now. This is our mission. Are you ready? What about your face? Is it—"

"It's fine."

It wasn't, really. It had been almost two full days since I stole Vycorax's face. My nose felt soft and blurry, my lips as if they might melt away. Another day, and they would be gone. I breathed in deep, holding the chilly, damp air in my chest. Then I exhaled. "Let's go."

We picked our way across the mire to the large barrow. Every few steps we paused, listening.

There was nothing. No birds, no frogs. Not even the hum of the tiny midges that had plagued us earlier. It was as if every living creature knew to beware this place. Every creature but us.

"No sign of the Bannon," I whispered. "So that's a good thing."

Vycorax frowned. "Maybe. I'm sure he's got something else up his sleeve." She waved for me to follow, and we scampered the last few yards to press ourselves into the shadows beside the entrance.

I leaned my shoulders against the stones, trying to take courage from the ancient granite. So fixed. So immovable. If only I could borrow some of that strength for what lay ahead.

"Okay, stay close," said Vycorax as she slipped inside. Moth scampered after her.

I stared into the darkness after them, willing my feet to move. But they wouldn't budge. It felt as if my blight had risen up and consumed me. That every part of me was fading away, in that unstoppable fog of fear. How could I possibly do this?

I closed my eyes, feeling my heartbeat thumping wildly. How fast had Trudi's heart raced when she was running from the Withering? Leading it away, giving us this chance?

You just do it, Fable. Not because you want to. Because it has to be done.

That was what Mum said to me when I was younger (or, well, last week) and complained about my chores. When I begged to put them off, to feed the chickens later. And I knew it was what she'd say to me now. Because this was so much bigger than any chore. This was my chance to save not just myself, but Elfara and Prince Rylain and every other person trapped by the curse.

I opened my eyes, then entered the barrow.

The thick shadows quickly strangled all other light, leaving us in a dim gloom. I could just barely make out Vycorax, moving in a low crouch, makeshift staff at the ready.

My own empty palms were sticky with sweat. I considered sweeping up a handful of rocks, but I'd never had very good aim. If the Withering caught me, my only hope was to run, or hide. I wasn't brave like Vycorax. I didn't know *what* I was, except that I was here. I hadn't given up yet. That was something.

We emerged into a vast, empty space. There was no sign of the Withering. A ramp spiraled along the inner wall, rising to a small, round opening in the very center of the domed ceiling. A thin, frail light pooled below. Dark niches pocked the walls, each holding a long bundle wrapped in pale cloth. I shuddered. It really *was* a barrow. A place of the dead.

"This is . . . strange," Vycorax said quietly. "It doesn't look like the den of any creature I've ever seen." She sniffed. "Doesn't smell like it either."

I breathed in. She was right. I smelled earth. Damp stone. The faint mustiness of old linen. "Do you think we're in the wrong place?"

She shook her head. "The trail was clear. Maybe the Withering is still out hunting. We should find a place to hide and—wait. Is someone *singing*?"

A moment later I heard it too. A mournful, slightly slurred voice. Low and strangely hollow.

> *"His voice stars could lull,*
> *His wit never dull,*
> *Until the foul day,*
> *For the prince he did play,*
> *Now he's—"*

The singsong voice broke off, muttering something I suspected was one of the curses Gavotte had promised to teach me when I turned fourteen. It might have been a relief, to hear another voice in this place of death and despair, this monster's den. But this voice was coming from *inside* one of the tombs. Vycorax and I exchanged a look. Carefully, silently, she tugged a candle and fire starter from her pack, handing them to me. With trembling hands, I lit the wick. Together, we advanced toward the dark niche that was now rattling off a series of seemingly random words.

"Mull? Cull? Adorable? No, no, no. Rubbish, all of it. I'd give my tongue for the right word. If I still had one." The voice broke off in a series of cackles that made my skin crawl.

In the shadows of the tomb, something shifted. A faint clattering came from within, like the clack of knitting needles. Except that I doubted anyone would sneak off to finish their winter woolens inside a tomb.

Vycorax halted, pressing herself against the stones just beside the dark niche. I leaned against the opposite wall, waiting. The voice was singing again.

> *"Renowned for his sweet virtuosity,*
> *Of talent no hint of a paucity."*

I thrust the candle into the darkness. The flare of golden light shimmered over rotting cloth and pale bone. The body was long dead. Only a skeleton. And yet a voice still came from its lipless, chattering teeth, crooning a singsong rhyme.

> *"But he sang for the prince,*
> *And the king saw him wince,*
> *Now he's a—"*

"Blighter!" Vycorax snarled, brandishing her staff.

The skull twitched, turning to look at us. Somehow it managed to look affronted, even without a mouth or a nose. "No, no, no, 'blighter' doesn't even come close to rhyming with 'paucity.' My honor as a bard would never allow it."

My pulse raced, but I held my ground. The thing looked horrible, but it hadn't actually attacked us. "What are you?" I asked warily.

"Don't talk to it!" Vycorax hissed.

"It doesn't seem that menacing," I told her. "It's arguing about poetry."

"Excuse me, I am not a *what* or an *it*," the skeleton announced, sounding aggravated. "I'm a *who*. A *he*, to be precise."

I blinked. "Oh. Er, sorry. Who are you?"

"I am"—he paused dramatically, empty sockets watching us closely—"DENDONDERUS VALE!"

Vycorax and I both stared at him. Moth leaped up onto the ledge of the tomb and began eyeing one of the skeleton's hands, which had fallen free from the bony wrist to lay against the stone like a strange, pale spider.

"Excellent! Judging by your awestruck faces, I see my prodigious reputation precedes me," said Dendonderus. "Alas. I am currently unable to sign autographs," he added, nodding to the disembodied hand. "Cursed prince. Chopping off my head was bad enough. Did he really have to chop off my hands?"

"Why did the prince chop off your head?" asked Vycorax. "Is your singing really that terrible?"

"Of course not! Surely all know that the voice of DENDONDERUS VALE is as sweet as honey falling from the lips of the sylph of dawn herself! Hmph."

"Er. Right," I said. I had never heard of anyone called Dendonderus Vale, but it seemed rude to mention that right now. "So why *did* he have you executed?"

"Apparently he didn't care for my *Ode to a Perfect Summer Morn, So Pure, So Pink, So Lovely*."

Vycorax snorted. "No. Really?"

"The prince?" I repeated. "Prince Rylain?"

The skull twitched. "Do not speak the wretched name! Oh, my poor fingers. Never again shall they draw forth notes so sweet the birds themselves swoon at their perfect—hey!" He broke off as Moth batted at the limp hand, setting the finger bones clattering.

"Moth!" I cried, horrified. "That's not a toy."

It is a toy if I toy with it. He swatted it again, and a knucklebone went clattering to the floor. I scooped Moth off the ledge, heedless of his protests, then bent to grab the errant knucklebone before he could pounce on it. Affronted, he stalked away, tail swishing.

I dropped the knucklebone gingerly onto the small heap of finger bones, then propped my candle next to them for good measure. "Er. Sorry about that. So, how did you end up here? And, um, still talking?"

"I presume one of my many ardent admirers saw fit to have my body properly interred," said Dendonderus. "As to speaking, I cannot say. It just . . . happened. One moment nothing, and the next here I was. In this state. A poor shadow of my former self. I really was quite handsome, you know. Though, of course, I've still got my charm. Nothing can take that away from DENDONDERUS VALE." He grinned at us, and there was a flare of crimson light in one empty eye socket, almost like a wink.

"It must've been the blight," said Vycorax. "I've never heard of it bringing back the dead, but that's the only reasonable explanation."

"And the Withering hasn't eaten you?" I asked. "Isn't this its lair?"

"Of course the Withering hasn't eaten me." The skull harrumphed. "I am DENDONDERUS VALE! Even a fell beast such as the Withering appreciates the genius of my work. I daresay it chose this barrow as its lair for that very reason."

"So we're in the right place, then," said Vycorax. "Now we just need to wait for the Withering to return and fall asleep."

"Wait? No need for that," said Dendonderus. "It's here right now."

CHAPTER ELEVEN

I stifled a shriek. Vycorax spun around, her quarterstaff raised. "Where?" she demanded, her voice pitched low. "Where is it?"

"You expect me to keep track of the thing?" Dendonderus snorted. "I've got more important things to think about. I've nearly finished my masterwork. The final glory of DENDONDERUS VALE. I just need the last verse."

He began mumbling to himself. Vycorax mumbled something too, but I didn't think it was poetry.

"Please," I said. "Can't you help us?"

"Certainly," he said. "Here's my advice. Leave. Get out of here, unless you want the Withering to eat you. I expect it will be waking soon. It's been asleep for hours."

"We can't do that," said Vycorax. "We need to steal its tooth before it wakes up, so we can use it to break the curse on this land and stop the blight."

"*Pff.* Such mundane tribulations are nothing compared to the noble calling of my art."

"Composing bad limericks about yourself is more important than breaking a curse that's endangering the entire world?" demanded Vycorax. "Someone has a pretty big head."

"It is, isn't it?" Dendonderus preened. "I do have a remarkably lovely skull."

Vycorax gave a growl. "Fine. There are only so many places it could be. We'll find the Withering without your help."

She started to march away, but I blocked her. "It was practically invisible, even in the middle of a sunny field. We might never find it in the shadows. And what if it wakes up? We don't have time to wait another whole day. If we can help Dendonderus—"

"I'm not a poet," said Vycorax.

"That's fine. I'm not either, but I'm pretty good at poetry duels."

"Poetry duels?" Vycorax tilted her head.

"You know, it's when you need to decide who's going to get the last slice of pie, so someone makes up the first line and everyone has to keep coming up with . . ." I trailed off. She was staring at me blankly. As if she'd never heard of such a thing.

"Haven't you ever fought a poetry duel?" I asked.

"No," she said stiffly. "If there's something to be decided, Father just decides it."

"Oh." She was looking at me strangely now. I flushed. "I suppose since there's just two of you—" I broke off. Had she flinched? "Oh, right, you have a sister, don't you?"

"No," she said. "Not anymore."

Blight. I'd seen the sheep dung and still stepped right into it. What did that mean, not anymore? Was she dead? Gone away?

"Go on, then," said Vycorax. "Help the blowhard skull. See if he can give us anything useful."

Right. Helping a skeleton with his masterpiece poem was

far better than accidentally poking at whatever wound it was that made Vycorax's mouth go all tight and twisted, made her shoulders hunch like she was expecting something huge to fall onto her.

I returned to the niche. "Okay, what if we help you finish your last verse? Then will you help us find the Withering?"

"*Hmph.* You really think that you can succeed where the splendiferous DENDONDERUS VALE has not?"

"Yes."

The black pits of his eyes bored into me. It reminded me of staring down our most cantankerous ram when it was time for him to return to his pen. You couldn't afford to back down, no matter how he tossed his horns and bleated. "Maybe you just need a fresh perspective," I told him.

"*Oooh.* You know the word 'perspective.' That's something. Well, I suppose it can't hurt. And I do give you credit for pluck and swagger. There are few who would dare set themselves the equal of DENDONDERUS VALE."

I fought the urge to roll my eyes, though I could see Vycorax doing just that a few paces away.

"It sounded like you were nearly there," I said. "What was it you were singing just before we, er, met you?"

Dendonderus made a noise that I would have taken as him clearing his throat, if he had a throat. Then he began to croon the stanza in his hollow, raspy voice:

> "*Renowned for his sweet virtuosity,*
> *Of talent no hint of a paucity.*

But he sang for the prince,
And the king saw him wince,
Death made him—"

He broke off there, with a rattling sigh. "You see? It's impossible. The first four lines are perfection, I know. Though if you feel like complimenting them, please do. I certainly won't stop you. But that last line! It's just been a fiendish trial."

I frowned, running options through my mind. There were plenty of short words that would rhyme with "city," but to preserve the pattern I should probably use another long word. Veracity? Complicity? Ah, wait, there it was! I bobbed on the tips of my toes.

"Death made him a skull-faced monstrosity?"

Dendonderus sputtered, clacking his jaw. "Monstrosity? Is THAT how you think I wish to be remembered? Outrageous!"

Oops. I held up my hands. "Okay! Okay! There are plenty of other options. Just let me think."

Vycorax had settled herself against the wall, watching me with a look halfway between amusement and disgust. I ignored her, still running through words. I needed something a bit more, well, positive. Dendonderus wasn't a monstrosity, after all. A centuries-old talking skeleton was actually rather remarkable.

That was when I had the flash of inspiration. "I've got it! *Death could not end his loquacity!"*

The skeleton stared at me. He'd been grinning this whole time, thanks to the whole not-having-any-lips thing, but somehow his bared teeth really did seem to be smiling now. "Aha! That's it! Lo, how they will sing my praises! Such brilliance! It will surely secure my legacy as greatest of all bards!"

"You didn't even think of it," said Vycorax. "It was Fable."

Dendonderus didn't appear to be listening. He was muttering, repeating the stanza with my new final line, emphasizing different syllables each time.

I coughed. "Dendonderus?"

"What?" he said, sounding peeved. "Did no one ever teach you not to disturb genius at work?"

"Sorry," I said. "It's just . . . we really need to find the Withering before it wakes up. And you *did* say you'd help us if I finished—er, if I inspired you to finish your poem."

"Oh, very well. The sooner we take care of it, the sooner I can practice my full recitation. You will be fortunate indeed! The very first people to hear my magnum opus, my master-piece!"

"So very lucky," Vycorax said dryly.

"Come on, then, I haven't got all day," said Dendonderus. "Pick me up!"

I had heard him wrong. Surely, he couldn't mean—

"Come, come," he snapped, sounding peevish. "I need to get closer. Can't see anything from in here."

"Oh, no," said Vycorax, when I looked at her. "This is your plan. You get to carry the skeleton."

"Just my skull will do," offered Dendonderus.

"Are you sure?" I asked. "It's not going to break the enchantment or anything? Make you stop talking?"

"Oh, what a tragedy," muttered Vycorax.

"Nonsense," proclaimed Dendonderus. "Death cannot end my loquacity! Snap to it, girl."

Right. I braced myself, then gingerly cupped my hands around the bard's skull, lifting him free from the niche. Then I turned toward the rest of the barrow. "Which way?"

"Hmm. Let me think. Yes, it always went over there, below that walkway. In the shadows. Just follow the sound of its snoring. The beast sleeps for days sometimes. I suppose it's hard work, destroying reality."

I carried my grim burden across the stones in the direction Dendonderus had indicated, trying to step as lightly as possible. Dendonderus's singing hadn't woken the beast, but I wasn't going to take any chances. Vycorax crept along beside me, holding the candle in one hand, her quarterstaff in the other.

As we passed the niches, I tried to breathe shallowly, afraid the musty scent of dust and decay would make me sneeze. Or lose my breakfast. I tried not to look too closely at the withered bundles, the ragged outlines of skeletal fingers. Shadows danced along the stones, making it seem almost as if the shrouded figures were moving.

Then my breath snagged. "There's something in there!" I jabbed a finger toward one of the larger niches. "Is it the Withering?"

Vycorax growled, brandishing the candle. Flickering gold fingers danced over the heap of moldering bones. One of the shadows dislodged itself, a slice of gray that leaped from the tomb and . . .

Began purring.

"Moth!" I sagged with relief.

His green eyes glinted accusingly at the skull in my hands. *You said the bones were not a toy, Fable.*

"Believe me," I said, "I'd rather not be playing this game if I could help it. But Dendonderus is going to take us to the Withering."

"What a strange sensation," mused Dendonderus. "To be without a body. But then, bodies can be *so* inconvenient. So confining. You see, that's the sort of enlightenment I've attained now. I am a being of pure intellect! You might say I've become one with my art!"

He cackled, and I could feel the horrible noise through the cool bone beneath my fingers. But if he could lead us to the Withering, this would all be worth it. Even if I had nightmares about laughing skulls for the rest of my life.

"Is this the right way?" Vycorax asked, sweeping the candle across the nearest niches.

"Ha!" crowed Dendonderus. "So good old Drofara the Droll finally kicked it, did she? *Hmph.* And the state of her. Some people just don't know how to decay properly, I suppose."

I looked away, trying not to breathe too deeply as we passed a particularly foul-smelling corpse.

"Though, you know, I do believe she smells better now than when she was alive. She had a horrible obsession with sardines pickled in— There! That's it!"

A shadow larger and darker than any of the others loomed ahead of us, far more than a niche. It was a tunnel, a wide passage that sloped downward, into the stone.

I stopped. So did Vycorax. Even Moth halted, though he pretended it was only because one of his paws was in desperate need of cleaning.

In the silence, I could make out a distant, low rumble. Like the breathing of a terrible slumbering beast. At least, I hoped it was slumbering.

"All right, then," said Vycorax. "Are you ready, Fey?"

The nickname warmed me briefly. And it gave me the courage to admit the truth. "No. Not really. We don't even have a plan."

How could we? What we were about to attempt was absurd. Impossible.

She took a step closer to me, her expression serious. "Fable, you can do this. I know you can. Mirachne chose us for this. We'll do it together. We'll figure it out."

Normally I didn't like it when people looked at me for too long. Even my family. Because I knew they were searching for something that wasn't there. No one could ever forget what I was. What I wasn't. But the way Vycorax was looking at me now was different. It was as if she could see something deeper. As if, maybe, somehow, she was seeing *me*.

It sent a hot flush creeping up my chest, my neck, my

face. Probably I was just imagining it. Maybe she was just looking at her own face.

"Right, I know. But it's pretty clear which of us is going to be doing the actual demon-stabbing, and it's not the one who nearly cut off her own finger last time she tried to chop carrots." I wiggled my fingers along the side of Dendonderus's skull, displaying the small, pale scar.

Her frown deepened into frustration. "That's enough of that. You act like you don't matter, Fable. But you do. With or without a 'real' face. I wouldn't be trying so hard to fix this if I didn't—" She broke off, looking away, and I thought she might even be blushing. "We found this place because of you, Fable," she said. "I couldn't rhyme my way out of a pot."

"Bah. An infant could manage that," muttered Dendonderus. "Sot, cot, lot, dot, tot." He continued on, humming.

Vycorax ignored him, still staring at me with disconcerting intensity. "You did this, Fable. You. Somehow you pulled those ridiculous words out of your ridiculously big brain, and you used them to convince that pile of bones to help us. That's something real, Fable. Something you did. *You.*"

I couldn't speak. All my words—the short ones, the long ones, the ridiculous ones—seemed to have gotten caught in an enormous lumpy tangle at the back of my throat.

"And now it's time to finish it," she said. "Together. Okay?"

Somehow, the look in her eyes almost made me believe it. I managed a small smile. "Together."

We entered the tunnel, creeping slowly and carefully

down the sloping stones. It felt like walking down the throat of a great, hungry beast. And with every step, the rumble of the Withering's breathing grew louder, until my skin prickled with each rasp. It was the only noise, aside from the faint drone of Dendonderus humming his masterpiece.

Finally the tunnel opened into a low, dim chamber. The rumble seemed to be all around us now, echoing from the stones. Vycorax lifted her candle. The light flickered, warping as it tried and failed to catch hold of the enormous beast in front of us.

Slowly, gingerly, Vycorax crouched, propping the candle on the stone floor. I knelt as well, tucking Dendonderus under my elbow as I looked into Moth's green eyes. "You should wait for us outside," I whispered.

Why?

"Because . . . this is going to be dangerous."

Where you go, I go, he said simply. *Unless it is wet. But it is not wet here.*

I reached out to skritch between his ears, to feel the solid warmth of him lean into my palm. Real. Moth was real, and he loved me. No matter the chill of oblivion tugging at me, I knew this much.

I stood, and together we advanced upon the Withering.

It was as hard to see as ever. The filmy, shivering nothingness was like the air above a flame. I had to squint to force my eyes to follow the outline of its haunches, the four great paws tipped with shimmering claws, each as long as my palm.

Even sleeping, it was utterly terrifying. Especially knowing it could wake at any moment. Snap us up in two bites, swallowing us to oblivion. The creature's great shaggy head lay across the stones, lolling open just enough to reveal the tips of two enormous canine teeth.

Vycorax pointed the tip of her quarterstaff at one of them, arching her brows at me.

"What now?" I asked. Surely she wasn't going to just thwack it with a big stick.

"Now I use an old blighthunter trick." Vycorax drew back the staff, gripping it tightly as she narrowed her gaze at her chosen quarry. I tensed, all my nerves coiling tight for whatever happened next.

She jabbed the quarterstaff, smacking the base of the tooth with a loud *crack!*

"That's your old blighthunter trick?" I whispered. "Hit it with a big stick?"

"Do you have a better plan?" Vycorax grimaced, then struck the tooth a second time. *Crack!*

Dendonderus broke off his humming to complain loudly, "At least try to keep to tempo if you insist on adding percussion."

"Shush!" I hissed, giving the skull a small shake.

"I will not be silent! True art will not quaver in the face of fear! The beast of oblivion shall not quell my voice! For I am DEN—"

His speech ended in an outraged sputter, muffled by the thick canvas of my pack as I jammed the skull hastily inside.

I tucked my bedroll over him for good measure. I didn't fancy the idea of sleeping on a blanket covered in bone dust, but it was better than getting eaten by the Withering.

My heartbeat thundered in my ears as Vycorax and I both stared at the Withering. But the beast hadn't stirred. Its heavy breathing hummed in the air, prickling my skin.

Vycorax rolled her shoulders, then drew the quarterstaff back again. "I think I felt it give, that last time. One more hit ought to—"

She broke off, the words falling into silence. Complete silence. Because the Withering was no longer snoring. And in the blur of its face, two silver slits had opened.

Eyes. And they were staring right at us. Awake. And *hungry.*

Chapter Twelve

*R*un!" shouted Vycorax, scrambling back as the Withering uncoiled itself with a low growl.

I ran, pelting back up the tunnel with Moth darting beside me. As I burst out into the upper chamber of the barrow, I glanced back. "Vyx!" I shouted. Where was she? My chest had gone hollow, as if the Withering had already clawed out my heart and left only chilly despair.

And then, a streak of scarlet. Vycorax flung herself out from the shadowy tunnel, breathless and gasping. "Go!" she shouted. "It's right behind me!"

Something huge and gray slashed across the air between us. I gasped, wrenching myself back.

The Withering crouched in the center of the barrow. A terrible, shaggy void, a maw of utter extinction. And it was blocking our only way out.

No. Not the only way. There was the sloping ramp that spiraled up along the walls. It looked as if it went all the way to the open circle of sky above.

It was a slim chance. But it was better than literal nothing. And . . . maybe I could give Vycorax an even better hope of escaping. If I was brave.

The Withering rumbled, casting its head toward Vycorax,

then me, as if trying to decide which of us was the tastier morsel.

"Hey!" I shouted, waving my hands. "It's me. If you want a snack, come and get me. I'm the blighted one."

Across the chamber, I saw Vycorax's mouth open and her eyes go wide. She started to shout something, but her words were lost, consumed by the bone-shaking roar of the Withering. I could only hope that she would understand. The way she had before, with Trudibeth.

I spun around and sprinted for the ramp. And the Withering followed.

My lungs ached. My legs pounded. The flick of Moth's gray tail led me onward, gave me strength even as a horrible juddering howl echoed behind me. I didn't dare look back. I didn't need to. I could feel the chill of the beast chasing after me. The pull of its terrible emptiness trying to suck me in.

Good. Every step after me was a step away from Vycorax. A chance for her to get out of the barrow. To escape.

Higher and higher we spiraled, the ramp narrowing, until it became a set of steps. Moth raced up them.

I was about to follow, when I heard it speak.

Why do you run, girl?

Its voice hummed in my head, like Moth's, but sharper, the edges tearing at my thoughts painfully. I halted. Turned to look behind me, still not sure I believed that I had actually heard the words.

The Withering stalked up the ramp below. Its paws tore

gray gashes, leaving a trail of broken, ravaged stone. Slower now, but relentless.

You carry oblivion within you. You know it.

I hadn't imagined it. The voice of the Withering was as ancient and merciless as winter. Even my wildest fears had never sounded so chillingly bleak.

"No," I protested, though my frozen lips seemed barely able to move. "I deserve to live. We all do."

Perhaps, said the Withering. *But I do not measure merit. Justice is not my purview. This land is corrupt. Unbalanced. If the schism cannot be mended, it must be destroyed.*

"Wait," I protested, as the creature took another step. "That's why I'm here! That's why we need your tooth! Please, I'm trying to fix this."

For a moment I thought it had worked. The Withering halted. I could feel it staring at me. Then it gave a low rumble.

No. You are not. And so you will be consumed. As will all this realm. The beast crouched low, a coiling ripple of violence.

So much for conversation. I flung myself up the steps, aiming for that circle of sky. Freedom. Escape. Hope.

I stumbled out onto a high dome. My palms slammed onto rough stone, slick with mud. My knees jammed into lumpy rock. If I survived, I was going to be covered in bruises and scrapes.

Moth appeared beside me, hair bristling, tail lashing. *Hurry, Fable! It comes!*

I rolled over just in time to see a great gray paw hooked over the edge of the opening behind me. Claws like shards of gray glass tore at the stones, ripping them away, leaving a jagged patch of blank emptiness.

You cannot escape me, daughter of earth. You are as lost as this realm. And all that is lost belongs to me.

Another rip. More stones shredding. The Withering was going to eat its way through the roof of the barrow to reach me.

Each beat of my heart was like the distant toll of a funeral bell. I'd only barely managed to outrun the beast this far. What hope did I have slowed by sucking mud and heel-snagging stones?

Moth hissed, crouching as if to spring at the Withering, but I caught him in my arms, clutching him to my chest. Felt his soft fur, the living warmth of his small body. What was going to happen when the Withering took us? Would I even be aware? Or would we just . . . blink out?

I cuddled Moth closer, wishing desperately that I could protect him. The way I had that day I first found him, tiny and bedraggled and half-drowned, clinging to a branch along the river. *You're here.* Those were the first words he'd said to me. And they were still true. I was here. He was here.

And whatever happened next, we'd face it together.

A gust of wind whooshed past my cheek. The Withering growled. Dimly, I was aware of a rush of movement behind me. A soft *thwump* of something . . . landing?

I staggered to my feet, spinning to find myself staring into the enormous golden eyes of a giant owl. The bird was massive. As large as a horse. No, *larger*, I saw, as she stretched out great, night-dark wings. A boy perched atop the bird's back. He leaned low over the sleek feathers of her neck, reaching out his hand to me.

"Come on!" he cried. "Hurry!"

"You," I said, dumbfounded. "You're the boy from the mask shop."

It was definitely him. He was still wearing the same demon mask, with its fierce fangs and twisting horns. How had he found me? And why?

The boy on the owl made an impatient gesture. "Right now I'm the person trying to save your life. Unless you *want* to be consumed by the Withering?"

No. Definitely not. Much better to cast myself to the mercies of a strange boy and his enormous owl. There would be time for all my other questions later. If I survived.

I flung myself toward him. The boy's hand clasped mine, tugging me up. I slid into place behind him, Moth tucked tight to my chest. Feathers shifted around my ankles as the enormous owl spread her wings. Muscles bunched beneath me. She sprang into the air. *Whoom. Whoom. Whoom.*

A bellow thundered below, but the Withering was too late. It gave a last slash, slicing three ribbons of empty gray through the air beneath us.

Three beats, and we were spinning far beyond its reach. Moth and I were safe. But what about Vycorax? "My friend!"

I gasped, finding it hard to catch my breath. "She's still down there! Please, we need to find her!"

"You're the one the Withering's hunting," he said grimly. "Safer for her if we lead it away. And safer for you if I take you somewhere it can't reach you."

I gulped. I didn't want to leave Vycorax, but the boy was right about the Withering. Even now I could see how it lifted its head, tracking our movement as we canted right. Then it was charging down from the barrow, chasing after us.

I squinted, searching the mire. Please. Please let Vycorax have escaped.

A flash of crimson suddenly caught my eye, down amid the lumpy turf. The blur of a light brown oval, peering up. Relief melted the lump of ice in my chest. Could she see me? Did she understand I was trying to help and not just abandoning her?

But I couldn't make out her expression. We were too far away for her to hear me. I couldn't wave.

And then even that small red speck was gone.

I hoped she knew that I was safe. That we'd find each other again and finish what we'd come here to do. Somehow.

The words of the Withering whispered in my thoughts.

If the schism cannot be mended, it must be destroyed.

But why didn't it believe that I was trying to fix it? A schism was a sort of division, wasn't it, when two people disagreed? Gavotte had explained it to me, after she used it to win one of our poetry battles (she rhymed it with euphemism, which she also had to explain). And Mirachne had been very clear that we needed to destroy the demon prince in order to restore Rylain to power. Surely that would get rid of the schism?

I let out a long breath. Just thinking about the Withering sent a chill through me. A reminder that I was fading. I could feel it. I needed a new face.

And there was one, right in front of me. Though I couldn't actually see it, only his narrow shoulders and a silky fall of reddish-gold hair. He was still wearing that demon mask. Besides, it seemed enormously rude to ask a boy who had just saved my life if I could borrow his face. Maybe once we got to wherever it was that the Withering couldn't reach. Somewhere a bit closer to solid ground, I hoped.

Moth escaped my grip, scrambling up to cling to my shoulder. *Fable. The world is too far away. I do not like it.*

I didn't like it either. Being so high, with the whole world spread out below, made me feel tiny and insignificant. Easy enough to just fade away. My stomach gave a sickening spin that was only partly due to the swooping flight of the owl.

Something below caught my eye, distracting me from my thoughts. A large patch of grayness ate up the edges of a dark forest. And there was more. Trails of emptiness wove through the entire landscape. Woods, meadows, lakes, all of it ragged as a moth-eaten cloth. There were even fragments of houses along the edges in places. There were—or had been—people down there. Villages like Fenhollow. Farms, like my own home. How many of them were gone now?

"Is that all wither?" I asked.

"Yes." The boy's voice was bleak. His shoulders hunched. "The beast has destroyed at least a third of the realm."

"Do . . . ?" I hesitated, not sure if I wanted to know the answer to my question. "Do you know if that village with the festival is still okay? When we left, the Withering was nearby."

"Fenhollow is still there," he said. "For now. I believe the Withering was following your trail, even then."

"Why?" I asked. "Why me?"

"I don't know."

I waited for him to say something more, but he was silent, leaning forward over the owl's neck. Judging by the sun, we were heading northeast, toward the center of the Mirrorwood. Below, a thick forest spread over rolling hills. I saw no more patches of wither, but something about the impenetrable darkness of the woods made me shiver. Or maybe it was just the chill of the wind.

"Thank you," I said finally. "You saved my life. I'm lucky you happened to be nearby, I guess. And that you have a giant owl."

"I was on patrol," said the boy, his voice clipped, as if even giving away that detail was too much.

"I'm Fable, by the way," I said. "And this is my cat, Moth."

A muffled grumble came from my satchel. But there was enough going on right now without adding a self-important talking skull to the mix.

"A pleasure to meet you," said the boy.

Again, I waited. I didn't have a lot of experience with

introductions, let alone introductions while escaping a monster on owl-back, but I did think normally the other person offered their name in return.

"And you are?" I prompted. "You're blighted, like me, I suppose? Or else you'd be stuck like the people in Fenhollow. Timespun."

"Yes. I'm blighted." The words were bitter, sharp as thorns.

Maybe that was why he was wearing the mask. Because the blight had done something to his face. I could still see only the back of his head, the curve of the golden horns. They were exactly like the horns of the demon prince in Mirachne's vision. Were they even part of his mask? They looked too sharp, too solid to be papier-mâché.

But that was ridiculous, of course. The demon was evil. The cause of the blight. We had come here to banish him. A cruel, monstrous prince would hardly be interested in saving my life. No, the horns must be part of the mask. Just like the tips of the pointed ears I could see poking through his coppery hair. Surely.

"What's your name?" I said, not caring if it was rude, so long as it could stop the queasy flutter of panic that had started in my chest. "Where are you taking me?"

"To the one place that's safe from the Withering," he said, pointing to something on the horizon.

It was a castle.

Dark and beautiful, with tall, peaked towers flung up against the sky. It reminded me of the wrought-iron fence that bound our village graveyard, whorls and curves and sharp jutting peaks, somehow delicate and impenetrable all at once.

"Is there more than one castle in this realm?" I asked as the flutter of panic became a stampede.

"No."

The owl tucked her wings, taking us lower, stealing the breath from my gaping mouth. Moth hissed, retreating to my arms again, as we plummeted toward a wide rooftop terrace at the center of the dark palace.

We landed with a soft *thwump*.

"Welcome to Glimmerdark Castle," said the boy.

This had to be a mistake. I slung my leg over the owl's back, sliding down in a rough tumble to stand trembling on the cool, dark stones.

"But that's where the demon prince lives." I stared up at the boy, willing him to say something that would make sense, something other than the horrible, obvious answer.

"Yes," he said, with a strange heaviness in his voice now. He slid down lightly, gracefully, pausing to slip something from one pocket of his long velvet jacket. He offered it to the owl, who snapped it up so quickly I caught only a glimpse of brown fur. She gave a low hoot as he reached up to scratch a spot along her neck.

"Who are you?" I asked, my voice strangled. "Tell me!"

"Isn't it enough that I'm the person who saved your life?" he asked, still tending to the owl.

I took a step back. "No." Why wouldn't he just answer?

The boy sighed. Then he turned, seeming to brace himself as he reached up and pulled the mask away. The painted oval fell, cracking against the flagstones.

Golden horns still curved from his temples. The sharp-tipped ears still poked from the sweep of copper hair. And his face . . .

It was as if a sculptor had been trying to capture the sylph of dawn, using only a razor to shape their clay. He was beautiful. And horrible. Just like in Mirachne's vision.

Except this wasn't a vision. This was the demon prince. Right here, in front of me. Staring at me with his bleak, black eyes, as if I held the answer to some terrible question.

So I did what any reasonable person would do.

I turned on my heel and ran.

Chapter Thirteen

oth and I raced across the terrace toward the nearest exit: a tall stone archway that promised some sort of stairway down into the castle. Moth, faster than me, paused at the top of the steps.

Where are we running?

"Anywhere away from that monster!"

I thought you wanted *to find the demon prince.*

"Yes, but I don't have the magic demon-killing tooth," I sputtered, bounding down the stairway two steps at a time.

Why did you go with him if you were only going to run away?

"Because I didn't realize he was the blighted demon prince!" The stairs spilled us out into a chamber with three doors. I halted, staring at them, wondering which might be my best chance of escape. But my thoughts wouldn't settle. They were like chickens when a fox was nearby, fluttering and clucking uselessly.

I glanced back up the stairs and caught a shadow of movement. He was coming!

Right, the middle door it was. I wrenched the handle open and tore onward, racing along a narrow hall that I would have stopped to ogle had I not been running for my life. Pale blue walls, glittering with gold scrollwork. Soft, velvety carpets. Spindly wooden tables lacquered to glossy brilliance. Candles dripping with crystal, set into golden sconces along the walls.

Fable, I hear—

I careened around a curve and collided with something. No, some*one*. I fell, and so did she, in a tangle of limbs and crunching pottery and . . . fur? I struggled, desperate to pull myself free. My scrabbling hand connected with something warm and soft. Skin.

My blight surged up hungrily. A shimmering heat flickered over my face. The short hair I'd borrowed from Vycorax curled and slithered down to fall over my shoulders. My nose lengthened, tickling oddly, and something *very* strange was happening to my ears.

I scrambled up. A girl crouched on the floor of the hallway, surrounded by broken teacups and the ruin of what had once clearly been a very delectable cake. A teapot lay on its side, dribbling steaming amber liquid across the plush carpet. The girl yelped, grabbing the teapot, tipping it upright. Then she looked up, and it was my turn to yelp.

She looked mostly human. Round, cream-and-roses cheeks, bright hazel eyes, and a vast amount of tumbling red hair. But furry, dark-tipped ears poked from beneath that hair. And her nose narrowed to a sharp point, tipped with black, like that of a fox.

I reached up, gingerly feeling my own long nose. My own furry ears. I'd thought nothing could be as strange as borrowing Da's beard. But becoming a fox girl was definitely a new experience.

Oh, I like this face, said Moth. *You finally have proper whis-kers.*

The thud of a door somewhere behind me broke me out of my stupor. The demon! He must have reached the chamber with the three doors. I didn't have long before he figured out which one I'd fled through. I had to keep going, and hope this hallway led to an exit.

"Your face—" stammered the fox girl, lifting a hand to pat her sharp black nose, as if to check if it was still there. "You look like—"

"Sorry about the tea," I called as I dashed onward.

Vycorax would probably have some sort of clever plan by now. All I had was a desperate desire to get out of this cursed place. Nothing made sense here. It was so huge, so lush, so overwhelming.

The passage led to a large stairway, curving with marble banisters and lit by enormous chandeliers dripping crystals that cast a thousand rainbow gleams across the milk-white walls.

Another choice. Up, down, or straight ahead through that large, polished oaken door? Down was most likely to lead to an exit. But it was also the most predictable. I remembered the games of hide-and-seek I used to play back home. None of us could ever find Gavotte, because she always hid in some completely unexpected place. As opposed to Indigo, who always hid in the pantry, probably so they could sneak spoonfuls of jam while they were waiting.

Enough dithering. I ran to the oak door, gulping down

my breaths, pushed it open as quietly as I could, then tucked myself on the other side. Moth followed close behind. I let the door close with a gentle thump, then turned to see where I was.

My breath gusted out. Oh. *Oh.*

It was a library. But this was far more than the two bookcases we had back home, which held a motley collection of pattern references, cookbooks, a collection of bloodcurdling ghost stories courtesy of a very strange great-uncle I'd never met, and the entire collection of Bonny Crispin adventures.

There were hundreds of books. Maybe thousands. It was hard to tell because they weren't ranged neatly on shelves.

They were *flying.*

Flocks of books soared around the arches of the high, vaulted ceiling. They flapped their leather bindings as they swooped over my head, then flitted off to dart in and out of the lacy stonework that decorated the railings and stairways crisscrossing the enormous room.

But as strange as flocks of flying books were, the room itself was even more bewildering. It was as if someone had taken the great hall, with all its stairs and balconies, and then broken it into pieces and stuck it back together again, completely at random and against all common sense, ignoring the force of gravity itself. Some of the balconies hung vertically along the wall. Stairs marched along the ceiling. Just looking at it made my stomach spin.

I shook myself out of my daze. I wasn't here to gape at the blighted architecture. I needed a place to hide.

There was a distant *clunk*. From outside in the hall? Or was there someone in here with me? I held my breath, hearing nothing but the distant flap of the books.

"This way," I whispered to Moth, heading for a spiral stair to the left. Maybe if we could get higher up, I could see a good hiding place. Or maybe even a window leading back onto the roof. We crept up the steps, coming out onto a walkway that tilted dizzyingly to the side. I kept my gaze fixed on the smooth marble under my feet until I passed through an archway and the world suddenly righted itself again. I was on a wide platform, near the very center of the library.

And there was a girl sitting in front of me, cross-legged on the floor, with a large book open in her lap. She looked up brightly, as if she'd been expecting me. "Where's the tea? Don't tell me that blighted kettle has gone wonky again."

She looked my age—about twelve, or maybe thirteen. She had warm brown skin and a cascade of glossy black curls, and she was wearing round spectacles. I wouldn't have known she was blighted, if it weren't for the pair of small, white-feathered wings that swept out delicately from either side of her head.

I didn't know what to make of this. I'd expected the demon prince's castle to be full of horrors. Not fox girls balancing cakes and scholars asking me for tea.

"Phoula?" she asked. "What's wrong? Is it the Withering again? Another attack?"

Phoula. That must be the fox girl's name. The winged

girl thought I was her, because I was wearing her face. But she'd figure out the truth soon enough if I just stood there gaping at her.

I coughed. "Er. No. I just . . . tripped on the way and dropped the tea. It's okay. I'll . . . go back and get more."

The winged girl peered up at me. "Are you catching a cold? Your voice sounds strange."

Blight. I stole faces but not voices. And the winged girl clearly knew Phoula quite well. "I'm fine. I'll be back with tea before you miss me." I stepped away, toward the archway. At least Moth was still out of sight, probably stalking one of the fluttering book-birds.

The girl tossed her book up into the open air, where it spread its covers and flapped off to join one of the spiraling flocks. "Wait. I'll come too."

She clambered to her feet. It seemed to be an effort, probably due to the absolutely enormous boots she was wearing. They were strange, completely at odds with her fine yellow satin jacket with its long, swishy hem, worn over a pair of fawn-colored breeches. The boots were made of thick leather and . . . bronze? Blight, they must weigh almost as much as the girl herself! How could she possibly walk in them?

I tried not to stare. I was terrible at pretending to be other people. Allegra used to try to get me to switch places with her, to pull tricks on our older siblings, but I hated it. I needed to get out of here, fast. "You really don't have to come," I said, trying to pitch my voice a bit higher. "You were in the middle of reading."

"*Pff.* You know I've already read *The Histories* a half-dozen times." She heaved a sigh. "I just keep thinking there must be something I'm missing. Some clue that could help us fix everything."

She peered up, spectacles glinting as she tracked the movement of one of the flying books. It was large and bound in faded red leather. Unlike the other tomes, it never seemed to dive low or pause to perch at one of the inkwells.

The girl sighed. "If only I could convince *The Book of Powers* to land. Then maybe we could find an answer."

The answer to what? If she thought a book about the Subtle Powers would help, could her question have something to do with the curse? But I didn't dare ask. It would make her even more suspicious.

"Even so," I said, "you should stay. It won't take long. Besides, I have a surprise for you. You need to stay here, or you'll ruin it."

The girl's eyes went wide. "A surprise? For me?" She glanced away, her cheeks flushing faintly. "Well. I suppose then . . ." She broke off, frowning. "Why do you have a cat?" I tried not to flinch as Moth gave a loud purr and stalked over to the girl, winding himself sinuously between her legs.

"Oh. Ah. That's the surprise. Surprise! I adopted a cat!"

For a moment I thought it had worked. The girl stared down at Moth, the corners of her lips twitching up. Few people could resist Moth when he was in the mood to be charming. Then she let out an enormous sneeze.

"I *told* you I was allergic," she said, crossing her arms.

Moth, who had leaped onto a nearby balustrade, proceeded to very deliberately wash one of his paws. *It is not my fault, Fable. Some humans are simply overwhelmed by my magnificence.*

The girl sneezed again. From the depths of my pack, a muffled voice said, "Bless you!"

"Shush!" I hissed. Bad enough to have to explain Moth. I had no excuse for a disembodied talking skull.

"DENDONDERUS VALE does not SHUSH!" protested the voice from my pack. "His voice is the clarion call of truth and beauty across the land! I did not escape the lair of the Withering to be silent!"

Maybe the girl hadn't heard. Maybe I could still invent a story she'd believe. But when I looked into her eyes, there was no questioning the icy suspicion.

"You're not Phoula, are you?"

I didn't even bother to answer. "Let's go, Moth!" I sprinted away through the chaotic jumble of bridges and steps. I had to get back to the door before the winged girl could stop me. She didn't seem like a minion of evil, but that might just be some sort of trick. I couldn't trust anything here.

But just as I sprang down to the main floor, the door to the library burst open, heavy panels banging against the walls, and then he was there. The boy who had rescued me from the Withering.

The demon prince.

I yelped, retreating sideways to shelter behind a heavy oak desk where several smaller books perched around a large inkwell, like sparrows at a birdbath. I jerked my gaze left, right. Up, down. There was nowhere to run. The winged girl blocked the stairs up, and the demon boy blocked the door. I snatched the inkwell from the desk in front of me. If I could just get past the demon, maybe I had a chance.

"Get ready to run for the door," I told Moth, hefting the inkwell.

"I'm not your enemy," the boy said, taking a step toward me.

I hurled the inkwell at him with all my strength.

A flash of annoyance crossed his face, and he whipped a hand in front of him, fingers snapping. The air itself seemed to spin around the movement, swirling into a dark, gleaming shimmer. The twist caught the inkwell as it flew, and the heavy glass suddenly burst apart into a cloud of tiny black moths that fluttered away like tiny fragments of night.

I stared. Stammered. "Y-you made a twist. You just snapped your fingers and *made a twist*."

The boy crossed his arms, glaring back at me haughtily. "And you tried to brain me with an inkwell."

"I should have known you had something to do with this, Lyrian." The winged girl clomped the rest of the way down the steps to join the demon boy, glowering at him. "Is she another one you rescued from the Withering? Why did you bring her here? What did she do to Phoula?"

"I *did* rescue her," said the demon prince, Lyrian. "Not that she seems to remember. And Phoula's perfectly fine. Our guest"—he waved an accusing hand at me—"knocked her over and smashed tea cake all over the eastern hall."

The winged girl turned on me again. "But why does she look like Phoula?"

"A very good question, Odessa. Perhaps she can explain herself." Lyrian regarded me coolly.

I swallowed, pressing myself back against the wall. Moth crouched near my feet, his hackles puffed, tail lashing. At least they were asking me questions, not just . . . sticking me in a dungeon, or whatever the demon prince normally did to his enemies. "I—I took her face. It's my blight. I borrow faces. I'm sorry. I was scared."

Maybe I could convince them I was just some blighted villager with a talking cat. Who just happened to be poking around the den of the Withering for no good reason. Ugh. Still, I had to try, even if I was terrible at lying. If Lyrian realized Mirachne had sent me, he might just toss me back to the Withering.

Before anyone else could speak, a patter of footsteps came from the hall outside. Then the fox girl herself, Phoula, popped through the door. "Lyrian, did you find—oh!"

She came to an abrupt stop, staring at me. One of her sharp ears twitched as she tilted her chin. Her dark nose scrunched. "Is that really what I look like?"

"Yes," said the winged girl, Odessa. "You see, I told you the ears were adorable. Now do you believe me?"

Pink tinged Phoula's cheeks. She gave a small shake of her head. I noticed, for the first time, that she had a fox's tail as well, the fluffy white tip poking out from under the knee-length hem of her wide black skirt. She wore green leggings and glossy black boots beneath, and a soft creamy shirt. Simpler clothing than Odessa and Lyrian, but still nicer than anything I was used to.

I coughed. "Well, thank you for rescuing me, Prince Lyrian. I—I'm sorry I panicked. I—well—there are some frightening stories about you."

His black eyes transfixed me. His lips were tight, thin. Then one corner of his mouth quirked. "Indeed. I'm sure Mirachne has told you all about my terrible misdeeds and evil nature. She sent you here, didn't she? To destroy me."

CHAPTER FOURTEEN

I opened my mouth. Then snapped it shut, unable to find words. Because it was true. Mirachne had said that to end the blight, the demon prince had to be gotten rid of. *Killed.*

"Mirachne sent her? I knew it!" Odessa rounded on me, pausing only to shove her spectacles more firmly up her nose. "You can't believe anything that witch says. She's the reason we're all in this mess! Toss a bit of glitter and starlight around, promise a few wishes granted, and the next thing you know she's got you spun around her little finger. What did you wish for? Gold? Power? A lifetime of raspberry pies?"

"No!" I protested. "I don't want any of that!"

Well, actually, a lifetime of pies didn't sound bad, but it certainly wasn't why I was here. And how dare they act like *I* was the villain? I'd come here to *stop* this. They were the ones living in the blighted castle, summoning twists!

"I'm blighted!" I told them. "Do you think I *like* stealing faces? Not having one of my own?" My voice shook, but I plunged on, heedless. "And Mirachne didn't make me this way. You did!" I stabbed a finger at Lyrian.

He took a step back, lips parting, as if I'd struck him.

Silence. Phoula had retreated to Odessa's side, her ears

flicked downward, her tail curled around her knees. Odessa's mouth was a round O. She shot a quick glance to the prince, then drew in a breath. "That's not—"

"Let me handle this, Dess," interrupted Lyrian, his shoulders stiff and straight. "You and Phoula should go have your tea."

The two girls departed, Odessa's steps thunking heavily. Lyrian continued to watch me, saying nothing more until the oaken doors closed behind them. Moth, traitorously, had scampered off after one of the flying books, which was now circling just low enough to taunt him with the trailing end of its ribbon place-marker. *Cats.* I could never tell if Moth was being deliberately obtuse to danger, or just knew something I didn't.

Lyrian took three careful steps backward, putting even more space between us. "Sit," he said, waving toward one of the plush armchairs scattered throughout the library.

I didn't move.

He cleared his throat. "Or stand. As you wish."

If I didn't know better, I'd have thought he was embarrassed. Nervous even. Well, I wasn't going to make this easier on him. I'd just seen him conjure a twist—he'd just proved himself the source of the blight. This could all be a trick. I couldn't let down my guard.

I crossed my arms, holding my ground. "As I wish? I *wish* I'd never been blighted. But I am. Because of you."

He flinched. "I suppose that's fair. I'd apologize, but that's not what you want, is it? You want to kill me. That's why you were in the barrow. You were after the Withering's Tooth. You and that other girl."

A muffled protest came from my satchel. "Outrageous! Am I to be completely overlooked? You shall not obscure the name of DENDONDERUS VALE, who valiantly led the charge deep into the heart of the barrow to claim—*oof!* Hey! Careful! I'm more delicate than I look, you know!" I had unslung the satchel and dropped it, not particularly gently, onto the desk.

The mention of Vycorax squeezed my heart. She was still out there. Alone. In a world full of blights. I lifted my chin, to reassure myself as much as to defy Lyrian. "She's a blighthunter. Trained to destroy evil."

He gave a bitter laugh. "You mean like me?"

A loud huff from my satchel interrupted our conversation. "It really is quite rude to not even bother to introduce me, you know."

Lyrian arched a brow. I glowered. Then sighed, tugging open the pack and pulling free the skull. "This is Dendonderus Vale, famous bard. Dendonderus, this is—"

"You!" the skull suddenly sputtered. "You! You had me executed!"

The faint trace of amusement fell abruptly from Lyrian's face, replaced by a haunted, hunted look. He took a step back, nearly tripping over a pile of roosting books that took off in a flutter, scattering scraps of loose paper.

"No," he protested, his voice raw, sounding more like a boy my age than ever before. "That wasn't me!"

"Murderer!" croaked the skull. "Tasteless vulgarian! You wouldn't know a good poem if it jumped down your throat and—*mfff!*"

I clamped a hand over his mouth. "You're not helping!" Crimson glints sparked in the skull's black eye sockets. I waited a moment, then lifted my hand away.

"What's he going to do?" Dendonderus muttered. "Kill me again?"

"I told you," snapped Lyrian. "That wasn't me. That was *him*. Rylain." He spoke the name like a curse. Like it was full of thorns.

I shook my head. It had puzzled me when Dendonderus first told us his story. I'd assumed that the skeletal bard must've gotten confused, that the truth had rotted away along with his brain. Because otherwise . . .

"That doesn't make sense," I said. "Everyone says he was kind and generous and beloved."

"Of course they do." Lyrian glowered. He turned away, shoulders hunched. "Who could believe otherwise? So much easier to blame it all on the *demon*. I'm sure that's what Mirachne told you. But I'm not the villain here."

I gritted my teeth. Was Lyrian trying to trick me? "Then who is?" I asked.

He turned back, his gaze fixing me so fiercely it made my breath catch. "Prince Rylain. He's the one you need to destroy. And I can prove it."

"How? By blighting me into believing your lies?"

"No." Lyrian's lip curled. "Even if I wanted to, my powers

don't work like that. They don't change people's minds. But I'm not lying. I'll show you. And Odessa and Phoula, they'll tell you the same thing."

I hesitated. The girls hadn't seemed dangerous or evil. But yet they lived here in this blighted castle, with this demon. Were friends with him, even. None of it made sense.

"Why do you care what I believe?" I asked. "Why not just . . . shove me in your dungeon or drop me in the moat?"

"I care," he said, with chilly calm, "because only someone from beyond the thorns can end this. Only someone like you can claim and wield the tooth of the Withering."

"And you want me to use the tooth on Rylain? You really hate him that much?"

"Yes," said Lyrian. "And no. As much damage as Rylain could do, he's not the real threat to this land. You've seen that."

I shivered, remembering the vast swaths of gray I'd seen while flying over the Mirrorwood. The claws of the Withering, tearing away chunks of reality. Its cold voice in my head, promising oblivion.

But I was still here. I hadn't faded away yet, in spite of Lyrian's blight. "The Withering is here because of *you*," I said. "You took Rylain's place."

A quiver went through the demon. Dark purple shimmered at the tips of his fingers. Twists. But he clenched his hands into fists, quenching them.

"I'm what the Bannon made me," he said bitterly. "I was *created* to take Rylain's place. But Mirachne will not allow it. My presence corrupted everything she had set in place, the wish she meant to fulfill. And now the entire realm is in chaos. That's why the Withering is here."

The Withering had told me the same thing, more or less. I bit my lip. What would Vycorax do in this situation? Probably punch him in the face and run for it. But I'd tried running already. My best option now was to play along, try to learn more.

"The Withering told me this land was corrupt and unbalanced," I said.

Lyrian's eyes went wide. "It *spoke* to you? Did it say anything else?"

"Something about a schism that couldn't be mended and had to be destroyed. You think that's you and Rylain?"

He looked away, following the flight of the red-bound book that circled high above us. "Yes. One of us has to die, or the Withering will consume the entire realm."

Bird books swooped. My heart thumped. There was something chillingly sad in his voice.

"So." Lyrian turned back. He looked uncertain. Then he drew his shoulders back. "I have a proposal. I'll help you get the Withering's Tooth, so long as you give me the chance to prove my case. To show you that I'm not the monster Mirachne says I am."

I watched him closely. Was he lying? Was that why he kept his hands tucked behind his back and stood so stiff, like a word from me might break him? Maybe this was all some sort of ploy to get the tooth and use it on Rylain.

"And then what?" I asked.

"And then you use the tooth. On Rylain. Or on me. I won't stop you. I just . . . hope I can convince you otherwise. But in either case, you stop the Withering. You save my people. So. Do you accept?"

It must be some sort of trick. But I couldn't see the loophole. Couldn't find any hidden hook to catch me. I looked for Moth, only to find him halfway across the library, curled into a plush armchair. Sleeping, while I was making a decision that could change not just my life, but this entire realm! Didn't he have even a single warning?

"You don't trust me," said Lyrian. He sounded resigned.

"No," I admitted. "Also, I had a bad experience with my last bargain. The Bannon almost got me stuck forever in a swamp."

A spark glinted in Lyrian's eyes. "I'm not the Bannon. It's just a promise. Nothing more. Nothing less. And you don't have to agree tonight. You must be tired. Hungry. Be my guest for the night. And in the morning I'll show you something that might help convince you."

I still wasn't sure what to make of Lyrian. I certainly didn't dare trust him, not yet. But I couldn't deny that the room he'd given me was absolutely gorgeous.

The enormous bed was like something out of a dream, with a canopy stretched over the top, hung with lavish curtains of pale blue velvet. Piles of soft pillows lay there, just waiting for me to sink into them.

I'd already taken plentiful advantage of the bathroom, soaking away the grime of the last few days in the wide tiled pool that seemed to be endlessly full of perfectly hot water that smelled of lilies. Though it had been slightly unnerving when my towel began to dry me off all on its own.

Nearly everything in the palace was blighted, as far as I could tell. I'd even caught the painted gold flourishes on the walls shifting around when they thought I wasn't looking, rearranging themselves into fanciful new patterns. Right now they looked disturbingly like dozens of eyes, all watching me with curious, hopeful expressions.

Moth, of course, was taking the opulence as his fair due. He settled himself regally atop the best pillow, as if he'd been made for palace life. Gingerly, I sank down beside him, still not sure how much I should trust this luxury. Especially when so much of it was blighted.

But it was such very *comfortable* blighted luxury. I couldn't help sighing as I sank into the pillows. This must be what it would feel like to sleep on a cloud.

What are you going to do, Fable?

"I don't know." I peered toward the far wall, where two tall, diamond-paned glass doors led out to a balcony. If I wanted, I could probably climb down the convenient wisteria vine alongside the wall. Run away. Find Vycorax.

And then what? We still needed the Withering's Tooth. Maybe it would be better to stay here and take Lyrian's offer. Even if it was some sort of trick, it might give me another chance to get the tooth.

But what if it wasn't a trick? My thoughts flapped and spun like the books in the blighted library, but they found no perch. Because if Lyrian was telling the truth, that meant Mirachne had lied.

Could she be wrong? She was one of the Subtle Powers. Surely she ought to know who the real villain was?

For all that Lyrian looked like a demon, with his sharp teeth and eyes of pitch and curving horns, I owed him my life. He'd saved me from the Withering. And saved others, too, from what Odessa said. Would a villain do that?

"Do you think Lyrian's just trying to trick me?" I asked Moth, teasing him with a tidbit left over from the dinner platter that had been delivered to my door by something that was either an enormous turtle blighted into a tea cart or a tea cart blighted into an enormous turtle.

Humans lie so often they can't even tell when they are doing it to themselves, said Moth, staring at me until I relented and gave him the scrap of chicken. *Also, he rides a giant bird. Birds are for eating. Not for riding upon.*

"I suppose I could at least give him the chance to show me whatever it is he thinks will convince me to believe him."

I drummed my fingers against the coverlet. There was also the matter of Dendonderus. Bad poetry was no excuse to execute someone, and he'd blamed that quite clearly on Rylain. Maybe I should have taken the skull with me rather than leaving him in the library.

No, it was just as well. I could always question him later,

and right now I needed sleep. And besides, I'd left him propped up with a volume by his nemesis Drofara, so he could spend the night criticizing her use of allegory.

"Have you seen anyone else in the palace?" I asked Moth. "Other than Lyrian and Odessa and Phoula?"

No.

"That's strange, isn't it? I mean, there must have been hundreds of people living here, in a palace this size. Where did they all go?"

Moth curled himself against me, purring contentedly. *Why do you want to know?*

I leaned sideways, reaching for the pile of my clothes that lay heaped beside the bed, discarded in favor of a voluminous, cloud-soft nightgown. I pulled free the pocket watch that the Bannon had used to try to trap me, running a finger lightly over the inscription.

"I just wish I knew who to trust. Mirachne said one thing, the Bannon said another, and now Lyrian says it's Rylain who we need to destroy. And I'm just *me*. I'm nobody. How am I supposed to figure this out?"

Do you wish to leave? asked Moth.

The question shook me out of my woeful mood. "No," I said. "I'm not giving up. I guess I just . . . hoped this would be easier. That we'd get the tooth and Vyx would destroy the demon and things would all be fixed. But I don't even know where she is now. If she's . . ."

My throat tightened, not letting me speak the words.

I could hunt for her.

My fingers brushed his soft warmth, feeling the reassuring drone of his purr. "How would you even find her?"

He didn't deign to respond, only flicked an ear.

I cuddled him closer. He was my Keystone Star, a fixed point that pinned my sky in place. Could I really send him away from me now, when I was in the castle of the demon prince himself?

Moth was clever and crafty. I had to be strong enough now to trust him. To endure fear and loneliness. "Okay," I said. "Yes. Find Vycorax. Bring her here."

I took a breath, releasing him. He sprang down from the bed, then stalked toward the half-open door out to the balcony. He paused to look at me, green eyes glinting.

Do not fear, Fable. I will be back soon.

Then he was away.

I rolled over in my soft, empty bed, feeling the warm space where he'd been. It was a long time before I fell asleep.

CHAPTER FIFTEEN

Prince Lyrian was waiting for me at the base of the grand marble stairway the next morning. I hesitated at the top step. He hadn't seen me yet, and part of me was shouting that I should run back to my room and hide there until Moth returned with Vycorax.

No, I told myself. I had come here to break my curse, to end the blight. I might not have the Withering's Tooth, but I had my wits, and I might as well learn what I could. I couldn't stop my face from fading, but my fear, my determination, those were mine to control. Lyrian had made me an offer, and I was going to take him up on it.

I drew a bracing breath, then marched down the steps. Lyrian glanced up, then jerked his gaze more sharply to me, his coppery brows pulling together as he watched me descend.

My cheeks went hot. Was something wrong with how I looked? It had taken me some effort to dress, partly because the grouchy armoire in my room refused to open until I tickled it. But once open, it had revealed yards of lace and silk, dozens of outfits ranging from smart riding jackets and breeches to a gown of what looked like spun snow. I'd chosen something in between, a shorter dress in shades of violet that cut away in the front, worn over darker purple leggings embroidered with small green leaves. There were even matching ankle-high boots of dark green with toes that turned up just slightly at the tip.

I tried to look down casually to check that my buttons were fastened properly, then anxiously patted the long red hair I'd borrowed from Phoula. There hadn't been a mirror in my room, and it had been tricky to comb it around my foxy ears.

"You really do look exactly like Phoula," Lyrian said finally. "It's remarkable."

"No," I said sourly. "It's not remarkable. It's a curse. Do you even know what they do to blighted people where I'm from?"

He cleared his throat. "You're the first person from outside the thorns that I've ever met."

"They hunt us. They lock us up," I told him, glowering. "Or worse."

He looked down abruptly, staring at the marble floor. "And that's why you're here. To get rid of your blight."

"Yes," I said.

"And Mirachne told you that destroying me would do that."

"Yes. But you said you could prove she was wrong."

It still seemed impossible, that one of the Subtle Powers could be wrong. But there was too much at stake not to learn more. I took a breath, hoping I wasn't making an enormous mistake. "I'm willing to listen. To accept your proposal."

I waited, expecting him to say something. To look pleased, or at least relieved, since he was the one who had made the offer in the first place. But instead he was staring at the tips of his black boots, lips pressed tight, as if he had mistaken a vial of red dye for cherry cordial and snuck a sip. Not that I would know anything about that.

"So," I prompted. "What did you want to tell me?"

"Not tell you." He shook himself, then strode off toward one of the doors. "Show you. This way."

I followed him along a series of corridors that grew less lavish as we went. Eventually, we came out into what I took to be a large indoor riding barn. I wrinkled my foxy nose, overwhelmed by the strong smell of hay and horses.

Lyrian halted at a wooden door on the far end. "You saw what it was like in that village, Fenhollow. You know what's become of anyone not blighted."

I nodded. "There was a woman there who helped us. She called them timespun. She said they were stuck reliving the same day, over and over. The day of the masked ball, on Prince Rylain's birthday eve."

Lyrian bared his sharp teeth briefly at the mention of Rylain's name. "Yes. The Bannon's curse fell just before midnight, when he would have turned thirteen. All the realm was caught by the magic. But it's stronger here, closest to the source. As you'll see."

He pushed the door open. "Walk softly," he said, his voice low. "They don't notice, so long as you stay in the shadows and don't speak."

Well, that was ominous. But I was too curious now not to follow.

I crept after Lyrian. We were in the stables, which were dark and dusty, the whiffling breath of horses. We passed several. They looked unblighted, watching us with soft dark eyes, stamping their great feet. It reminded me so strongly of home I had to stop to catch my breath. To close my eyes and tell myself to be strong. I was doing this so that I could go back to my family.

Low, ghostly voices sounded ahead. I slid into the deeper shadows of one of the empty stalls, close beside Lyrian. Too close. I started to edge back a step, wary of the sharp glint of his curving horns, but he hissed a warning. There was someone in the stall next to us. Along with a strange, high-pitched squeaking noise.

Lyrian gestured to an open knothole along the wall separating us from them. Warily, I peered through.

I'd been expecting something horrible. Instead, all I saw was a pink-cheeked boy with curling, honey-colored hair. He was sitting cross-legged in the straw, surrounded by four gamboling puppies, looking as if he couldn't have been happier had someone handed him the keys to the golden realm. The puppies scrambled over his legs, trying to wrestle each other but more often than not toppling into fat, furry piles.

I looked away, at Lyrian, arching a brow. Puppies? This was the dark and dire proof of Rylain's villainy?

But the haunted look in Lyrian's eyes turned me back. There must be something more.

Steps approached. The boy went tense, darting a look

toward the entrance to the stall. A moment later a man stepped inside. Like the boy, he wore plain but well-made clothes. They must both work here, in the palace stables.

"Best I take her now," said the older man, crouching beside the boy and reaching for one of the puppies.

But the boy caught her up first, clutching the pup to his chest. "No, Da. We can't. He'll hurt her. Just like he hurt Mist."

The man sighed heavily. "He's the prince, Will. You know we've no choice. He doesn't understand what happened to Mist. That's his blessing. He sees no pain, no sorrow. Nor can he."

He smiled wearily, skritching between the ears of the puppy in Will's arms. "This one looks like enough to the other. He'll never realize the truth."

"Maybe he should," snapped Will, looking mutinous. "Maybe someone should tell him what he did. Or better yet, toss *him* out a window to see if he can fly. Let *him* feel what it's like to break his legs."

The older man shook his head wearily. "Enough, Will. This is the way of things. It cannot be changed." The puppy gave a piteous squeal as the man plucked her from Will's arms.

"Please, Da," the boy begged. "Please don't take her."

But the man was already walking away.

I shoved myself back from the knothole, feeling ill. I spun toward Lyrian. "I'll go," I told him. "I'll . . . get the puppy back."

"Unnecessary," he said, nodding toward the stall.

Will's pleas had stopped. When I peered back though, I saw he had returned to playing with the puppies, as if nothing had happened.

Wait. There were still four puppies.

"Timespun," said Lyrian, his voice low. He stood again, retreating from the stables. I followed, feeling slightly foolish now. Of course. This had all happened years ago. The puppies, Will, his father, they were all trapped, just like Elfara and everyone else in Fenhollow. Except . . .

"The village repeated an entire day," I said, as we passed back into the palace proper. "But that was less than ten minutes."

"Yes," said Lyrian, walking ahead. He was dressed in black breeches, boots, and a coat of some dark, shimmery fabric that swirled with faint patterns of crescent moons and stars. His coppery hair was bound back in a low ponytail, which only seemed to make his curving gold horns and sharp-cut ears more noticeable. "It's stronger, the closer you get to where it happened."

"Where what happened?"

"Where the Bannon's curse fell. Where I was . . . created."

Created. I suppose there weren't a lot of good words to describe the moment a demon was cursed into existence. I hadn't really thought about what it might have been like for Lyrian.

I knew what it felt like to have no control over who you were. Because one of Lyrian's twists had somehow escaped the thorns and found me. But he hadn't had much of a choice in who he was either. The Bannon had created him.

I shrugged off the uncomfortable feeling, refocusing on Lyrian as he turned down a wide hall. The walls must once have been painted with a scene of autumn oaks. Now, leaves fluttered down in a soft crimson rain.

My feet scuffed them as we walked, stirring blood-colored drifts. I kept hearing the puppy's cries. Will's protests.

"I don't understand," I said. "Prince Rylain was blessed by Lady Mirachne to never know pain or sorrow. That should be a *good* thing! How did he turn into a monster that would throw puppies out of windows?"

"*Is* it a good thing?" Lyrian halted, crossing his arms, looking at me as if I'd suggested picnics should always be held on top of anthills. He cocked his head. "How did *you* learn not to jump out of windows?"

"Because it hurts, of course. Oh." I was starting to understand. I glanced up into the high painted branches above. "When I was seven, I broke my arm falling from our old walnut tree. Mum had warned me to be careful, but one of the branches snapped."

"Did you stop climbing trees after that?" asked Lyrian.

"No," I admitted. "I was a lot more careful to check for dead branches, though." I shuddered. "So you're saying Rylain didn't feel pain?"

"Yes. And he didn't understand that everyone else could. I don't even know that he realized other people were people. I think they were just . . . shadows to him. At least, most of them."

For a moment, the demon prince looked like just a boy. A strange, sad boy with black eyes that fixed on me with a shade of desperation.

It made a horrible sort of sense. If you didn't feel pain or sorrow yourself, if you didn't realize that the people around you could suffer them, then yes, you might become a monster.

"How do you know all this?" I asked. "You weren't here, not until after the curse."

He looked away. "I know because I have the prince's memories."

"How?" I shook my head, unable to fathom it. "Why?"

He shrugged. "The Bannon created me to replace the prince."

That didn't seem like an explanation to me, but Lyrian had already moved on again. "There's more," he said, leading us out of the autumn hall and into another grand corridor.

"But why didn't anyone *stop* him?" I asked. "His parents must have seen what he was turning into. Couldn't they have explained?"

"The queen died when the prince was still very young," said Lyrian. "And as for the king, well, he'd wished for a child who would know no pain or sorrow. And Mirachne gave him one," said Lyrian. "He was bound by that wish."

I remembered Moth warning me about wishes and felt a shiver of foreboding. I'd given Mirachne a wish too. But surely wishing for my true face couldn't do me harm?

"What about Lady Mirachne?" I asked. "Couldn't she see that the wish had gone wrong?"

Lyrian gave a bitter laugh. "The Subtle Powers don't care about right and wrong. This is all just a game to them."

I could believe that of the Bannon. But Lady Mirachne wasn't like that. Maybe she just hadn't seen what Rylain was like. Maybe I could find a shrine, call to her, and she could help us fix this.

We'd come to an enormous set of doors. They were also clearly blighted, overgrown with a fierce tangle of vines that twisted in and out of the walls and carpet, as if the stone and wood were earth. Dark leaves and red-brown thorns bristled everywhere, broken by clusters of pure white roses.

The doors were propped half-open, leaving barely enough room to squeeze past. Lyrian slipped through gracefully. I was about to follow when I noticed a figure, half-hidden by the vines. At first I thought it was a statue.

It wasn't. It was a man, dressed in a pale blue coat, standing stiff and attentive beside the door. His eyes were open, staring, but every so often he blinked. A woman in a matching coat stood on the other side of the entrance.

I hurried on through the narrow gap in the door. "Lyrian, what are—"

My question broke off as I saw the room we'd entered. It was vast, large enough that our barn could have fit inside with space to spare. But like the doors, all of it had been overgrown in thorny vines heavy with sweet-smelling white roses. They twisted up the gold-painted walls, slithered around gilded lamps, turned the second-story balcony into an enormous trellis. They cascaded from the chandeliers and nearly obscured the wall of gleaming windows, filtering the sunlight so that a thick green mist seemed to hang in the air.

I might not have recognized it as a ballroom, except for the masked dancers crowding the open floor. Unmoving. Frozen in pairs, with arms sweeping wide, bodies tense. One dancer even seemed to float, lifted in the arms of their partner. It was like a painting, a single moment of some glorious waltz, caught out of time.

"This is where it happened." I spoke in a hush, some part of me half-convinced the dancers were sleeping, that I might wake them if I spoke too loudly. "The curse."

Lyrian nodded. "We're very close now. This way."

He led us across the room, weaving between the dancers. They all wore masks, but I could still see their eyes, staring endlessly into the moment that trapped them. Could they see me, even just for a heartbeat? Were their thoughts as frozen as their bodies?

I shuddered, turning my gaze up, away. There was a large clock hung high on the far wall, all cream and gold with sharp hands like black daggers. It didn't move either, frozen at eleven o'clock.

Just like the gold watch. I slid a hand over the pocket in my skirt, where I'd tucked the thing earlier. Would it be safe to show it to Lyrian? If it had been part of the curse, it might just make things worse. Maybe I should wait to hear the rest of Lyrian's story first.

"Out here," he said, pushing open a set of glass doors along the wall.

We exited onto a terrace scattered with marble statues. Some were pale, streaked with gold. Others were black, streaked with silver. Like an enormous set of chess pieces, except that our chess set back home was made of pawns and knights and queens, not turtles and owls and wolves.

The terrace itself was a checkerboard of black-and-white marble. Lyrian crossed it, heading for a large stone chair set at the far end. In the chair slumped a person. A boy.

Chapter Sixteen

Prince Rylain sat as motionless as the rest of his court. Though in Rylain's case, he truly looked as if he'd fallen asleep, his chin tucked to his chest, his coppery hair falling loose over his shoulders. He wore no mask.

I glanced between Rylain and Lyrian. I could see the resemblance. Looking at Lyrian was like seeing Rylain cast in shadow, the beautiful lines all slanted, cut sharp, turned to something harsher and fiercer.

Gingerly, I leaned closer to the sleeping prince. A bit of his velvet cloak hung over the arm of the chair. I brushed my fingers against it, and they passed right through the fabric, as if it were made of mist. I gasped. "He's—he's like a ghost. A dream."

"Yes," said Lyrian. "Mirachne's ensured that no mortal weapon can harm him."

Which was why we needed the Withering's Tooth. I tried to imagine myself holding the thing, standing there between the two of them. Using that sharp, world-slicing blade on one of them. Just thinking about it felt like a great rock crushing my chest.

But I didn't need to think about it yet. We hadn't even gotten the tooth. And there was still so much I didn't understand about the curse.

"Do you remember what caused it?" I asked, thinking again of the pocket watch. "Why the Bannon's curse fell?"

Lyrian's lips pressed together. "In a way. It was . . . confusing. I was suddenly here. My mind was full of someone else's memories. Terrible things. And there was magic everywhere, bursting out of me."

"The blight," I said.

"Yes. I couldn't control it. It was like trying to catch a waterfall in a sieve. So I ran." He pointed off into the garden beyond the terrace, and I saw what he meant. Most of the hedges were neat geometric shapes, spheres and squares. But here and there, a bush rose in some enormous fanciful shape. A giant mushroom, a pair of spectacles, something that looked like a winged hedgehog.

The bizarre topiaries formed a sort of ragged trail, leading off toward the distant woods. "I might have run all the way to the sea and blighted it into wine if the Subtle Powers hadn't created the thorn wall. Even that isn't perfect, as you know." He glanced at my foxy ears, my borrowed whiskers. "Once I'd learned how to control the twists, I returned. I still didn't understand what I was, why I had such terrible memories. It was Odessa who explained."

"Odessa? She was here too when it happened?"

Lyrian's face went still. His black eyes shifted away. As if he were embarrassed. Or guilty.

"Yes."

"Well? What happened?"

"I— You should ask Odessa. It's not my story to tell."

I threw my hands up. "I thought the whole point of this was to show me why Rylain is the one we need to destroy."

Lyrian frowned. "I did. You heard for yourself just what sort of monster he was. What he would be again if you strike me down and release him. But there are other stories. Dozens of them. Believe me, I've had plenty of time to hear them all. I'll show you. There's a scullion down in the kitchens who he forced to chop off—"

"No," I said quickly. "That's fine. I don't need proof Rylain was a horrible person. It's just . . . Lady Mirachne told me one version of the story. You're telling me another. Now I don't know what to believe. And meanwhile the Withering is still out there somewhere."

And so were my friends. Was Vycorax tracking it, trying to claim the tooth? Or was she trying to reach me?

"You're thinking of your friend," said Lyrian. He was watching me.

"Yes," I admitted. "I just wish I knew she was safe." And Moth, too. Both of them were out there, in a blighted realm hunted by a monster that could consume them utterly.

"I'll look for her," said Lyrian. "When Vesper and I patrol later."

"Thank you," I said, a flood of warmth filling my chest. Though I could only imagine how Vycorax would react to being rescued by the demon prince.

"In the meantime, we should go check with Odessa. She said she thinks she found something that might help you to get the Withering's Tooth."

We entered the library to the sound of raised voices. Phoula and Odessa stood in the center of the room, looking up at the circling books. Or rather, at one particular book: the large, red-bound tome that never seemed to land, but only spiraled high above, serene and inscrutable.

"You can do it, Dess," Phoula was saying. "Fly up there and grab it."

"No," Odessa said sharply. "I can't control it."

"Because you haven't tried. Maybe if—" Phoula broke off, her foxy nose twitching. She turned, spotting us. "Tell her, Lyrian," said Phoula, setting her fists on her hips. "She doesn't believe she can do it."

"Do what?" I asked.

"Fly up there and get *The Book of Powers*."

"Fly?" I glanced at the fluffy white wings that fluttered just above Odessa's ears. At the heavy bronze shoes she wore. And at the way she held her arms, wrapped around her midsection. Like she was embarrassed, or afraid.

"Dess's blight makes her lighter than air," said Phoula. "So she can fly."

"No," said Odessa, her voice rough, maybe even panicky. Her eyes darted up, not to the book, but to the wide-open windows set into the walls above. "I can't *fly*. I can float. I can only go up."

Only up. Now I understood those heavy bronze boots. My chest went tight with sympathy, but also a sort of relief. I wasn't the only one with a blight they couldn't control.

"We could use a rope," Phoula offered, her voice softer but still insistent. "I promise I won't let you go."

Lyrian stalked over to join them. "She's said she doesn't want to." His brows knit together, making him look even more fearsome. "She doesn't need you nagging her."

"And she doesn't need you coddling her either," said Phoula, her fox tail swishing. "Just because you made her those shoes doesn't mean she needs to be locked into them for the rest of her life!"

Lyrian didn't raise his voice, but his black eyes glittered dangerously. "Those shoes are to keep her from floating away. And she *asked* me to make them for her. I thought they turned out rather stylish, actually."

Odessa stamped one of her heavy bronze boots with a loud *clonk*. "Will both of you please be quiet and let me say what I *actually* want?"

Lyrian and Phoula fell silent, glancing at each other almost guiltily. In spite of the tension, my heart gave a jog of homesickness. It reminded me of the arguments I had with Gavotte over the best way to rake the soil in the garden each spring. Or how Thespian and Sonnet held that old grudge over the name of our dog Quick, because Sonnet had wanted to name her Sir Barksalot. It was the sort of disagreement that you had with people you loved. Your family.

"Good," said Odessa in the silence. "We don't know if *The Book of Powers* even says anything about the Withering. But I do know somewhere else we can get answers."

"Where?" I asked.

Odessa tilted her head, regarding me with an intensity that made my cheeks flush. "Right here. You, Fable."

I lifted my hands, uncomfortable with the way all three of them were staring at me now. Whenever people stared, it always made me even more aware of whatever stolen face I wore. And the emptiness beneath it.

But I resisted the urge to turn away. "I want to help," I said. "I came here to break the curse. But the last time we tried to get the tooth, the Withering woke up and tried to eat me. I don't have any answers."

Only lots and lots of questions. Not just about how to get the tooth, but what I was going to do with it after. It felt as if Mirachne and Lyrian had each given me a handful of threads, but I still couldn't see the full tapestry.

Odessa waved a dismissive hand. "People always know more than they think they know. Just wait. I have a whole list of questions. I'm sure there's something that can help us."

"The Withering spoke to Fable," said Lyrian. "Has it ever done that before, Dess?"

"Oooh!" Odessa bounced, as if she'd just discovered a secret room full of kittens and cupcakes. She dug a pencil and notebook from one pocket of her dress. "What did it say? What did you say? Try to remember the *exact* words. It might be vital. Oh, and what did its voice sound like? In *The Tale of Sir Hildegard* the Withering speaks with a voice 'like the scrape of eternity's claws against the stones of a long-forgotten shrine,' but I thought that must be artistic license."

I took a step back, overwhelmed by the stream of questions. I wasn't sure I could remember *exactly* what the Withering had said.

"Well?" prompted Odessa, peering at me with furious focus over the top of her notebook. Then she blinked, glancing to Phoula and Lyrian. "I'm doing it again, aren't I?"

Phoula grinned. "Only a little."

"You're passionate about your research," said Lyrian. "That isn't a bad thing."

"But it's lunchtime," said Phoula. "There should be a picnic laid out in the Rose Garden. You can ask Fable all your questions there, *and* we can have scones."

Which was how I ended up sitting on a red-and-white-checked cloth laid out across a perfect velvety green lawn, having a picnic with a fox girl, a winged scholar, and a demon prince.

What would Vycorax think if she saw me here? Probably that I was consorting with the enemy. But it was getting harder and harder to believe that Lyrian *was* my enemy. Especially when I watched him carefully setting free a large bumblebee that had gotten trapped in the sugar bowl. The insect was clearly blighted, its fuzzy body about three times as large as a normal bee, and striped purple and orange. It settled onto Lyrian's palm, feasting happily on a single pink sugar cube.

"So then it said this realm was corrupt and in chaos," I said, continuing my account for Odessa, who was somehow managing to utterly ignore the buttery, raisin-studded scones in favor of her notebook. "And that it was going to obliterate it all because there was a schism that couldn't be mended. No, wait, that wasn't quite it."

I tapped the rim of my teacup, trying to remember exactly what the monster had said. "It said *if* the schism couldn't be mended, the realm had to be obliterated."

"We know how to fix that," said Lyrian. The bee had flown off. He sat stiffly, slightly farther away from the rest of us. "This realm has two princes. One of us needs to be destroyed." He very deliberately avoided looking at me when he spoke, but even so, I shivered. The cupcake I'd been nibbling suddenly seemed too dry, the crumbs catching in my tight throat. I took a gulp of hot, sweet tea. One thing at a time. I needed to get the tooth before I could decide how to use it.

"It's strange, though," I said, remembering something. "I told the Withering I was trying to fix things, and it said I wasn't. The Bannon said something like that too. He tried to stop us from getting the tooth and said that it would only make things worse."

Lyrian's expression darkened at the mention of the Bannon. He flipped a scone between his fingers but didn't eat. "The Bannon can't be trusted any more than Mirachne. The Subtle Powers are only here to play games with our lives. None of this would have happened if they hadn't meddled in the first place."

"But . . . the Bannon created you," I said.

"As a tool. Not a real person."

A dark ripple twisted around his fingers as he spoke, and abruptly the scone shimmered, sprouting translucent buttery wings. Lyrian grimaced, releasing it to flutter away.

"You *are* a real person, Lyrian," said Odessa, lowering her notebook for once as she peered through her spectacles at the prince.

Lyrian gave a small shake of his head, as if he didn't believe her. I watched him out of the corner of my eye, not wanting to stare. I knew that feeling all too well. Even the Withering had sensed it. *You carry oblivion within you.* Of all the things it had spoken, that was the one I remembered with perfect clarity.

Phoula coughed. "Dess, didn't you say you found something in the legend of Sir Hildegard you wanted to ask Fable about?"

"Right! Yes, let me check my notes." Odessa riffled through her notebook. "Here. When Sir Hildegard goes to rescue the Swan Prince from the blighted land, the legend says that she used something called the 'Song of Oblivion' to put the Withering to sleep. And you said the Withering was asleep when you first found it, didn't you?"

I nodded. "Yes. But there wasn't any song playing. Well, actually, Dendonderus was humming. But that was just his song about how wonderful he is. Nothing about oblivion."

Odessa tapped her pencil against her chin. The small wings above her ears twitched. Suddenly she jabbed the pencil at the sky with alarming vigor. "Death!"

She began flipping through her notebook, frowning at the pages.

"Don't worry," Phoula told me. "She does this sort of thing. She'll explain once she works it out."

"I mistranslated the passage," said Odessa a few moments later. "It's not the song of oblivion. It's the song of death! Or the song of the dead."

"Wait. You mean Dendonderus? But that doesn't make . . ." I trailed off, remembering how I'd stuffed the skull into my pouch to silence him. "Oh. No. That makes *perfect* sense. The Withering only woke up when I made him stop humming."

"Which means we might have a way to get the tooth," said Odessa. "We just have to find the Withering and get your skull to sing to it."

"He's not my skull," I said. "But I'm pretty sure he'll take any opportunity to perform."

"All we need is to find the Withering, then," said Phoula.

Lyrian stood. "I'll take Vesper out again. We'll find it. We'll get that tooth, and then"—his eyes fixed on me—"Fable can end this. One way or the other."

CHAPTER SEVENTEEN

*I*t *was taking too long.* Lyrian returned from his search late with nothing to report, except that the barrow had been completely erased, lost in the same gray nothingness that had consumed so much of the Mirrorwood already. The Withering's hunger must be growing. If it had devoured its own home, what else would be next? It could be anywhere now. And there was still no sign of Vycorax or Moth. Lyrian only stayed long enough to rest and feed Vesper, before flying off again to continue the search.

It was well into the next day and he still hadn't returned. I paced the halls of Glimmerdark Castle, pausing at each window to peer up into the sky, searching for wide, soft wings. My chest juddered like a wagon rolling over a rocky, rutted path. I'd been trying to help Odessa in the library, where she was preparing Dendonderus, but she said my pacing was making the books nervous and banished me.

So now I marched up and down the velvet corridors, trying to sort through the whirl of my thoughts.

I'd come here to get rid of my blight, so that I could return to my family and live a normal life. So they wouldn't be in danger. But for the past two days I'd barely thought about my face. I'd been so focused on the Withering. On the fact that an entire realm was in danger of fading away.

But I was still blighted. My foxy nose had started to blur. My sharp ears were softening. Mirachne had promised my wish would come true—that I would have my true face—if I destroyed Lyrian. What would happen if I chose to destroy Rylain instead? Would I still be blighted? And what might Mirachne do if I went against her?

Quick steps approached. I turned to see Lyrian stalking toward me, windblown and breathless. He must have just returned. "I know where the Withering is," he said. "But there's a problem."

He looked even more grim than normal. I braced myself. "What?"

"It's heading straight toward that village. Fenhollow."

I leaned forward, trying to see past Lyrian as Vesper flew us above the green patchwork of fields and woodland toward Fenhollow. There was no sign of the Withering yet. I hoped that meant we still had time.

"How long will it take Odessa and Phoula to get there?" I asked.

"Not much longer than us," said Lyrian. "The carriage dragons are almost as fast as Vesper." He patted the owl's neck, and she gave a low hoot. "But, Fable, the villagers are all timespun. You know what that means."

I did. And the knowledge sat in my stomach like a lump

of ice, slowly turning me cold. "They can't leave." I forced myself to say the words. Mum always said there was no way to solve a problem if you ignored it. "Even if they try, the magic will bring them back."

I couldn't see Lyrian's face, only the way his shoulders stiffened, then slumped. "Dendonderus," I asked, "how long do you think you can keep performing?"

"What a ridiculous question" came a slightly muffled response from the satchel slung over my shoulder. "DENDONDERUS VALE is a consummate artist. His very life—er, unlife—is a performance! An endless profusion of poetic genius and pure delight that can charm even the Withering itself!"

I groaned inwardly. The bard had been insufferable even before I explained how he might be the only one who could save us. Now I was surprised his skull wasn't the size of the moon.

"We don't know how long the song will work for," said Lyrian darkly. "Or even if it will work at all."

"It will," I said. "It has to." But Lyrian was right that we couldn't count on it, not forever. Maybe not even for more than the length of Dendonderus's masterpiece, which Odessa had timed at eleven and a half minutes.

Vesper gave a low hoot, drawing our attention to the world below. We were flying over a meadow, vivid and bright with flowers. I recognized it. I'd walked through it just a few days ago, on my way north from Fenhollow with Vyx and Trudi.

"Look," said Lyrian, pointing north, to what should have been the willow-fringed edges of the tall grasslands.

It was only green tatters now, swimming in a sea of gray nothing. And out of that emptiness stalked the Withering.

I hunched down, cowering even though I knew we were safe here in the sky. There was something about the relentless advance of the shimmering monster that made me shrivel inside, as if my bones had turned to nothing but screams and shadows.

"How long before it gets to Fenhollow?" I asked.

"A quarter hour," Lyrian said grimly. "At most."

I could see only one solution. A solution I never in a thousand years would have considered. But it *would* save them. And right now that was what I cared most about.

"Then we need to change that," I said. "If they were blighted, they'd be free to escape."

"What?" He glanced back over his shoulder, inky eyes wide with alarm. "You're not saying I should—"

"Blight them. Summon your twists and blight them all. It's the only way they can get out of the Withering's path."

"No," he protested. "I can't."

"Why not? So they sprout rabbit ears or turn blue—at least they won't get eaten. And besides, once we break the curse . . ." I trailed off, remembering my earlier doubts.

Silence. Only the faint swish of Vesper's wings.

"Fable. There's something you should know."

Vesper swooped. My body tensed. I didn't want to hear

whatever he was going to say. "You have a secret plan to lure the Withering away with a giant invisible bone?"

"No. Fable, you came here to free yourself from your blight. And the blight comes from me. I know I asked you to give me a chance. To consider sparing me. But I can't promise that doing that will free you from your blight."

I wanted to say something, but the words jumbled in my throat.

"I'm sorry," he went on bitterly. "I wish I could change things. But this is what I am. What the Bannon's curse made me. I twist things. I make them strange and terrible."

Strange and terrible, like a girl who was lighter than air or wallpaper with eyes. Like a cat who could talk, who was my best friend. Something wrenched deep inside me. Like a rusty key turning. A door locking or unlocking. I wasn't sure which.

"No," I told him. "Not everything." I breathed deep. "This doesn't change anything. It's still better to be blighted and alive than timespun and eaten by the Withering. We'll figure the rest out later. So let's do it."

Moments later we were spiraling down onto the village green of Fenhollow, surrounded by colorful festival tents and crowds of curious villagers. Including four that I recognized: Elfara, her two little girls, and . . .

"Trudibeth?"

I practically fell off Vesper in my rush to reach her, afraid it might just be some other villager in a festival mask. But no. There were those familiar purple ears, those jaunty tusks. Which actually looked rather menacing right now as she noticed me.

"It's me," I said, halting a few paces away. "Fable. You helped me and my friend Vycorax. I know I look different—that's just my blight."

"Fable?" Trudi blinked, her expression softening.

"I thought you were gone," I said, my voice rough.

Now she smiled, lips curving around her tusks. "To be honest, so did I. The Withering nearly had me. Chased me for over a mile. But then that fool crow flew past, and the beast took off after it instead."

Crow? Could it have been the Bannon? But why? Surely he didn't care about some blighted villager.

"Powers bless me, I'm glad to see you alive as well," said Trudi. "But why are you here?" Her gaze shifted past me as Lyrian dismounted. She muttered under her breath, "The demon prince!"

"It's okay," I said hastily. "He's here to help. Trudi, the Withering is on its way. We need to get everyone out of the village."

"And we need to hurry," said Lyrian, joining us. "We don't have long. A quarter hour at most."

Mutters began to filter through the crowd. "Is that the prince?" someone called out. "What's that on his face? A mask?"

"Did she say the Withering?" asked another. "That monster Sir Hildegard fought?"

Elfara, who had been watching us with a puzzled expression, shook her head. "Trudi, what's going on? Who are these people?"

I could hear the edge of mistrust and uncertainty in her voice. I wished there was time to properly explain. But with each moment that dragged past, the Withering slunk closer, trailing a path of oblivion through the world.

"Please," I said to Trudi. "Please trust us. Lyrian and I are here to help. We can get everyone away, out of the village. Stop them from being timespun."

Trudi reached for Elfara's hand, desperate hope flashing in her eyes. "How?"

I gestured to Lyrian, who still stood a few paces away. You might not think someone with horns and fangs could look nervous, but he did. It was going to be up to me to make this work. If only I were like Indigo, who could talk a fish out of water. I tried to remember what they'd told me, how to speak loudly, not to rush, to make every word count.

"This is His Royal Highness," I said. "Your prince."

"I thought the prince was supposed to be beautiful, Mama," said one of Trudi and Elfara's girls. Out of the corner of my eye, I saw Lyrian wince.

"Yes, as you can see, the prince has been enchanted and granted magic by the Subtle Powers. Magic that he can give to you, so that you can escape a terrible monster that is on its way here to destroy this village."

"Is it the curse?" Elfara swept her daughters against her, eyes wide. "The Bannon's curse?"

More dire mutterings and growls rose from the crowd of villagers.

"Yes," I said. "But we're here to break it." I waved to Lyrian.

He gave me a dour look, lips pressed tight. Finally he took a single step closer to Trudibeth and her family.

The younger girl gave a small wail, her eyes darting to his sharp teeth, his horns, and ducked behind Elfara. "Mum, I don't like the monster."

Elfara stiffened, then ducked her head. "I'm so sorry, Your Highness." She was trembling.

Lyrian saw it too. He looked pained. Ashamed. He drew back instantly. "Don't apologize," he said curtly.

It wasn't fair. No more fair than Telmarque hunting me. But then, I'd feared Lyrian myself. Because all I knew of him was a twisted fairy tale.

"It's okay," I said, crouching, peering at the girl where she still huddled behind Elfara. "We both look pretty strange, don't we?" I twitched my foxy whiskers, and the girl actually gave a small smile. "And your mama, too."

"Mama's wearing a mask," said the girl.

Trudibeth coughed, her cheeks flushing deep purple. She tugged at one of her long ears. I remembered what she'd once said. That she couldn't bear the thought of her family looking at her and seeing only a monster.

But if you loved someone, you loved someone, didn't you? Like my family and me.

"No," said Trudibeth, her voice rough. "This is my face,

Lill." She glanced toward Elfara. "But I'm still me. I just look a little different."

I forged onward. "Because she's magic. We all are. Do you want to see the prince do something amazing?"

"Yes." The girl clapped her hands together. Elfara looked befuddled and Lyrian suspicious. The crowd of villagers hummed with interest.

I grabbed the nearest convenient object, a potted geranium sitting in front of one of the tents. I set it down between us. "Go on," I told Lyrian. "Make it something magical."

"Fable, I can't just—" He leaned closer, lowering his voice. "I can't control what the twists do. I might turn it into a pot of venomous snakes."

"Just try," I said. "We need them on our side."

He arched a brow. "*Our* side?"

I flushed. "If you're going to be their prince, you don't want them terrified of you, do you?"

"No. But, Fable, what if I just make it worse?"

"You won't," I said bracingly.

He looked unconvinced but turned back to the potted geranium. His shoulders rose as he drew in a deep breath. Then he snapped his fingers, conjuring a twist that wriggled through the air, glinting purple.

The girl gasped. So did several people in the crowd. The wild magic spun around the flowerpot. Several buds swelled at the tips of the plant, bursting open within seconds to reveal not geranium flowers, but pink-and-white-striped taffies. The little girl squealed in delight, picking one and popping it into her mouth.

I looked over her head to Lyrian, grinning at him. He didn't exactly smile back, but something in the tight set of his jaw softened, and he gave me a small nod.

"See?" I said. "Not so scary."

The girl watched me, still wide-eyed, chewing busily.

I turned to Elfara. To all the villagers crowding around us, ogling the scene. "Now it's your turn. Are you ready?"

Before long Elfara sprouted frothy stalks of asparagus among her blond curls. One of the girls could snap her fingers, filling the air around her with a fall of glittering light. The other seemed completely unchanged, until she stepped back into her own shadow and disappeared.

"You should go south," I told the villagers. "Our friends will meet you there with carriages. They'll take anyone who wants back to the castle. Or if there's somewhere else you can go that's safe."

Trudibeth shook her head. "Nowhere is safe. Not while the Withering is here."

"We're working on that," I told her. "We have a plan. We just need to make sure folks here are safe before—"

A low, bone-rattling roar thrummed through the air.

Someone in the crowd screamed, pointing north, toward the meadow that bordered the village.

Or what would have been the meadow. It was gone now. Only tattered green rags and gray mist. And the shimmering, half-seen monster stalking out of the ruin and heading straight toward the village.

Despair clutched at me, tugging me toward defeat. Just the sight of the monster had set me shaking. I remembered those agonizing moments at the barrow. The horrible emptiness of its maw.

Then I stuffed it away. I had to do this. Dendonderus and I had to stop the Withering for as long as we could. It was the only chance these villagers had to escape. I turned to Lyrian, finding his black eyes. Holding them for a heartbeat.

Then I took off, sprinting across the green to meet the Withering.

CHAPTER EIGHTEEN

*E*ach *breath tore my lungs.* My legs burned. But I ran, and ran, and ran. Past the striped tents. Past booths filled with plush toys. I hurdled over a stone wall and tore through a patch of bramble, heedless of the thorns.

My chest ached, but I drove my heels faster, harder, heading straight toward the Withering. The monster had halted, lowering its wolfish head, silver eyes fixed on me.

Its voice tore through my mind. *Have you come to embrace your fate, daughter of earth?*

"No," I snarled. "I told you I was going to fix this realm, and I am."

The schism tears deeper than ever. This realm is lost. And you, with it. The Withering tensed, coiling itself low, ready to spring.

"Tell that to my friend," I said, and pulled the skull out of my satchel. "Maybe you've heard of him? The renowned and loquacious DENDONDERUS VALE!"

As soon as the bard was free, he began to sing. Even I felt the spell of it. It wasn't the words but his voice. The richness. Like one of Mum's finest tapestries, threaded with every color, every emotion, every experience. An entire life, spinning out through the air.

I held my breath, gripping the skull, not daring to move as slowly, slowly, the Withering's eyes closed. Its great gray bulk melted down, curling onto the grass.

You still do not understand, its chill voice whispered in my thoughts.

Then it breathed out. In. A long, low rumble. And did not move again.

"Well, that's just rude!" Dendonderus sputtered, breaking off mid-verse. "Sleeping during a performance."

"Keep singing!" I hissed, as the Withering twitched, one paw scraping deep gray gouges from the meadow. "We want it asleep, remember?"

Dendonderus continued, though with an air of great injury.

It took me two verses to work up the courage to approach the Withering. Unseen fingers plucked the raw edges of my soul, trying to unravel it. *Don't think about it,* I told myself. *Lock it away.*

I imagined Vycorax standing beside me. She'd been so brave, marching right up to the monster last time. But she wasn't here now. Which meant it was up to me. Time for me to be the hero I'd wished for.

I knelt beside the Withering's jaws. A chill wind rippled over me. No, not wind. Slow, slumbering breaths. I shuddered. The tooth was right there. I could reach out and touch it. But what if it cut me? Every muscle in my body cramped tight, quivering as I reached out for the fang. It was slightly crooked. Vycorax must have loosened it. I ran my fingers along the base. It was like ice, so cold my skin wanted to stick to it. Tightening my grip, I pulled.

A low rumble came from deep within the monster's maw. But its eyes remained closed. "Keep going," I called to Dendonderus. And to myself.

Another tug, and this time something gave way. It was working! I abandoned gentleness and began yanking with all my might. Dendonderus was almost to the end of his song.

No, actually, he was singing something entirely new. A verse I didn't recognize.

> *"None other can match the bard's might,*
> *But even he cannot sing through the night,*
> *He needs a break,*
> *And a nice slice of cake,*
> *So let's get ready to run from this fright."*

I coiled all my strength into one great heave. Suddenly I was flying back, tumbling away from the sleeping monster with a shard of shimmering nothingness clutched in my hand.

I stared at it. The tooth! I had it. The plan had worked!

"Well done," said Dendonderus, his voice crackling, even more raspy than normal.

"Thanks," I said, feeling as limp as wet wool.

"Not *you*." He gave a huff. "I was talking about myself, of course. Did you not hear that performance? My range? My depth of emotion? Ah, I see you're so overwhelmed you can't even speak."

But it wasn't the bard's performance that had silenced me. It was the eyes of the Withering. Awake. Open. Fixed on me with a cold and ruthless intensity.

Foolish girl. You think my tooth will save you? It will not. It will only make things worse, no matter how you use it.

I recoiled, my mind tangled with its words. What did that mean?

"Fable!" Lyrian's shout broke me from my confused thoughts. A shadow of wings passed over me. The prince landed Vesper with a soft *thwump*. "Hurry!"

Scooping Dendonderus up from the grass, I stuffed him back into my satchel. Then I launched myself onto the owl's back. A heartbeat later Vesper was in the air, wings beating mightily.

The Withering bellowed. In my hand, the tooth seemed to quiver in response, thrumming up my arm and rattling my teeth. I looked down, stomach spinning from the height, to see ancient empty eyes fixed on me.

No matter. Oblivion claims all things in the end. You know that better than most.

I didn't stop shivering until I'd had a hot bath, three cups of hot cocoa, and an enormous slab of toast slathered in butter. Even though I'd hidden the Tooth in the deepest recesses of my grouchy armoire, I could feel it. A chill pressed against my fingers, as if it were still in my hand, waiting to be used. My mind wouldn't stop spinning the words of the Withering over and over. *It will only make things worse.*

I dressed in a frothy pink gown and made my way down to the large drawing room, where the refugees from the village had gathered. Phoula was moving among them, helping the turtle cart distribute tea and cocoa, while several of the villagers made more toast over the large hearth.

They seemed to have adjusted well enough to their change in circumstances. Or, more likely, they were still in shock from having learned that they'd been stuck in time for a hundred years and now suddenly had asparagus growing out of their hair. But I was glad to see Elfara and Trudibeth standing together by the hearth, heads bent close. Trudibeth gestured to Elfara's ferny hair, and they both laughed. It was almost enough to make me forget the Tooth waiting for me back in my room.

Almost.

If only Vycorax were here. She saw things so clearly. Maybe if I laid out all the tangled threads of my thoughts, she would know what to do. I missed Moth just as fiercely. His pragmatic questions. His steadfast surety.

But neither of my friends had returned. Which meant it was up to me to find my answer. To decide what to do with the Tooth, now that I had it.

There was no sign of Lyrian, but I found Odessa at a desk in one corner, bent over something that looked like a map of a building. Of Glimmerdark Castle itself, I realized, noticing the four round towers at each corner.

"What are you doing?" I asked.

She sighed, adjusting her round spectacles. "Trying to figure out where we can put everyone."

"It's a castle," I said. "Doesn't it have hundreds of rooms?"

"Yes," she said. "But two-thirds of them have timespun people in them. And the rest are all blighted. This one"— she jabbed a finger at a lavish guest room near the south tower—"has pillows that try to swallow anything that touches them. And this one here has a bathroom that runs with blood instead of water. This one might be all right," she added speculatively, "so long as whoever stays there doesn't mind spiders."

"Where's Lyrian?" I asked. "Can't he help?"

Odessa crinkled her nose. "He's run off. Said he had to make sure the Withering was keeping away, but I know he's really just avoiding them."

"Them?"

She hooked her thumb in the direction of the villagers.

"Are they afraid of him still?" I asked, remembering the little shadow girl. She was sitting on the floor over by one of the windows with her sister, carefully watering the taffy-geranium, looking delighted.

A strange look tightened Odessa's face. "No. It's more the reverse. They were trying to toast him earlier. For saving them from the Withering. And they keep bowing to him."

"So he ran away because people were treating him like a prince?"

Odessa gave a small shake of her head. "No. Because they were treating him like *the* prince. Even calling him by his name. But Lyrian is nothing like *him*." She bit off the word, like it tasted bad.

"You mean Rylain."

Odessa nodded. "They don't know the truth. What an absolute *monster* he was." Her hand tightened on the map of the castle, crumpling the corner.

"I know. Lyrian showed me some of it." I hesitated. She already looked fierce and flushed, like someone trying not to cry. But this was important. "He said you were there, when the curse fell."

Odessa breathed in. Not a gasp of surprise, more like a bracing breath, as if she'd been expecting the question. Carefully, she smoothed out the crumpled edge of the map. "I was."

Her fingers traced a path along the paper, down one of the ink-sketched hallways, toward a large rectangle labeled BALLROOM. "Rylain was my cousin," she said, keeping her eyes on the paper. "My father was the queen's younger brother. Rylain and I were born only a few months apart. We grew up together. Played together. It"—her lips twisted—"it wasn't all bad. He could be sweet. And he always had some new game, some new adventure planned. We were Bonny Crispin and Lady Scarlet, questing for danger and romance. Well, mostly we stole chocolate cake and cherry tarts from the kitchens, but we did it with dash and style." Odessa grinned, but the smile fell away almost instantly. "But that wasn't enough," she said. "Bonny Crispin had a sword. So Rylain had to have one too."

The cocoa and toast turned queasy in my belly.

"The games weren't as fun after that," she said, her voice gone distant, hollow. Like she was talking about something that had happened to another person, not her, never her. "I tried to hide. That's when I first met Phoula. Her grandfather is the head gardener, and she used to help me hide out in the hedge maze. But Rylain always found me."

"That's ridiculous," I exploded. "Couldn't your parents do anything?"

She shook her head. "I heard them talking once, late at night, about taking me and my little sister away. But the king wouldn't allow it. He said the prince would be devastated. He said it was my duty to be Rylain's friend, his best friend. That it wasn't his fault. That it was just the way he was, and I couldn't expect better."

"Yes, you could!" I said, furious for her.

Odessa rubbed her thumb over the map, brushing away a bit of dust. "I tried, Fable. I tried so hard. But I made a mistake. I triggered the Bannon's curse."

My mouth opened. A faint huff came out. "You? How?"

"I was only trying to give him his birthday gift," she said. "It was a lovely thing, a golden pocket watch. I picked it out myself, at the market."

A pocket watch! I pressed a hand to the smooth lump in the pocket of my gown as Odessa continued.

"Rylain thought it was boring. He threw it back at me."
She shook her head. "It was such a stupid thing. It didn't
even hurt all that much. But it had all ballooned inside me
for so long, and that little, tiny pinprick was all it took to
just . . ."

"Pop," I said.

"Pop." Her face scrunched. "And then I did the one thing
I'd promised to never, ever do. I cried. Rylain begged me to
stop. He didn't understand, and that just made it all worse."

I frowned. "How did he see the mirror? Was it in the
watch?"

"It must have been. I guess I didn't notice it." Odessa
drew in a ragged breath. "Rylain was shouting at me to stop.
He looked so strange. His eyes. It was . . . it was like he saw
me, for the first time. Really looked at me. And I told him he
was a monster." Her gaze went distant, her lips pressed tight.

"And then?" I prompted.

"And then everything changed. Like a thunderstorm,
right over my head. Like falling into water when you can't
swim. I heard him—or maybe it was Lyrian by then—
screaming. But I couldn't see anything except the twists.
They were everywhere. I tried to run, but the next thing I
knew I was floating, and I had these." She gestured to the
small white wings fluttering above her ears.

"It was horrible! I've always hated heights, and it seemed
like I was going to just float all the way up into the sky. But
I managed to catch hold of one of the windows and pull
myself inside. If I hadn't . . ." She trailed off, shuddering.

Then she tapped one of her heavy bronze boots. "Now I need to wear these every moment of every day. Or I might just float off forever. I guess it's a fitting punishment." She heaved a great sigh, finally lifting her brown eyes to meet mine. "It's all my fault, after all."

"No," I told her hotly. "*None* of this is your fault. The Subtle Powers mucked this all up, not you. The king let it happen, *not* you."

There was a clunk as Odessa shifted in her seat.

"What about your parents?" I demanded. "Why weren't they with you?"

"They'd traveled outside the realm with my little sister, to visit my mama's family in Thessequa. I suppose—"

Her voice cracked, and she looked away. "I suppose they're all dead now. It's been a hundred years, even if it doesn't feel like it in here. I can still remember my father waving from the carriage. How Gilly made a face at me and said she'd bring me back some Thessequan spicecake. Do they still make that now?"

"Yes," I croaked, the sadness of it sitting in my throat like a clod of mud. My father had promised to make one for Allegra and me next month, for our birthday.

I'd come here to free myself from my blight. To win back my true life. Now everything had changed. There was more, so much more at stake than just my own face. There was an entire realm full of people in danger of being snuffed out. And even if we could stop the Withering, there were things I could never repair. Odessa was right. It had been a hundred years or more. If what Lyrian told me was true, I might never find a way to end my own blight. But at least I still had my family to return to. Odessa had lost that forever.

A shriek jerked my attention back to the villagers, but it was only Trudi and Elfara's girls and the handful of other kids playing the Floor Is Fire over on the far end of the room, hopping from one silky sofa to the next. One of the boys, sprouting blighted velvety ears like a rabbit, managed an enormous leap that set all the others giggling with delight. He looked five or six, about the same age I was when I first found out I was blighted. The lump returned to my throat.

"If you're looking for Lyrian," said Odessa, "he's probably in the north tower. It's his favorite place, especially at night."

I tugged my gaze from the rabbit boy. "Thanks."

"Fable," she said, watching me pensively, "Lyrian told me about your agreement. He said he was going to let you decide what to do. With the Tooth."

I coughed. "Yes."

"He isn't a demon," she said abruptly. "I know he looks like one. I know he never smiles and he's grim as a tomb. Believe me, when I first met him, I thought the worst. Phoula and I were trying to reach the thorns. We thought maybe if we could get out, we could find a way to fix things. But we couldn't get through. Not with fire, not with Phoula's claws. We even tried to climb it. I thought it would be easy, with my blight making me float, but I lost my grip. I would have floated away if Lyrian hadn't spotted me. He and Vesper saved me."

"And what about climbing the thorns?"

"They just kept growing taller and taller. Even Vesper couldn't fly high enough. But Lyrian kept trying. He's a good person. He cares. Maybe too much. There's this one timespun farm he visits every day, just to catch the farmer's little boy when he falls out of the hayloft, so he doesn't break his arm. He takes care of the blighted beasts in the menagerie, including the tiger that breathes fire. He even refuses to put the insulting portrait of our great-aunt Marion in the oubliette."

"It's really that bad a painting?"

She winced. "Not just bad. *Literally* insulting. She called me a waffle-livered goosepenny with the handwriting of an arthritic crocodile. But Lyrian visits her every day. My point is . . . he deserves a chance."

"And I want to give him that," I said. "Honestly, I'm not sure I want to use the Tooth on anyone. I think maybe it's more complicated than that."

Odessa tapped her pen against the desk, looking troubled. "What are you going to do, then? We can't keep blighting villages and bringing them here." She gestured to her map, giving me a wry grin. "Not unless some of them really like spiders."

"I know. I'm going to figure it out."

"Fable," said Odessa as I started to step away. "I know you came here because of your own curse, not to save us, but . . . I'm glad you're here. Thank you."

Heat warmed my cheeks. "I haven't done anything yet."

"Yes," she said. "You have. You've been a friend. It's been lonely here, with just the three of us trying to fix things."

I swallowed, choked by a bittersweet lump of responsibility and happiness. "I'm glad I'm here too."

Then I left Odessa to her work and set off to find Lyrian.

Chapter Nineteen

He was in the tower, as promised. It was night by then, and there were no lamps lit, only a frail silvery starlight to guide me up the stairs. It took me a moment to find him. Elbows propped on the stone ledge, chin resting on one hand, dark eyes turned up to the stars—a strangely wholesome pose for someone I'd known as the demon prince up until three days ago. At the scuff of my steps, he straightened abruptly, tucking his hands behind his back, chasing away all hint of the dreamy stargazer.

He nodded formally. "Fable."

Now I felt awkward too. With all my siblings, I was used to being around people—sometimes too many people packed into one not-so-large farmhouse. But they were all entirely familiar. I'd known them my whole life. I knew their habits and quirks as well as my own. The closest I'd ever come to having to make a new friend was when I rescued Moth five years ago.

With Vycorax, it had been easier in a way. We'd started off enemies. At least I'd known where we stood. And even once that changed, once it started slipping sideways into friendship, we had a common enemy, a common goal: to end the blight.

And now here was Lyrian, foiling all my expectations.

Taking that entire goal and turning it inside out. If I used the Tooth on Lyrian, I might banish the Withering *and* cleanse the blight. But what would become of him? Would he just . . . wink out? Would he turn into a slice of nothing, like the rents left behind by the Withering's claws?

A tired, petulant part of me couldn't help but feel a bit frustrated by it all. If only he'd been exactly what Mirachne promised. Just a horrible, nasty, nightmare-spewing demon that Vycorax and I could destroy, releasing the true prince and setting everything right, tra-la-la. But he wasn't, and now I had a muddle to sort.

Lyrian drew back his shoulders, as if bracing himself. "Have you made a decision?"

No. Not even remotely. I still had so many questions. Should I use the Tooth on Rylain? Did I dare risk a choice that might anger Mirachne and leave me blighted forever? Or was there some other option, something I was missing completely?

But when I saw what stood behind the prince, propped beside the broad ledge of the tower wall, a different question popped out.

"Is that a telescope?"

He blinked, clearly not expecting that. "Er. Yes?"

I couldn't help myself. I'd traced the trails of light in the sky for years, trying to teach myself the constellations from one of our old encyclopedias. Da had taught me the few he knew: the Weaver, the Archer, the Serpent. But there were *so* many others! And I had so many questions.

Why did the Keystone never seem to move, when all the other stars spun slowly through the seasons? Why were some stars brighter than others? Why did they seem to twinkle?

Before I knew it, I was standing beside the telescope, peering at it hungrily.

"Do you want to take a look?" asked Lyrian, somewhat stiffly.

"Yes, please!"

He gestured to the eyepiece. "It's pointed at the Seven Sisters right now."

Gingerly, I peered through the copper tube. Then gasped. "I can see all seven of them!" I pulled back, checking with my eyes alone. Without the telescope, they were only a hazy blur above the Archer's bow. But squinting through the lenses again, I could see each distinct gleam. Could even see how one sister was more yellow, while another was tinged almost blue.

I turned to Lyrian, feeling as if I'd swallowed a star myself, something gleaming bright that glittered inside me. "I never thought I'd ever see a telescope! I read that the university in Morena has one, and of course the Golden Empire invented them, but they're thousands of miles away."

Lyrian fidgeted with the cuff of his twilight-blue coat. "I doubt there was anything my—the king wasn't willing to do to keep Rylain happy. He built a water garden, a gaming lawn, even a menagerie. Though I don't think Rylain cared much for stargazing. This hadn't even been taken out of the case when I found it." He cleared his throat. "How did you come to have an interest in the stars?"

It was my turn to flush. "It started when my father showed me the Keystone. I just . . . It was nice to know there was something up there that didn't change. Something you could always count on. I know that probably sounds silly."

"Not at all," he said, with no trace of humor in his voice. His black eyes seemed to have devoured part of the night sky, to be holding pieces of it in their inky depths as he watched me.

For some reason, it made me want to keep talking. To tell him the rest. "I wish I could go to the university," I said in a rush. "And study them. But . . . it's impossible. I mean, so long as I'm like this." I gestured to Phoula's foxy face. It must be starting to fade, which meant I probably should be figuring out where I could borrow another, not idling around on top of starlit towers making awkward conversation with a prince.

"I'm sorry."

"You don't need to apologize," I said. And I truly meant it.

"Don't try to make me feel better. Unlike Rylain, I intend to face my mistakes. I know what I am. I know the harm I've caused."

"You didn't harm those villagers," I said. "If it weren't for you, they'd be withered by now. And so would I."

He turned away, running thin brown fingers through his shaggy copper-gold hair. "They're blighted. I may have done it to save their lives, but that doesn't mean I haven't done harm. I'm a curse come to life, Fable. Sometimes I wonder if I even . . ."

"What?" I prompted, when he trailed off. The sharp, tense lines of his shoulders made my own hunch, as if bracing for a blow.

"If I'm anything more than just a shadow. I have Rylain's memories. I live in his castle. I've taken his place, but who am I, really? Just a twisted reflection sent by the Bannon to thwart Mirachne's plans. No one."

The words tugged at something in my chest. I reached out to touch his shoulder. "You're more than that. I know, sometimes I feel—"

I broke off. He'd startled at my touch, turning. Something warm brushed my hand. His cheek. Heat bloomed over my skin, rushing up to my own face. My foxy ears tingled, melting away. My nose thinned, my cheeks lifted, my jaw spread.

I tried to pull away, but it was too late. My blight, hungry, eager for a new face, had done its work. I'd stolen Lyrian's face.

Except . . . not entirely? I ran my tongue over my teeth, feeling only the normal ridges of incisors and molars. No sharp fangs. My ears were round. No horns curved from my temples.

And Lyrian was staring at me in absolute dread and horror.

"W-what did you do?" he stammered, eyes wide enough to swallow the sky. "That isn't—that's *him*. Take it off! Take it off!"

I staggered back, frightened by the fury in his voice. "I'm sorry. I didn't mean to take your face!"

"That *isn't* my face!" Lyrian shouted, a wildness in his sharp movements. Something shuddered in the air around him. The air twisted into shivery magic, spinning away heedlessly.

Dozens of twists were pouring off him! I ducked as one of them slithered over me and struck the telescope. The tripod legs twitched, growing long and jointed, like the legs of an insect, and it began doing a sort of spidery jig.

Lyrian's eyes were wild. His lips curled back, showing his fangs, as he flung a hand at me, releasing another twist. It was as if he didn't know who I was. Like he was trapped in a nightmare and I was the monster tormenting him. I had to get away.

I ran for the steps, zigzagging to avoid the twists. They blighted bits of the tower instead. A patch of black stone to my left turned to chalk. To my right, the pavers suddenly exploded with a ring of bright red mushrooms. Part of a nearby wall jiggled alarmingly, like a molded blackberry jelly.

I'd leaped down five steps when I nearly collided with Odessa, who was clunking upward, accompanied by a floating lantern. When she saw me, she shrieked, her mouth an O of fear, her entire body tense, curling in on itself.

"It's me!" I said. "Fable! I took Lyrian's face by accident, and now he's gone wild!"

At the sound of my voice, some of the wildness in Odessa's

own eyes melted away. She peered at me more closely, shuddering slightly. "You don't look like Lyrian," she said. "You look like *him*. Rylain!"

Oh. Oh no. "I'm sorry," I said. "I don't know what to do."

"Take mine. My face." She stepped closer, taking my hand as I stared at her in confusion, then pressing it to her own round cheek. Another tingling rush, and curls were suddenly tumbling to my shoulders, as something ticklish burst from above each ear. The world turned blurry, but I could hear Odessa sigh. "There. Come on. Let's sort this."

I stumbled, squinting to find my way. I had Odessa's eyes now, but no spectacles. She grabbed my hand, pulling me back up to the tower. To Lyrian.

He was a dark blur huddled against the parapet, but I could make out the golden-brown oval of his face. The two dark slashes of his eyes, fixing on us. Even my muddied vision could see the glimmering shivers gathered around each of his tight fists.

"Stop it, Lyrian!" shouted Odessa. "Get ahold of yourself. *Look.* Look at her! It's only Fable!"

"Odessa? Fable?" He groaned, spinning to fling the twists out into the night sky. Then he sagged, slumping against a bit of the tower wall that was still stone. A choked noise came from him as he stared out into the night. It might have been a sob, or a laugh.

A wary silence stretched out. Then his shoulders stiffened. He lifted himself wearily. Spoke in a broken, painful voice. "I'm sorry."

"That's okay," I said. "No harm done. I mean, who doesn't need an entire wall of blackberry jelly?" I'd gotten some on my hand somewhere along the way. I popped it in my mouth now. "It's quite tasty! You should try it." But my bright chatter had no effect. He kept his back to us.

"Lyrian," said Odessa. "If Fable took your face, why did she—"

"I'd like to be alone," he said, cutting off the question.

Odessa glanced at me. I squinted back at her. "Come on," she said. "I've got an extra pair of spectacles you can borrow. We'll finish this conversation in the morning." She shot the boy a sharp look. "Right, Lyrian?"

He said nothing, only stood there, staring into the sky as we left.

CHAPTER TWENTY

I woke at dawn from a fitful sleep, sitting bolt upright in my extravagant bed, my breath still quick from a nightmare in which a giant gray wolf chased me through a maze of shimmering silver mirrors. Shadows flitted beside me in the dream. I caught glimpses of faces glaring at me, none of them familiar. At last one final mirror rose before me. A dim gray shape stood within, more girl than ghost. She faded into nothing even as I watched, screaming for her to run.

I sat huddled in my blankets, staring at my hands. I fumbled on the bedside table for Odessa's spare spectacles, propping them on my nose and letting out a long, slow breath. It was only a dream. I was still here.

Skff.

I jerked my gaze to the open glass doors that led to the balcony. It was light enough outside that I could see the shadows of the wisteria vines. They swayed gently in the morning breeze. Maybe that was all it had been. I held my breath, listening. Then, suddenly, something leaped onto the bed beside me. Something small and soft and purring.

"Moth!"

I swept him into my arms until he wriggled in protest, slipping free to regain his dignity. A larger shadow stepped into the room. A shadow with a sharp smile and a patched crimson coat.

Vycorax peered about at the splendors of the room. "Huh," she said. "I have to say, this is nicer than I'd expect for a demon prince's prison."

"Vyx! You're alive!" I flung myself out of the bed to hug her.

She went stiff at first, then relaxed slightly, even managing to pat me lightly on the shoulder in return. "Of course I'm alive."

"Oh. Sorry." I pulled back quickly. "I'm just really, really glad you're here."

Vycorax adjusted her crimson coat. It might only have been the rosy light of dawn, but she looked a bit flushed. "That's okay. I don't mind. I mean, I'm glad you're all right." She gripped my shoulders, staring at me with her bright eyes crinkled at the corners, her lips a thin, worried line. Her gaze flicked to the feathery wings I'd borrowed from Odessa. "Whose face is this? *Are* you all right? If that monster's hurt you, I'll do more than kill him. I'll rip out his—"

"I'm fine," I said quickly, not particularly interested in hearing the rest of that sentence. "Really. Lyrian isn't what we thought. None of it is. I got this face from Odessa. She's Rylain's cousin, and he's the real monster. Lyrian is only trying to save his realm from the Withering. He even helped me get the Tooth."

I'd been talking faster and faster, aware that Vycorax's frown was only getting deeper and deeper the entire time.

As if what I was explaining was only making her more confused. But at my final statement, she blinked, gaping.

"The Withering's Tooth? You have it? Here?"

I nodded, padding over to my grouchy armoire, tickling the handle to convince it to open. The doors swung wide. I shoved aside the lace and silks to reveal the Tooth.

Even just lying there, it felt like a threat. Like a stormy sky promising thunder. I wanted to slam the doors shut, but Vycorax was too quick. She gave a cry of triumph, then seized it.

Stepping back into the moonlight, she turned the weapon, examining it. "You see?" she said, grinning at me. "I told you that you were a hero. Where's the demon prince?"

"We can't use the Tooth on him, Vyx."

She stared at me. "You're going to have to repeat that, Fable. Because I think I just heard you say that you don't want to use the Tooth on the horrible demon prince who caused the blight. Which would be complete rubbish."

"It's not," I said. "What's rubbish is that story Mirachne told us. She lied!"

Vycorax crossed her arms. "What's he done to you? Is this some sort of glamour? He's twisted your mind just like he twists magic."

"No, nothing like that. He just told me his side of the story. Please, Vyx. Just listen. Let me explain. Let me show you."

I took her to the ballroom, then out to the terrace, where the slim, beautiful boy forever slumped in his stone throne, surrounded by polished marble and distorted topiaries. Fortunately, it was still so early none of the others were up. I didn't want Vycorax meeting anyone else until I'd had a chance to explain.

I told her all that I'd learned. The story of my arrival, of meeting Odessa in the magical library with its flying books. About Lyrian's proposal, the puppies in the stable, Odessa's description of how the curse fell. Picnics and bumblebees.

Vycorax listened with a sort of deepening, darkening silence that made me nervous. It was like my words weren't even reaching her. Moth, bored of our conversation, had disappeared into the hedges, probably stalking the songbirds that had begun their morning trills.

I plunged on. "And Lyrian helped to save Trudi's village. The Withering was going to destroy it, but he blighted all the timespun so they could escape! And Trudi's alive, Vyx! She and Elf and their daughters. They're here in the castle. Safe!"

Vycorax gave a bark of laughter. "Safe? You mean *cursed*. Powers, do you even hear yourself? We came here to end the blight, not to go spreading it around entire villages."

"It was the only way," I protested. "And anyway, there's more important things than getting rid of the blight."

Vycorax said nothing, only lifted the Tooth, staring at its gray, shimmering edge. Her lips were a thin, tight line. She looked sad. As if I'd . . . disappointed her.

"You don't believe me," I said after the silence had spun out into something thick and thorny.

She shook herself. "I do believe you, Fable. But we came here to fix *you*. To stop the blight. I'm a *blighthunter*. That's my job. And now you're telling me you don't care about that anymore?"

"I *do* care," I said. "Of *course* I care. I don't want to live my whole life having to steal faces. But, Vyx, there's more at stake, than just me. This entire realm could get eaten by the Withering."

Vycorax paced, her steps carrying her back and forth in front of the stone chair. "Because the realm is in chaos. Destroying the demon will fix that."

"But I *like* Lyrian, Vyx. He's a good person. It's not his fault he makes the twists. And I'm not even sure using the Tooth on anyone is the right decision. The Withering said almost the same thing as the Bannon. It sounded like maybe there was something else. An entirely different option."

"Okay," said Vycorax. "What's the different option?"

"I—I don't know. I haven't figured it out. But now you're here. We can do it together, like we agreed."

Vycorax turned away from me. All I could see were her stiff shoulders. "That wasn't our deal."

I let out a gusty breath. "Vycorax," I said. "I can't believe you'd rather—"

She whirled toward me, her pointed chin jutting, her expression fierce. "We were going to fix you. Fix all the blighted."

"Maybe I don't need fixing!" I snapped back, feeling trembly, like I might rage or burst into tears or both. "Maybe none of us do. So if the only reason you're here is to make your father proud of you, then tell me right now. Because I thought it was more than that. I thought you actually cared about *me*."

"I do!" she exploded. "Of course I do! Do you think I want you to get locked away? Or—" Her voice caught raggedly. Her cheeks were flushed, and her eyes glittered. Surely she wasn't crying. Not Vycorax. "I don't want anyone else to die!"

"Anyone *else*?" I said, confused. A queasy feeling had begun to bubble inside me. "Who are you talking about?"

She dragged in a long breath. Adjusted the collar of her scarlet vest with fingers that trembled slightly. Her eyes were distant. "My sister."

I waited. It was a few more heartbeats before she went on. "Velichor was my father's first apprentice. And she was amazing, Fable. So much better than me. She could run like a deer and fight like a lion. She even bested Father once." Vycorax was staring into the distance now, a small smile on her face. "She was a brilliant cook, too. Our mum taught her how to make these walnut pastries from the Golden Empire—that's where her family was from—and Veli used to make them for my birthday. She promised to teach me too, since Mum died when I was only a baby. But she never got the chance."

The smile vanished. "She was out on patrol with Father. There'd been a report of twists along the western border of the Mirrorwood. I remember begging them to let me come too. Father had finally agreed to let me become his apprentice, since Veli had been promoted to full-fledged hunter. But he said next time. Next time I'd come with them. Except there wasn't a next time. Not for Veli."

"What happened?" I asked softly.

"She got blighted." Vycorax clenched her jaw, as if she didn't want to speak anymore, but the words jerked out. "It was an accident. But blighted is blighted. That's what Father told me when he came back. Alone."

"He killed her?" I couldn't stop the question. It was just so outrageous. So unbelievable. I tried to imagine my own father, his soft eyes going hard, his hand raised. No. *No.* Impossible. How could Telmarque do that to his own daughter?

"Yes. Or another hunter did. It doesn't matter. She's gone. And I'm not losing anyone else I care about." She fixed me with her dark brown eyes, her narrow body coiled tight.

And just then I heard it. A light footstep. Someone else approaching. Not the clunk of Odessa's enormous boots or the quick dart of Phoula's feet. A measured, solid step I had already learned to recognize.

"Fable? Is that you?" asked Lyrian, as he stepped from between two of the enormous marble chess pieces. "Are you—"

It felt like we were all timespun, held fast in that horrible moment. Lyrian, his coppery brows arching in surprise, eyes going wide. Me, raising my hands, opening my mouth to call out, *No. Wait. Listen.*

And Vycorax, leaping at the demon prince with the fierce

expression of a girl utterly convinced of the terrible righ-teousness of her duty. She had never looked so much like her father as she did plunging the Withering's Tooth into Lyrian's chest.

There was no blood. Only a terrible, soft gasp, as Lyrian's eyes widened, staring down at the shimmering gray blade sunk deep into his flesh. He took a step back. Lifted his head. Found me. Opened his mouth as if to ask something.

And then he was gone.

Winked out, as if he'd never been. Like thistledown, blown to tiny fragments in the breeze. Catching one last bit of sunlight, then gone, gone, gone. I couldn't feel myself. I wasn't here. This wasn't happening.

"Is it morning already?" said a voice, resonant and familiar, from somewhere behind me.

I spun, eager for it to be a mistake, for Lyrian to pop out of the shadows and reveal that he was perfectly fine. But it wasn't Lyrian who'd spoken. It was the boy in the stone chair.

Rylain was awake.

CHAPTER TWENTY-ONE

*I*t *felt as if* I'd swallowed an entire thistle bush, and it was tearing me raw from inside. I couldn't bring myself to look at Vycorax, but I was aware of her, turning to face the awakened prince. To see what she'd done.

He sat upright, brushing back locks of coppery hair so that the first rays of the risen sun lit his beautiful, impossible face. He wasn't smiling, and that felt like a tragedy.

I shook myself. No. I had to remember what he was. It didn't matter how pretty he was. He had thorns inside his heart. Sharp ones. I'd seen the scars they'd left behind.

"Is it my birthday yet?" asked the prince, sounding slightly dazed.

I shuddered. That voice. It was exactly like Lyrian's. In every other way the two princes had been warped reflections of each other, but Rylain spoke with the exact same voice that had invited me to look at the stars. The same voice that had spoken my name just moments ago.

But everything else about Lyrian was gone. Vanished as if the Withering had torn him out of the world. My insides spun, sick and dizzy. If only we *were* timespun. If only I could snatch that moment back! But it was over. Lyrian was gone, destroyed by the dagger I had worked so hard to claim.

And the true prince was awake.

Rylain blinked, finally seeming to take notice of what was around him. The empty terrace. The blighted topiaries. The frozen silence of the ballroom. The two girls standing there goggling at him.

"Odessa?" His brown eyes fixed on me, going wider. "I remember . . . you were . . ."

"Just a dream, my prince."

I gasped. Beside me, Vycorax startled. That voice. That sweet, honey-drenched voice.

It was Lady Mirachne. Even more brilliant in the dawn than by starlight. She skimmed toward us out of the light of the newly risen sun, trailing her gleaming gown over the marble. "A dream that is over, or will be very soon now."

"Who are you?" the boy asked her, still sounding sleep-dazed. "Where is my father?"

"I am the lady Mirachne," she said gently, a soft smile curving her lips. "Your godmother. I'm afraid your father had to go away, but I promised him I would take good care of you."

"Away? But he said there was going to be a tremendous surprise at midnight. Is it very long now?"

"No," said Mirachne. "Not long. That nasty Bannon tried to keep you from your party, but fortunately these heroic young ladies were able to set things right." She gestured to Vycorax, who still stood stiffly, as if she'd just reported for training. And to me.

"That's not a hero," said Rylain, laughing. "That's my cousin Odessa."

"No, this is not your cousin," Mirachne told him. "Poor Fable here was cursed by that wicked pretender, but she is brave and wishes to set things right. That's why she helped to wake you and banish the monster who tried to steal your kingdom."

I shuddered. No. I didn't want credit for this. This wasn't what I wanted.

Except it *was*. This was *exactly* what we'd come here to do. What Mirachne had told us we *must* do to make our dearest wishes come true. How sure I'd been, just a few days ago, that I knew what I wanted. How foolish I'd been, not to think what the cost might be.

"Well done, daughters of earth," said Mirachne. "I knew I was right to trust you in this. That you would have the strength and the courage to do what must be done."

"Of course," said Vycorax resolutely. "We had to do our part to end the blight." She glanced toward me, then away so quickly I didn't have to decide whether or not to meet her gaze. "Lady Mirachne," she went on. "You said that once the Bannon's curse was broken, the true prince would be able to get rid of the blight. Can he do it now? Fix Fable?"

I felt the tickle of Odessa's wings at my temples. In spite of everything else, a bubble of hope rose inside me. I could be free. At last.

Then I swallowed, shoving the feeling down. If anything good was to come of this, there were more important things than my blight. "What about the timespun?" I asked. "And the Withering?"

"The sleepers will wake soon enough." Mirachne gave us a star-bright smile. "Now that I've released my hold, time has already begun to catch up. Tonight, the midnight bells will finally toll. And then all will be as it should be."

"You mean we'll be cured of the blight then?" I asked. "That's when I'll have my true face back?"

"Yes," said Mirachne. "The chaos that has consumed this realm will be purged at last. There will be no more need for the Withering to cleanse it. All will be joy and bliss."

She smiled so very brightly, but her words crawled over my skin. Invisible spiders, spinning me into her web.

"Joy and bliss?" I asked. It sounded sweet, but then, so did a child who would never know pain or sorrow. But maybe there was still a chance. "Please, Lady Mirachne, I know you think that what you gave Rylain was a blessing, but it's not. And Lyrian, he wasn't evil. Isn't there some way you can bring him—"

"The king's wish must be fulfilled," proclaimed Mirachne. "Unbreakably this time." She swept over to the stone chair, ignoring me. "Rise, Prince Rylain. Today is your birthday eve, and you must prepare for tonight's ball. All the realm will celebrate with you."

The prince blinked, then smiled. "Of course they will. I am their beloved prince. Will there be sweets, godmother? And dancing?" He sounded strangely childlike for a boy about to turn thirteen. But then, he'd spent his whole life getting exactly what he wanted. Never being disappointed. Never losing anything he cared about. *Could* he even care about things? Love them? Or was that too great a risk for pain and sorrow?

"Yes, all those delights and more," said Mirachne. "And at midnight, when you turn thirteen, I will give you my birthday gift."

"What is it?" he asked, looking delighted, bright and eager as a puppy.

Mirachne showed a mouthful of pearly teeth, a triumphant smile. Like a queen striding out from the ruin of a great battlefield to claim her crown.

"I will grant you the power to purge your realm of the blight, along with every pain and sorrow. It will be glorious! You will all live happily ever after. Isn't that wonderful?"

I stared at Mirachne as the weight of her words crashed over me. I would be free of my blight. I would have my true face. But only if I became like Rylain.

Maybe it wouldn't be as bad as I thought. I only had the stories from Lyrian and Odessa to judge by. And Rylain was one single boy. Plenty of people in the world were cruel and heartless without any interference from the Subtle Powers. Maybe I was panicking over nothing.

Fear of my blight had ruled me all my life. Always, that gray nothing, eating away at me, hungering, demanding to be fed with the faces of my parents, my siblings, strangers, anyone who could keep it away for another day. I could be free of that. Finally free.

A gasp broke me from my thoughts.

"R-Rylain?"

Odessa stood on the edge of the terrace. Her skin had gone ashen.

But Rylain only smiled, stepping toward her. "Cousin! There you are! Come, you have to meet my godmother, Mirachne. She is going to give me a marvelous gift tonight for my birthday."

Odessa looked dazed. Like someone who'd just woken from a dream to find the world a cruel and shabby place. Or else someone who hoped she was dreaming yet and that this was all a nightmare.

"Isn't this lovely?" crooned Mirachne. "Family reunited at last. Poor girl, it must have been such a trial to endure that demon pretender. Acting as if all this were his, when he was nothing but a twisted shadow."

Odessa made a small, desperate noise. Her eyes turned to me, lancing me with all her confusion, her fear. I saw it plainly, even if Rylain did not.

"What happened? Fable, where is he? The Tooth, did you . . . ?"

She trailed off, spotting Vycorax for the first time. "Is that your friend?" she asked, her voice turning cold. "The blighthunter?"

I could tell Vycorax had heard us. She cleared her throat, clasping her empty hands behind her back. As if trying to find something to do with them, now that the Tooth was gone.

"Yes," I said.

Then there was no more confusion, only bleak despair.

Briefly, I saw a ghost of Lyrian in her face. He had been her friend. And I had taken him away and set loose a monster instead.

I should have stopped Vycorax. The Bannon was right. The Withering was right. The Tooth had only made things worse.

"Oh, yes," Rylain babbled on cheerfully. "Have you met the brave heroes? One of them looks like you. Isn't that a great joke? Lady Mirachne says it's them we have to thank for freeing me from the Bannon's curse. They banished that horrible demon."

I cringed, feeling Odessa's gaze sharpen on me.

"And now all will be as it should! Tonight I will fix it all, at midnight, once I have my gift. Then everyone will be happy forever! Won't that be grand? So you must wear your prettiest dress, and we will dance to . . ." He stopped, frowning at Odessa's feet. At the heavy bronze shoes Lyrian had made her.

"Why are you wearing those ridiculous shoes? They're horribly ugly! Take them off at once!"

"No," said Odessa. "I can't."

Mirachne tsked her. "Of course you can, child. You see how happy it will make your princely cousin to do so. And it is a small thing."

"I can't," said Odessa, her eyes wide behind her spectacles. "I'll float away."

"Oh, but I am the Lady of Wishes," said Mirachne. "I know what you have whispered in the dark. Your dreams of slippers of silk, beaded with pearls, fit for a princess."

"Yes!" Rylain cried. "Oh, yes."

Mirachne smiled. "Let us have it, then." She gave a small wave of one hand, setting a drift of glimmers in the air. They spun away, circling around Odessa, clinging to her heavy boots. There was a faint pop, and abruptly the leather and bronze were gone, replaced by delicate slippers beaded with pearls like drops of dew on a cobweb.

Odessa began to drift upward. She twisted, scrabbling at the air, trying to seize something to hold her, but it was too late. She rose like a soap bubble, softly but surely. Her shriek was more of a gasp, as if her lungs were held too tight to release it. But I saw the look of utter terror on her face.

And Rylain could do so much more, so much worse. Should I do something? Surely Mirachne wouldn't let this get out of hand. I shot a glance at Vycorax. She swallowed, her expression uncertain.

"Oh, Dess, what a trick!" cried Rylain. "You're like a balloon! How high can you go?"

"Please!" she cried. "I want to come down! Help me!"

Rylain cocked his head. "Perhaps I could shoot you down. Like a bird. Fetch me my bow and arrows," he commanded, to no one in particular.

Enough. I didn't care if it meant risking Mirachne's wrath. This wasn't right. This was torment. And if I didn't act now, she would be too high to save. She was almost out of reach.

I leaped for her, putting every bit of my strength into the jump. My straining finger slid over silk and pearls. An ankle! I grabbed hold.

I thought she might carry me away too. My feet hung in the air. My breath folded itself into my chest. And then my toes thudded back against the flagstones.

"No!" Rylain was shouting. "You're not playing properly!"

But I refused to let go. We fell together, in a tumble, a few paces from the others. There wouldn't be much time to speak privately, but I needed Odessa's help now. I had to undo this.

"Fable," croaked Odessa. "Lyrian. Is he—"

"He's gone. But it's not midnight yet. We can still bring him back. If we can find another mirror, maybe we can trigger the Bannon's curse again."

Odessa's fierce eyes met mine. "Haven't you done enough? Isn't this what you and your friend over there wanted?"

"Not like this," I said. "Please, Odessa. I want to fix this. Help me bring back Lyrian."

I thought she was going to refuse. And honestly, I wouldn't blame her. I'd brought back her tormentor. I might not have struck the blow, but I'd given Vycorax the weapon.

"There might be a way," she said at last. "But I need to get to the library."

An ember of hope was better than nothing. I scrambled to my feet, careful to keep a grip on Odessa's arm, grounding her.

The others were watching us. Vycorax looked wary and Rylain petulant. Mirachne beamed like the sun, so certain everything would keep spinning around her, that none of her planets could possibly go astray.

"No. You must let her float," demanded Rylain. "I want to shoot her down. She even has wings now, like a pigeon." He laughed. "Go on, Dess. It will be an excellent caper!"

Odessa shuddered. I moved in front of her, my mind scrambling for some excuse, some distraction.

But it was Vycorax who spoke. "I'd like to see you shoot, Prince Rylain. Would you show me? We could see who can shoot the most targets."

She met my gaze then, giving me the smallest of nods, her jaw tight. Could she finally see the monster we'd unleashed?

I held my breath, but Rylain was like a stream of water, eager to take whatever course ran easiest. "Yes," he crowed in delight. "I should like that. Come, you can use my old bow. It is not so pretty, but it will do. Mine is black yew, and it gleams like obsidian. Come and see!" He smiled, and for a moment, just a moment, I seemed to see a different face. One crowned by curling horns, fierce with sharp teeth and sharper bones. Lyrian. Was there hope in my madcap plan? Could we bring him back and stop Mirachne and Rylain from cursing us with heartless happiness?

Whatever we did, if Mirachne suspected us, she would do anything to stop our plan. And she was one of the Subtle Powers. Immortal. Powerful enough to stop time itself. With a wish at stake, she could do nearly anything.

Rylain had started to move away, Vycorax following him,

but he paused after a few steps. "You must come too," he told Odessa and me. "We'll have cakes and tea. It will be such fun."

Odessa's smile frosted over her lips. Her eyes darted to mine. Then something in her seemed to grow sharper. As if she'd found an old, uncomfortable coat, one she thought she would never need to wear again.

"We'd love that more than anything, Cousin," she said brightly. "But we have to prepare for the ball. So that everything will be perfect."

I caught Vycorax's eye. I wished I could speak to her with my thoughts, like Moth did. There was so much I wanted to say. Did she understand the terrible thing we'd done? Was that why she was distracting Rylain? But I couldn't ask her, not in front of the prince and Lady Mirachne.

"Of course it will be perfect," said Rylain, looking slightly baffled. "It is my birthday ball."

Mirachne smiled. "Yes, indeed, my love. And I promise you, this time I will let nothing interfere with it." Her bright eyes transfixed me, the threat clear as sunlight. "We must ensure that *all* our wishes come true."

CHAPTER TWENTY-TWO

*E*ven after we'd reached the library, the back of my neck crawled, as if somehow Mirachne could see us. Did she suspect we were plotting against her and Rylain? Was that why she'd looked at me like that?

The only good news was that Phoula had been waiting in the library when Odessa and I arrived. I nearly had to tackle her to keep her from tracking down Rylain and tearing out his throat after she heard what he'd done to Odessa. Thankfully, she agreed to stand guard at the door instead. That way she could warn us if anyone else came, and we'd have time to make some excuse—that we were searching for a song to sing for the prince's birthday or the recipe for a new cake.

As opposed to finding a way to bring Lyrian back. If that was even possible. I had too many doubts to lock away—the moment I stuffed one into my mental box, another took the opportunity to slip out. They hissed at me, a nest of venomous serpents, promising failure.

Courage, Fable. I'd stolen a tooth from the mouth of the Withering itself. I could do this. "Okay," I said, looking toward Odessa. "How do we find a mirror to trigger the curse again?"

We stood on the balcony in the center of the room, the same place we'd first met, scattered with a few squashy armchairs and an incongruous birdbath, where several books of the flock were perched, their papery wings fluttering. Moth sat nearby, having rejoined us on our way to the library.

Why did you break the curse if you want to trigger it again? he asked. *Is it like when you catch a mouse and play games with it?*

I shuddered. "No, definitely not. We made a mistake, Moth. Or . . . I did. But we can still fix it."

"*The Book of Powers*," said Odessa, pointing to the lone crimson-bound book that still circled high above. She clung tightly to the balcony railing. Without her heavy shoes, she risked floating away if she didn't hold herself down.

"Isn't that the one Phoula wanted you to fly up and grab?" I asked. "You think it has something in it that might help?"

"I hope so. It's the only book in the library I've never read. But there are references to it everywhere. It's full of stories about the Subtle Powers. Including one about how the Mirrorwood got its name."

I frowned. "I thought that was just what we called it since the curse. Because of the king destroying all those mirrors."

Odessa shook her head. "It's always been the Mirrorwood. Ever since the Subtle Powers granted the first queen a magic mirror that would show her the faces of her true enemies. Or . . . something like that. See, this is why I need that book. Maybe it will tell us what happened to the first queen's mirror. Or maybe we can figure out how to get another."

"But first we need to get the book," I said, peering up.

Odessa made a face. "Yes. If it were a normal book—well, a normal *flying* book—I'd lure it with ink." She nodded to the birdbath. Several books perched along the rim, bending over the pitch-black ripples within. Each sip sent squiggles of inky text across their pages.

"Why is that one different?"

"Because it's not written in ink," she said, her lips twisting in distaste. "*The Book of Powers* is written in blood."

The skin along my spine prickled. "You mean we need to—"

"No," she said hastily. "It's not human blood. It's dragon blood. So unless you're hiding a dragon somewhere, we can't lure it."

I glanced at Moth. Indigo had told me a story once, about how the last dragon had hidden himself away in the body of a housecat, to escape the hordes of knights that were constantly besieging him.

No, he said, very simply. I wasn't sure if it was a denial of being a secret dragon, or a denial of giving up any blood. And maybe I was better off not knowing.

"Then we have to catch it," I said, frowning as I followed the book's flight. Just because it appeared high above us didn't mean we couldn't reach the thing, what with the topsy-turvy architecture of the jumbled library. "If we can get up to that walkway over there, maybe I can grab it," I suggested.

Odessa shook her head, lips pressed into a grim line. "No. I've tried that. I've tried everything we could think of.

Except . . ." She trailed off, looking down at her feet, floating a few inches above the floor.

"Are you sure?" I said. "You're not worried about floating away?"

"I am. But some things are worth facing your fears over. Like this."

Keeping one hand on the railing, she tugged at the sash around her waist. "Hopefully, this will be long enough," she said, holding it out to me. "But I'll need your help."

Her determination was contagious. It reminded me, a bit, of being around Vycorax, or my sister Sonnet. Odessa's bravery made me feel braver.

I took a firm grip on the end of the sash. Odessa kept her gaze fixed on the book as it circled above. On the railing, her fingers clenched tight, the knuckles pale.

"Whenever you're ready," I said.

She gave a dry laugh. "That's going to be never. But since we only have until midnight to fix this, I can't wait to be ready. I just have to"—she took a breath, then leaped away, up, sailing into the air—"go!"

I clung to my end of the sash, watching as she floated higher and higher, closer to the circling book that might hold the key to saving Lyrian. Saving all of us from Mirachne's curse of happiness.

Odessa reached out, straining. Almost! But the book swept past, inches from her grasp. I tried standing on the tips of my toes, my arms aching as I held them as high as I could, but it wasn't enough. The line was taut.

"We can try again," I called. "I'll pull you back. We can get more—"

"No. I can do it." She tugged at her waist, freeing the sash to hold it in one hand, using the extra length to drift another few inches higher. She snatched out with her free hand. Catching hold of the large red book, she clutched it tightly to her chest. Her gasp of relief echoed through the library.

I reeled Odessa back down as fast as I could. When she reached the balcony, she was shuddering, trembling as if she'd spent all night out in the snow. But her expression was triumphant. A smile to melt away the winter. "I did it!"

I grinned back as I helped tug her down. "That was amazing!"

"Let's just hope what's in here is worth it," she said. Her expression darkened. "Who knows how long we have before Mirachne's time magic wears off completely?"

We both bent over the book. Odessa paged through, her spectacles glinting as she skimmed the text. It was exactly as she described: stories of the Subtle Powers and their dealings with humankind. I glimpsed delicately engraved images of a gorgeous maiden stepping out of the sun. A crow, shimmering feathers melting into a cloak for a tall man with mischief in his eyes. And others too. Didarae the Huntress, with her silver wolfhounds. Tormach the Smith, who my sister Sonnet had left gifts for after she was offered her apprenticeship.

All those and more fluttered past, until Odessa finally

came to a page that held her attention. She spread it open before us. "Here! 'The Queen and the Mirror.'" She flipped a few pages forward, then let out an exasperated breath. "That's no help."

"What? Doesn't it say what she did with the mirror?"

"Only that she returned it to the place where it came from originally. Somewhere called the Grove of Reflection. Ugh. This is useless. We don't have time to go traipsing all over the realm looking for that."

"Good, because you wouldn't find it in any case," said a booming voice from one of the empty armchairs.

No. Not empty. A leering skull sat wedged in among the pillows, half-hidden behind an enormous volume titled *Who's Who in the Bardic College Today*.

"Dendonderus?" I said. "Have you been there this whole time?"

"Where else would I be?" he drawled. "Out on a morning stroll?"

"It's just that you're not normally so . . . quiet."

"You weren't saying anything particularly interesting."

Odessa rolled her eyes. "But the Grove of Reflection is interesting?" she asked. "You know something about it?"

"Of course I do," he scoffed. "Am I not the greatest bard in all the realms? I know far more secrets than could be contained in any pitiful tome. And as you know, even death cannot stop my loquacity!" Sparks flared in his empty eye sockets. "Ah, such a perfect turn of phrase. The world is not worthy of my genius."

"Great. Will you share some of that genius?" I asked hopefully.

"There is no map to guide your way," he began in a sing-song voice. "For it stands apart from night and day. Seek the wisdom of the greatest bard. For he shall—" The skull broke off, muttering, "Card? Lard? Ugh, no. All right, let's try this instead. The greatest bard can offer advice, if you—"

"O great Dendonderus Vale," I said, interrupting. "Please share the precious bounty of your knowledge and tell us how to find the Grove of Reflection!"

The skull wore a perpetual grin, but at my words he seemed to smile even more widely. "Of course! The mighty DENDONDERUS VALE is always willing to share his wisdom. So. You seek the Grove of Reflection. I shall tell you the tale, for it is a story of great valor and mighty deeds. It begins—"

"Sorry," I said. "Could we skip to where it actually is?"

Dendonderus huffed. "Skip to the end? But you haven't even heard about the flying donkey. He's very amusing."

"Please," I said. "Unless you really want Rylain to rule forever and force us to live happily ever after."

The skull made a choking noise. "Happily ever after? No tales of true bravery and courage ever came from that false promise." He sighed. "Very well. The Grove of Reflection can be found on no mortal map, because it lies within the Subtle Realm itself. The birthplace of the Powers, perilous and strange, where no mortal dare trespass long."

His warning prickled my skin with gooseflesh. An entire

land that belonged to the Subtle Powers. It sounded absolutely terrifying.

But I had once thought that about the Mirrorwood. And still, I had found my way here. I had survived. So far. I drew in a breath. "Right. How do we get there?"

"You ask one of the Subtle Powers to take you there, of course," Dendonderus said matter-of-factly.

I sagged back against the stone railing, all my hopes turning soggy and sodden as overcooked oatmeal. Just ask a Subtle Power for help. As if they were waiting at the market for me to stop in and buy some tarts.

"Mirachne would never do it," said Odessa. "She wants this. She stopped time to keep Rylain as he is."

"You're right," I said, as the truth of what I had to do drummed over me like cold rain. "Not Mirachne. We need someone else. Someone who wants to stop her as badly as we do."

Odessa frowned. "Who?"

Someone I never wanted to see again. Someone I didn't trust. I pushed myself upright again, forcing myself to speak his name. "The Bannon."

Odessa goggled at me. Moth made a spitting sound.

"It's the only option we have left," I said. Then, before I could lose my courage, I flung the words out. "Bannon! I want to make a bargain!"

CHAPTER TWENTY-THREE

*M*y *challenge echoed* across the stones of the library. It seemed the entire hall was frozen, even the circling books, even Moth's swishing tail. Then a tall man in a cloak of feathers stepped out from a nearby archway that should have led to a set of steps but now showed a sliver of some dim, green-gloomed wood. He paused at the threshold, the feathers whispering secrets, even as his crimson eyes promised lies.

Odessa gave a muffled yelp. Then she tugged her notebook and pencil from one pocket and began scribbling notes. "It's really him," she whispered to me. "Oh, I need to record *everything*. There are so few reliable firsthand accounts!"

"Yes, take notes," I said. "That way he can't slide out of any promises."

The Bannon smirked, as if he'd heard the entire exchange. "Greetings, daughters of earth," he said, dipping his head.

I nodded in return. "Thanks for coming."

"But of course. Though I did think you had lost your taste for my bargains." The corner of his thin red lips twisted up. His eyes gleamed hungrily. I shivered. How many witless bargains had other mortals made with the Bannon? Maybe I was a fool. But I would do it, if it would save us.

"I want you to give me safe passage to the Grove of Reflection and back again," I said.

The Bannon cocked his head. "Hmm. Not an insignificant request. It takes considerable power to open a path to the Subtle Realm. What would you offer in return? Perhaps you might promise me a favor? I'm sure I'll think of something I need someday." He smirked.

"No," I said. "I think there *is* something you want."

"Oh, really? You claim to understand the wishes and desires of the Subtle Powers?" He seemed more intrigued than offended. Good.

I took a breath. "You want Lyrian back. Your curse set him free in the first place. I don't know why—I don't really care; maybe this is all just a game between you and Mirachne—but I know you didn't want us to use the Tooth on him."

"No," said the Bannon, and for once he seemed utterly serious. "I did not."

"Then, please, help us bring him back. He was created by your curse. We just need a mirror, so we can trigger it again. Rylain will turn thirteen tonight, at midnight, but there's still time. Please."

I hadn't meant to add the last bit. I didn't actually think the Bannon cared for mortal pleas. But all the pent-up desperation and hope was too much to keep it unspoken. I would beg if I had to.

Something changed in the Bannon's sharp face. Bloodred eyes held me. I felt as if I were being measured. Weighed. Gone over like a hank of wool that might hide some thistle or burr.

Maybe he was right to judge me. I'd made mistakes. But this wasn't one of them. I just needed the Bannon to see that. To understand what I was willing to do. Bringing Lyrian back meant I might never be free of my blight. But I'd do it all the same, to stop Mirachne.

Finally he nodded. "We have a bargain, Fable, daughter of earth. I will open the path to the Grove of Reflection. When you have found what you need, a way will open for your return. But be warned, for there is but one mirror that will break the curse now. You must find it and not be tricked by any other. Choose wisely, and use it to show the prince his true self. Is that clear?"

I glanced to Odessa, who was recording the Power's words in her notebook. "Do you see any loopholes?"

She bit her lip, shaking her head. "But, Fable, that doesn't mean they aren't there. This is the Bannon."

"I know. It's a risk, but I have to do something. We're running out of time." I turned back to the Bannon. "How soon can I go?"

He slanted a sly smile, gesturing grandly to the archway and the glimpse of that dim green wood. "Whenever you wish."

Had he known what I wanted from the start? Had he expected this? My mind was too slow, too stuffed with worries to puzzle it all out. I had to focus on my task now. The one thing I could do to fix this.

"I don't know how long it will take," I told Odessa. "Can you keep Mirachne from noticing I'm gone? We can't let her suspect what we're doing. She might try to stop us."

"What about the girl?" asked Odessa. "Your friend. The blighthunter." Her voice turned frosty on the last word.

I hesitated. Vycorax had distracted Rylain earlier, kept him from tormenting Odessa. But she'd also been the one to unmake Lyrian. Vycorax wanted to get rid of the blight more than anything. Yes, she was my friend. But friends didn't always agree on what was best for each other.

"Don't let her know either. Just play along."

Odessa smiled wryly. "I've got a lot of experience with that."

"Thank you." I glanced down at Moth. "Moth, you should stay here. It might be dangerous."

"It will *certainly* be dangerous," said the Bannon. "And it will not be easy."

Moth padded closer, winding himself between my feet. *I have been to many dangerous places. Where you go, I go.*

I drew in a long, steadying breath, peering through the archway. Maybe it wouldn't be as bad as I feared. It looked almost peaceful, from what I could see. A flat open wood of silvery birches and pale green ferns. And here and there, the shimmer of small pools. "At least it's not as bad as sneaking into the Withering's lair," I said.

"No," said the Bannon. "It is worse. The Grove of Reflection is not a place to travel lightly. Be careful what you look upon, or you may never leave."

The Bannon's warning haunted me as Moth and I stepped gingerly through the ferns. The mossy earth hushed my steps. It was a strange, silent place. Scattered throughout were dozens of small pools, each utterly still, reflecting a watery silver-green light. Cautiously, I peered into the nearest one.

Odessa's face stared back at me, faded slightly, gone blurry around the wings and chin. Then she flinched. Or, rather, I did. I'd never cared much for seeing my own reflection. It was never really me looking back.

I crouched, plucking a pebble from the ground, then tossing it into the pond. Ripples spread, shattering the image. It was only water, then. Nothing dangerous.

"What do you think?" I asked Moth. "Is one of them really a mirror, not water? Do I have to toss pebbles in all of them to find the right one?"

Aren't they all mirrors?

"Maybe that's what the Bannon meant about there being many to choose from," I said. "But he said I needed to choose the right one. Blight, I hope it's one of the small ones. It's going to be hard to get close to Rylain carrying a mirror bigger than I am."

I was about to move on, to check another pool, when something caught my gaze in the distorted ripples of the first. It was hard to tell, but the reflection looked different now. Larger, maybe? I held my breath, waiting for the image to clear again.

But when it did, all I saw staring back at me was Odessa's reflection.

Silly goose. I was spooking myself. Wasting time I didn't have.

I moved on, following a spiraling path away from the large split oak that held the archway I was counting on to return me once I had the mirror. Over and over, I tossed pebbles into ponds, watching ripples distort the reflection of Odessa's face.

"This is ridiculous," I said, after the dozenth pond. "They're all the same! We don't have time for this. It must be getting close to midnight."

Moth prowled to the edge of the pool I'd just plopped a stone into. *Are you sure you're looking for the right thing?*

"No," I admitted, groaning and slumping down against one of the birches, wrapping my arms around my legs. "I don't feel very sure of anything anymore."

Moth's warm weight leaned against my leg. Purring, he slipped himself under my arm. I stroked his back, trying to ignore the angry, hot itch in my eyes, the weariness that clung to me like spiderwebs I couldn't brush away.

Are you giving up, Fable?

My breath caught in a tiny sob. The question wasn't accusing. It wasn't angry or woeful. Moth, like most cats, was too pragmatic for that. It was only a question. A simple, terrible question.

"No," I said. And I almost believed it. "But I am feeling sorry for myself."

Why? He flicked an ear.

I gave a hollow laugh. "Because even if I do somehow manage to find the mirror and fix Lyrian and stop Mirachne and Rylain, I'm still . . . nothing, Moth. I came here because I thought I could be free."

Free from what?

I opened my lips, certain I knew the answer, certain it was something I'd been aching for all my life. Except now, suddenly, I had no words. Free from what? What was it, really, that I wanted to escape?

"Fear," I said, after a long moment.

The smiling prince can help you, if that is what you seek. He will take away all fear and sorrow.

He was right. If all I wanted was to be unafraid, I had my answer. I didn't need this. Easier to let midnight come. Mirachne would take away all my sorrows and pains.

"It's not that," I said finally. "I just hate being so terrified that I'll never have the chance to really live. I hate feeling like my life is a bit of dandelion fluff that's going to blow away and be forgotten."

Moth twisted himself up, settling his paws on my chest so that his green eyes in their white mask stared into mine. *You're alive now, aren't you?* He sniffed, whiskers tickling my neck and cheek. A prickle of pain burst along my collarbone, as his front claws unsheathed, digging into my skin.

"Ouch! Blight, Moth! What was that for?"

He arched back, giving a low rumble of satisfaction. *You bleed. So you are definitely alive. Dead things stop bleeding.*

"Of *course* I'm alive!" I sputtered. "That's not what I meant about *really* living."

Moth twitched an ear. *I do not understand the difference. You bleed. You are alive. You* are *really living.*

I sighed, not feeling qualified to argue with feline logic. But Moth did have a point. Feeling sorry for myself wasn't going to change anything.

I shoved myself upright and stalked over to the next pond. I'd scooped up the pebble, ready to toss it in, when I saw the reflection staring up at me. It wasn't Odessa.

It was my father.

Which made no sense whatsoever. I checked my face, just to be sure, running a hand over the curve of her cheeks, the fluffy feathers of the small wings, the curls that fell to my shoulders. I still wore Odessa's face.

So if it wasn't my reflection in the pool, then what was it? Could it actually be—

"Da?" An ache burst in my chest, all the barbs of home-sickness I'd tried to lock away bursting out and tearing me raw with memories. Indigo singing me to sleep when I was sick last winter. Gavotte tossing me an apple she'd saved, one of the yellow ones I loved best. Da, wrapping me in a warm bear hug, his beard tickling my forehead.

I leaned closer, reaching out a tentative hand. Was it really him? Was this some sort of magic, showing me my home?

Da reached back, smiling. My fingers brushed the surface of the water between us.

Icy cold swept over my hand. A slippery slickness coiled around my palm, tugging me down. I gasped, trying to pull free. The reflection still smiled, but fiercely now, and with too many teeth. I shrieked, jerking as hard as I could.

I tumbled back into the ferns, panting, damp, and horrified. I scrambled to my feet, keeping well back from any of the nearby ponds. The Bannon's warning came back to me. *Be careful what you look upon, or you may never leave.* "Right," I said. "New rule. No more reaching into pools."

But something had changed. As I walked on, each shimmering pond showed me a new face. My mother. Allegra. My other siblings. A small girl with curly black hair. Phoula. I had to brace myself each time. Their eyes were so accusing, demanding something I couldn't even name.

Finally I came to a pool that stared back at me with Rylain's face. The one I'd worn after I touched Lyrian's cheek. Which still made no sense. Why would Lyrian's stolen face look like Rylain? The Bannon had created Lyrian to replace Rylain. They were completely different people.

Except that they had the same voice. And . . . Lyrian had Rylain's memories. They weren't different; they were opposites. Reflections of each other. Was that what the Withering meant about a schism? But then how could it be mended?

Fable, Moth interrupted my thoughts. He had already moved on and now crouched at the edge of another pool. *This one is different.*

I certainly hoped so. Because as far as I could tell, we'd reached the last pond in the wood. Beyond lay only ferns and birches.

I peered into the pool gingerly. It held a stranger. A girl. Her hair was a dark golden brown. She had creamy skin scattered with freckles and a tip-tilted nose. I couldn't see her eyes, though. She was turned away, as if looking over her shoulder.

No. She was looking at a *mirror*. She held it in one hand, a silver disk in a polished frame. And in that disk was the reflection of a single blue eye, watching me.

My breath caught. Prickles raced over my skin.

"Moth," I said. "Is that *me*?" If only she'd turn around. Show me her full face. If I could see her clearly, surely I'd know. Surely I'd recognize my own true face.

How can that be you? Moth asked. *You are here. You are not in the water.*

"I don't mean it like . . . Never mind." He couldn't understand. And it didn't matter. I *knew*. Knew in my bones that the girl was me. That this was my face, the one I'd lost so long ago. I felt light. My bones were air. My stomach was a cloud. I'd wished for this moment practically my entire life.

She has a mirror, Fable.

I shook myself. Right. The mirror. That was why we were here. So I could bring back Lyrian and stop Rylain and Mirachne from cursing us all to be heartless monsters. And surely this was it. A mirror that could show me my true face must be the one that could restore Lyrian.

I grabbed hold of a bit of root that twisted among the ferns near the edge of the water, then stretched out my other hand toward the water.

You said no more reaching into pools.

"I know. But I need that mirror."

My fingers slipped into coolness. So far so good. I moved slowly, trying to keep the ripples from spreading. The girl in the pool ignored me, still turned away.

Something tangled my fingers. I'd caught a tendril of her hair. It would be so easy to reach for her face. Maybe that was all I needed to do. One touch and her face would be mine. Maybe that would be enough. My own true face. Would it finally feed the hunger of my blight? Stop the ceaseless melting away, the daily shifting?

I knew it was dangerous. A warning thrummed inside me. But the thought was there in my head, and then suddenly I was doing it. Reaching out, not for the mirror, but for the girl's cheek. Round and freckled, so much like Allegra's, but not quite.

The moment my fingers brushed her skin, the girl in the pool spun around and I realized my mistake. Her face was no longer sweet, no longer even human. Her eyes were black and empty, her hair a tangle of slimy tendrils like the roots of water lilies.

The mirror fell from her hand, drifting down into darkness. I started to scream, but it was too late—my mouth had already filled with muddy water. Clawlike fingers stabbed into my upper arms, dragging me down, down, down. Far deeper than such a small pool should allow.

The creature's grip was like iron. I wrenched and twisted, fighting for my life, but I could feel a chill seeping into my arms, my chest. Then, suddenly, something else. A blur of gray, slashing. Green eyes, bright against the gloom, against the white fur that spread over his face in the shape that had given me his name.

Moth!

I tried to call to him, but only swallowed another mouthful of muddy water. Then suddenly I was bobbing up, tumbling free, gasping as I crawled onto the ferny shore. The monster, or whatever it was, had released me.

"Moth!" I croaked. *"Moth!"*

He wasn't there. The forest was utterly silent, except for the gentle slosh of water behind me. No. No, no, no.

By the time I turned around, the water had nearly stilled.

I glimpsed a pair of green eyes set against white fur, trapped within the water's mirror. Heard a whisper so faint my own panicked heartbeat nearly silenced it. *It's you, Fable. Always you.*

Then nothing. No mirror. No golden-haired girl. No brave gray cat. Only a dreary, faded girl with sad, stolen eyes, who looked as if she had lost her best friend.

Chapter Twenty-Four

Somehow, I managed to get myself back to the archway. To shove myself through the portal. I tumbled free, emerging not into the library, but my frilly extravagant bedroom, with its staring walls and canopied bed. I sank onto the mattress, too exhausted to question why. Maybe the Bannon had taken pity on me, sending me here, where no one could see that I'd failed.

I had no mirror.

And no Moth.

I stared at my hands, covered in mud, black under the fingernails. I'd clawed at that last pool, torn up chunks of mud, but there was nothing inside. Whatever magic the water had held was gone, and it had taken Moth with it. My friend. My heart. My Keystone.

In the silence, I heard a loud *tick*.

I tugged the pocket watch from my coat with shaky fingers. Then I opened the case to stare at the black hands. They were moving.

Tick. The second hand leaped again. Again. No longer frozen at eleven, but marching on toward midnight. And it was dark, I realized. It hadn't even been noon when I left, but now it was full night.

So. There was no more time. I'd had my chance, and I'd failed.

Now my wish was going to come true at last. I'd be free of my blight. And so much more. What else would I lose? I summoned images into my mind. Moth leaping after crickets. Moth purring on my chest, his heat melting into me. Moth staring back at me from that dark, dark pool.

The memories were full of pain now. Pain that Mirachne was going to take away. I'd lose even that once midnight fell.

No. There had to be a way to get Moth back. I clenched my dirty hands into fists. The Bannon had sent me to the pools. He was one of the Subtle Powers. Surely he could help. I'd pledge any bargain he asked.

"Bannon!" My voice scraped my throat, full of grief, like burrs tangled in wool. I stood, quivering on legs that still felt like jelly.

"Fable?" The door creaked open. "Are you here? I've been looking everywhere."

It was Vycorax. She stepped into the room.

"If you came here to try to stop me, you needn't have bothered." I slumped face-first onto the bed, staring down at the plush carpet. "I messed everything up."

Sometime later—seconds, years—Vycorax's boots appeared in front of me. I heard her draw in a breath. I wondered, dimly, what she was going to say.

She let out the breath. Took another.

"You'll have your wish," I said bitterly. "Everything you

wanted. No more blighted. I'm sure your father will be very proud."

"This isn't what I wanted, Fable. Not this way. What Mirachne wants to do, it's horrible. And . . ." She trailed off.

"Fable. What is it?" Another breath. Then, "Where's Moth?"

My mouth made a noise, something like a whimper. "He's gone."

The boots shifted. Suddenly her face was in front of mine, brown eyes wide. "Gone? What do you mean gone?"

"I went to find a mirror. A mirror that would show Rylain his true self. I tried to get it, but I—I couldn't. And Moth . . . He . . ." My voice cracked. "He got stuck. He's trapped. Gone. I don't know. I guess it doesn't matter now." I pulled the pocket watch out, flipping it open. "It's almost midnight. For real this time. And then I suppose I won't even know to miss him."

Vycorax was silent for a long moment. "Can I sit?" she asked.

I couldn't think of a reason to stop her, so I shrugged.

She sat beside me, not close enough to touch, but close enough that I could see her brown fingers, laced together in her lap.

"Are you sure?" she said.

"About what?"

"That there's nothing we can do to stop Rylain and Mirachne."

"Why do you care?" I didn't even have the energy to be angry. I was just sad. "The blight will be gone. That's all you care about."

"No," she said. "It's not. I care about you. And about me! Do you think I want to be like Rylain?"

"It would make it easier to vanquish evil," I said. "If you weren't afraid of anything. If you didn't feel pain. You wouldn't even need that box to shove all your feelings in."

"It *shouldn't* be easy," said Vycorax. "I couldn't kill you even when my father wanted me to. Because I didn't want to hurt you. Maybe part of that was because you looked like me. But I think it's more than that. I don't want to not be able to understand pain, Fable. If I do, I'm more of a monster than anything I've ever hunted."

I finally looked up. Vycorax was watching me, fierce and hesitant at the same time.

"Don't let Mirachne hear you say that," I told her.

"Mirachne can go swallow live eels," said Vycorax. "She's wrong. I'm sorry I ever believed that she wanted to help us, Fable. And if there's a way to stop her, I'm in. There must be something we can do."

A faint ember sputtered deep inside me, too frail to be hope. Everything still seemed utterly impossible.

But. We had already done impossible things.

"There's no other mirror. The Bannon said so himself."

There is but one mirror that will break the curse now. You must find it, and not be tricked by any other. The words echoed in my thoughts like scraps of a song you couldn't stop hearing.

Vycorax shook her head. "That doesn't make sense. I mean, you can't get rid of every single reflection. Dinner plates, still water, polished steel. Even another person's eyes, if they get close enough. There must be something else we can use."

I gripped the pocket watch, remembering Odessa's story of how the curse had first been triggered. How she couldn't remember there being a mirror in the watch. She'd just assumed it was there. And so had I. But like Vyx said, there was more than one kind of mirror. *He looked so strange,* Odessa had said. *It was like he saw me for the first time. Really looked at me. And I told him he was a monster.*

The idea bloomed into my thoughts like a witch's magic beans bursting into full-grown vines overnight. And just as dangerous. But it could work. It had to work.

"Me," I said, sitting straighter. I pressed my palms into the coverlet, breathing deep, testing out the word. "*I'm* the mirror. I can steal Rylain's face."

Vycorax's brows arched. "You really think that will be enough?"

I hesitated. "Yes. I think so. I stole Lyrian's face. And it was . . . strange."

"You mean the horns and the fangs and the funny ears?"

"No. That's the thing. I didn't have any of that. According to Odessa, I looked like Rylain. Not Lyrian."

Vycorax drummed her fingers over the hilt of the dagger. "Hmm. Well, he's basically a sort of version of the true prince. Just twisted with the Bannon's magic. Right?"

"Maybe." Lyrian had called himself Rylain's shadow. But what if they were something more? Two faces of the same person? Maybe that was what I needed to make him see.

"It doesn't really matter," said Vycorax. "So long as Lyrian's back at midnight. It's worth a shot. But, Fey, Mirachne won't be happy. Are you sure you want to risk it?" Her worried eyes were fixed on me, making my own fears flutter.

"I have to do this, Vyx. Look." I showed her the pocket watch. It was twenty past eleven now. "We don't have much time left."

I shoved myself up from the bed, marched over to the armoire, and flung it open. Silks and satins flashed under my hands as I riffled through them, searching through the gowns. No time to worry about favorite colors now. I grabbed the first one that I came to, white satin embroidered with silvery butterflies. No, I realized. They weren't butterflies. They were moths.

My throat closed tight, and I gripped the sleeve. My Keystone. He was still with me. I pulled the gown free and retreated behind my changing screen. A quick trip to the bathroom and I was more or less presentable.

"I'm ready," I announced as I stepped out again. Vycorax was waiting, dressed in a dapper silver jacket and black breeches, her shoes decorated with silver buckles.

She hesitated, running her gaze over me. "No, you're not."

I frowned, checking myself for loose ribbons or pond muck.

"Your face," she said. "It's fading."

"It's only been a day," I said, though I did feel more drained than normal since walking in the Subtle Realm. Since losing Moth. "I'll be okay."

She drew in a breath, as if bracing herself. "Borrow mine."

"Vyx. No. You're joking." She must be. It was the last thing in the world she'd ever offer.

"No," she said. "You need every bit of strength you can get." She took a step closer. Close enough that I could have reached out to trace the line of her proud cheek. The sharp jut of her chin. The softer curve of her lips, slightly parted.

"So. Go on, then." She leaned closer.

"Are you sure?"

"Yes. I know what I'm doing."

I lifted my hand. My fingers trembled, hovering a few inches from her cheek. "Thank you."

The corner of her mouth curved. "You're welcome. It's a good face. Take care of it, will you?"

I couldn't speak. But I nodded and met her eyes as steadily as I could while I touched her cheek.

Warmth. A prickling rush. I gasped, pulling back.

Vycorax sagged, but she caught herself against one of the pillars of the bed. "Oof. I forgot what that feels like. No, I'm okay." She breathed deep, then straightened. Grinning, she bowed and extended her arm. "Now, are you ready to go save the realm?"

We entered the ballroom to a fanfare of trumpets. Vines still wove strange and secret patterns over the walls, but the masked guests and servants were no longer silent. They danced. Swayed. Laughed.

The room was *full* of laughter and smiles. It made my skin

crawl, but I forced myself to be part of the crowd, stitching my lips wide and bright as we advanced toward the far end of the room. Rylain awaited, lounging in an ornate gold chair that somehow managed to look more like a gold-taloned hand grasping him. Mirachne stood nearby, a pillar of diamond, her sharp gaze sweeping over us as we approached.

I curtsied before the prince. Odessa and Phoula stood over to one side, but I didn't dare meet their eyes, in case I gave something away. If Mirachne guessed my plan, all would be lost.

"Your Highness. Lady Mirachne," I said. "Thank you so much for all you've done. And all you will do for us."

Rylain beamed. "It is a fine ball, isn't it? And later there will be dancing bears! You must have some of the ginger sweets. They're the best thing I've ever tasted."

So much joy. And like this, it did no harm. But it wasn't all sweets and amusements. I glanced up. The great black hands of the clock were relentless. Only ten minutes to midnight now. The musicians were just finishing a minuet. I glanced at Vycorax. She gave me a small nod. It had been her idea. The best way to get close to Rylain, without anyone suspecting.

"Yes, my prince," I said. "But a ball is for dancing. Please, Highness, would you give me the honor?"

I curtsied again. Under the fringe of my dark bangs, I thought I saw Mirachne frown. But Rylain clapped his hands together in delight. "Oh! Excellent! I am a very fine dancer. Everyone says so."

His smile was so bright and joyful as he stepped toward me that I felt a twinge of guilt. I couldn't forgive him for what he'd done. His thoughtless cruelty toward Odessa. His disregard for any other living creature. But at the same time, it wasn't his fault. He was a monster, but Mirachne had made him. His father had nurtured him.

And now I must unmake him.

Rylain bowed in return, all grace, as if he were formed of song and starlight, rather than flesh and blood. And perhaps he was. He extended his hand. I took it. And we swept together into the spin of the waltz.

I'd only ever danced with my siblings. It wasn't safe for me to go to the village dances, any more than I could risk fairs and markets. But even if I had gone to a thousand village dances, none of them could possibly have prepared me for dancing with a cursed prince in an enormous ballroom tangled with rose vines, under the eyes of a Subtle Power who could probably destroy me in a wink of one glittering eye.

I tried to keep my smile fixed, my eyes bright, as we spun out into the center of the dance floor. I didn't know how long it would take to bring Lyrian back, or how it would even work. The farther I could get from Mirachne the better.

"I remember you," said Rylain, as we swung past the other dancers, who still moved almost as if in a dream, caught by the dying breath of Mirachne's time spell.

"What?" Was he talking about Vycorax, the face I wore?

Rylain watched me, his brows drawn together, as if I were a puzzle. A book set back out of place on the shelf.

"You looked different." He shook his head. "Maybe it was a dream?"

I stared at him, my breath snagging in my throat. For a moment his eyes had seemed darker than just brown. For a moment he'd been staring at me with pitch-black eyes. Eyes that belonged in a different, harsher face.

"Lyrian?"

I didn't mean to say it. It just slipped out.

Rylain stumbled to a halt. The other dancers swirled on around us. But Rylain didn't move. "What did you say?" His voice quavered. Uncertain, or maybe even fearful.

Blight, I should have made my move sooner. "Nothing. I didn't say anything important."

I reached for his hand again, but he recoiled. "That name. That's the demon's name. Wh-why would you call me that?" He looked away, toward the dais. Toward Mirachne.

And high on the wall above, the clock gave a loud *tock*, as the minute hand joined the hour hand, both of them pointing to the number twelve.

Gong.

My blood turned to ice. Then to flame. Midnight! I was out of time. It was now or never. We stood in the center of the ballroom. The masks of the dancers surrounded us. The air was heavy with the scent of roses and a promise like thunder.

Rylain tried to back away, but the other dancers were

whirling faster and faster around us. There was nowhere to run.

Gong.

I threw myself at the prince, reaching for his face. A slide of silky hair brushed under my fingers. Then lace at his throat. And then . . .

A prickle, like thorns bursting under my skin. Pain, exploding at my temples as something curled up, away. And Rylain, trying to jerk free. Shrieking for me to release him.

Gong.

"No!" I shouted, gripping his arms. He cowered, turning his head away. "Look at me! Look at who you are!"

Gong.

Dimly, I was aware of a commotion. Mirachne crying out. Then Vycorax, snarling something about eels.

Gong.

When I'd stolen Lyrian's face, I hadn't sprouted horns and fangs. I'd transformed into Rylain, all golden-brown gleam and loveliness. But now the horns curved heavy from my brow. The sharp teeth pricked my lips, making me taste blood. I had stolen Rylain's face, but it was Lyrian who he saw.

Gong.

Because they were the same. There was only one cursed prince. Rylain. Lyrian. He was *both*. And I had to make him see that, accept that, before the final toll of the bell. I had to mend the schism, or all was lost. I could see the glimmer of Mirachne's bright hair at the far end of the ballroom. She was trying to reach me, but a smaller figure blocked her way, brandishing what looked like a carving knife from the buffet table. Vycorax. Giving me time. I had to make it count.

"You do remember me," I told him fiercely. "Not the face I'm wearing but me. Because you saved my life, Lyrian. Rylain. You sat out in the Rose Garden with me, eating scones and feeding bumblebees. We watched the stars together. We saved a village together. You have to remember it all."

"No." He shook his head. "No!" The words were raw with horror. "I can't. I'm not him. When I'm him, it *hurts*. He—I—we did terrible things."

Gong.

He thrashed, trying to pull free, but I clung to him, digging my fingers tight. I wasn't letting go. I'd lost Moth. I wasn't losing Lyrian. I wasn't losing myself to Mirachne's dangerous bliss.

"Good!" cried someone. Odessa. Phoula was at her side, holding one hand, keeping her grounded. The winged girl floated, her expression fierce. No longer muffled. No longer hidden. "It *should* hurt!"

I remembered what Vycorax had said. "She's right," I told him. "You hurt people. You need to understand that. You can't just forget. It can't just go away."

Gong.

The prince groaned, shoulders bowing. Then he cast back his head, as horns curved from his temples. "I didn't mean to!"

"No, of course you didn't." Mirachne stalked toward us, bright and furious as the sun. The air around her quivered with the force of her glamour, sending every other dancer fleeing from her path. I shuddered as her outraged eyes fell on me. But when she spoke to the prince, her voice was as sweet as ever. "My darling godson, you knew nothing of pain or sorrow. You were perfect! Just as your father wished."

"That was a curse, not a blessing!" I snapped.

Gong.

The prince shuddered. His face was flickering, drifting between demon sharpness and celestial beauty. His fangs sharpened, then retreated. His horns burst, then diminished. And all the while the bell tolled toward midnight.

"Do not listen to these wicked girls, Rylain," Mirachne commanded. "It is nothing but the Bannon's curse. And you are *mine*. My creation alone. The promise of a grand and glorious wish. I will not allow you to be tainted."

"No, Lyrian!" I cried. "Remember. Remember it all. You've done good. You can still be a good prince. But you can't do that if you don't see the suffering around you. If you don't recognize what you've done." I gripped his shoulder, turning him toward Odessa. She flinched as his eyes settled on her.

Gong.

"Dess!" The prince gasped. "Dess, I'm sorry. Can you forgive me?"

Odessa floated closer, her face tense and haunted. "I don't know," she croaked. "But try, Lyrian. Rylain. Try to give me the chance."

Gong.

The prince sighed. It was as if all the air gushed out of him. His head, heavy with the curve of his horns, fell. But not in defeat. It was relief.

Gong.

An enormous shudder rippled through the ballroom as the final bell tolled. Midnight. It was a new day. The first truly new day that this land had seen in a hundred years. And its prince looked up to greet it with eyes that somehow held both hope and sorrow.

CHAPTER TWENTY-FIVE

The music had stumbled to a halt. The dancers stood about us in confusion. Time had returned, with the clock's slow *tock, tock, tock* echoing through the silent room. And yet it still felt like the world was waiting.

"Lyrian?" I held his shoulders, gripping him as if I expected a storm to blow him from my grasp. Did I dare believe it was over?

"That's my name," he said, sounding endlessly weary. "Or, at least, one of them. Maybe now I need another." He met my gaze. "Thank you, Fable."

"Thank her?" demanded Mirachne. The bright lady seemed to have dimmed slightly. Her sweet lips pulled back, baring sharp white teeth as she met my gaze. "After such torments? These wicked girls only want to make you feel sorrow." Mirachne swept a hand at me, Odessa, Phoula, and Vycorax, who had appeared beside me, now armed with two long metal skewers, one still dripping chunks of fruit.

"Wouldn't you rather play a game, my prince?" Mirachne purred. "I can bring out the bear. You could have the girls dance with him. As always, your wish is my command." She lifted her hands, as if to clap for attention.

"No," said Lyrian sharply. "I don't want anything more

from you, Mirachne. I don't belong to you. I won't be bound by my father's wish. Not any longer."

The prince's words resonated, as if the ballroom were a great cavern, casting back echoes. Tingles prickled my skin. It felt like stepping out into the first spring morning after an endless winter.

"It's over," I said. "He's escaped your curse. He's free, and so is this realm. We won." I couldn't quite keep the note of victory out of my voice. Indigo would probably warn me that mortals who crowed too loudly over besting one of the Subtle Powers ended up regretting it. But I was just so relieved that I couldn't help it.

My blight had saved the prince. It had saved *me*. I had wanted to lock it away, to rip it out of me, but I couldn't do that, no more than Lyrian could rip Rylain out of his life. We were what we were. All we could do was learn to live with it. To turn our blights into blessings whenever we could.

And then I noticed something that made me shudder.

A gleam in Mirachne's eyes. It looked far too much like triumph.

"Yes, indeed. You've won. Enjoy your victory. For as much time as you have left."

"What?" I demanded. "What do you mean?"

"Dear girl, do remember who I am," she drawled. "Lady Mirachne. Bestower of wishes. And your wish hasn't yet been granted. What was it again? Oh yes. *I wish I had my true face.*"

Her smile was poisonous. "I would have cleansed you the

easy way, but you made that impossible. So. We have to do it the hard way."

I shook my head. "No. I don't want that anymore. I take it back."

"I'm afraid it doesn't work that way. You wished. It will be granted." She stepped back a pace, gesturing toward the wall below the clock.

"What have you done?" shouted Vycorax, whirling on Mirachne, her skewers at the ready. But the Subtle Power was already rising, floating up until she perched atop one of the great glittering chandeliers.

"Only what I was asked," said Mirachne. "Consider this your . . . reward . . . for thwarting me."

And then I heard it. A low rumble that wasn't thunder, but something crueler and more perilous. I opened my mouth to cry a warning, but my breath had vanished. I knew that sound. I knew the monster that made it.

It seemed to be inside the wall, beneath the white roses and latticed vines. Several panes of glass shattered with painful, discordant wails, almost as if the ballroom itself were crying out for mercy.

The wall below the clock began to shudder. Thin gray streaks sliced through the vines. The roses winked out, torn away in strips of empty gray void, as the Withering clawed its way into the ballroom.

It seemed larger now, filling the entire far end of the ballroom with its sickening half-seen bulk. Ancient eyes fixed on me.

I told you I would come again. The Withering's voice rippled through my mind. *It is time. Time for you to accept the truth, girl.*

It began to pace across the room, straight toward me. It made no move to attack the masked guests cowering in clumps along the walls and hiding behind overturned tables. But neither did it appear prepared to spare them, if they were unlucky enough to be in its path.

Like the old man in the rooster mask who had been crawling over to the glass doors. He gasped, trying to scramble away. Too slow. I opened my mouth to scream as one great gray paw descended straight toward him. But Vycorax was already pelting forward. She scooped an arm under his, heaving him to the side.

The Withering turned its wolfish head to watch them briefly. Then it returned its attention to me.

Come, Daughter. The schism has been mended. There is nothing more for me here. Except you. Do not make this world suffer.

"Run!" I shouted belatedly. "Lyrian! Odessa! Get everyone out of here!"

"But, Fable—" the prince started to protest, but I cut him off. The Withering was halfway across the room. It would be upon us in heartbeats.

"It's here for me. You need to go! You're the prince. Keep your people safe!"

His lips pressed tight. "You saved me," he said. "I should stay."

"No," I told him. "That's not your job. And I think . . . I think I need to save myself."

I heard Lyrian and Odessa and Phoula shouting for the guests to leave. Most had already fled. I saw Vycorax ushering the old man out the glass doors. Our eyes met. I nodded, hoping she understood.

Then I turned to face the Withering.

It loomed over me. Close enough that I could see the gap in its ragged maw, where a single tooth was missing. Chill breath poured over me. My legs trembled, knees knocking together. So that wasn't just a figure of speech. I'd have to tell Indigo.

A tiny sob burst from me. But I couldn't. I wouldn't see them ever again.

It is over now. You must accept it. You know the truth of it. You always have.

"What truth?" I demanded. If it was going to destroy me, I wanted to understand why. This was something more than Mirachne's vengeance. It had hungered for me from the first moment it saw me.

You are nothing, said the Withering. *You have no true face. All you have ever been, all you will ever be, is a reflection. The only way to be free is to accept that. To accept oblivion.*

I wanted to scream that the monster was wrong, but the words stabbed deep, cutting away all the lies I'd told myself. The dreams of walking into my home with my true face. Of going off into the world finally knowing who I was.

I whimpered, lifting a trembling hand to my face. I could

barely feel my skin. The horns and fangs I'd stolen from the prince were gone. I could trace only the barest lines of brow and nose and lip. A fading stubble on my scalp.

It was finally happening. I was fading away forever.

"She does not have to accept that!" A hand slipped into mine, warm and tight and sure. It was Vycorax. She gave me a single stern glance. "Don't listen to the thing. It doesn't know anything about you. You're *not* just a reflection, Fable. You're a *person*. You're my friend."

The words shimmered through me. I thought of Moth. Of Allegra and Indigo and my parents. Of everything that I had, all the sweet, vivid, joyful, painful, frightening truths of my life. *My* life.

My skin buzzed. I gripped Vycorax's hand more tightly. I could feel the tug of the Withering's nothingness tearing away my stolen face. It felt like my lips were melting, soft as wax, but I forced them to open. Flung the words out.

"I'm Fable," I told the Withering. "It doesn't matter what I look like. I'm more than that. I have people I love. People who love me."

The Withering gave a long, low rumble that set my teeth rattling. I stared into its eyes, into oblivion. But it no longer terrified me.

"My life is *real*," I snarled. "And you're not taking it!"

Deep inside me, something seemed to unfold. A new winged thing, ready for its first flight.

A long, low sound came from the Withering. Almost like a sigh.

No, it said, and now the voice was softer. *It seems I am not. Live, daughter of earth. Live and prosper.*

And then the Withering, force beyond the Subtle Powers, destroyer of all things, dipped its shaggy shimmering head and vanished.

I held my breath. The world was still here. I was still here.

"Is it over?" Vycorax asked shakily. "Has it really gone for good?" Then her breath caught. "Fable! Your face!"

"What? Is it horrible?"

"No! It's . . . You look like you did when I first saw you. Like your sister."

"That's not possible," I said, my voice cracking. "That's not how it works. I'd need to touch her."

But my fingers, roaming over my cheek, the slope of my eye, felt the familiar lines. I knew them well enough. A drop of hope bloomed inside me, like a drop of honey melting into tea. Was this it? My true face? After all this, I really was just a copy of my twin sister?

"Is that the face you were born with?" asked Vycorax.

"I—I don't know." My voice trembled.

"Try to change," she prompted. "Try to change to me."

I'd dropped her hand. We were still standing very close— so close I could smell the whiff of lavender that clung to her jacket—but I wasn't touching her. So it shouldn't have worked.

And yet the familiar buzz rippled over my skin. Vycorax laughed, clapping her hands. "There I am! Fable, I think your blight's changed. Or maybe you've just figured out how to control it? Can you do any others?"

My skin buzzed, shifting into Phoula's foxy nose and ears, Indigo's wry smile, Sonnet's strong jaw and curls. I could do all of them. Any of them. I only had to hold the image in my mind, and my face reflected it.

The drop of honey was, after all, just a drop. And yet, somehow, I was glad. I'd made peace with myself. I was Fable. No matter what face I wore.

"Fable?"

The prince's cry jolted me out of my thoughts. I turned to find him jogging back into the ballroom. He halted, staring at me in befuddled dismay.

Which was understandable, considering I was currently wearing my father's face. Including the beard.

"It's me," I said, hastily switching back to Allegra.

The prince paced forward. He looked almost the same as when we first met. A face full of angles, not all of them pleasant. Curving horns and pointed ears. But the bleak black eyes were gone. His brown eyes met mine, warm with relief.

"You're still here," he said. "And . . . the Withering?"

"Gone," I said.

"But you're still blighted." There was an apology in his voice. Regret.

"No," I said. "I'm still *me*. That's what matters."

He gave me a wry look. "Yes. So you taught me. Thank you, Fable. You gave me my life back. You saved my realm. I can never repay you."

"Well," I said, flushing under the intensity of his gaze.

"I had to get you something. It was your birthday, after all."

I saw the smile in his eyes, but it fell away before it could reach his lips, as a familiar voice echoed from above.

"Wicked girl. Foolish boy. You think this is how it ends?"

"Blight, hasn't she given up?" muttered Vycorax, as we all squinted up to see Mirachne, hovering above us, haloed by a crackling nimbus of light so bright it almost hurt to look at.

"I am not finished with you," she snapped. "You mortal creatures, do you really think you'll never wish again? Impossible. You want too much. You feel too much. You cannot stifle your desires, and all it will take is one tiny, insignificant wish and—"

"No," said a new voice, deeper, full of dark wings and sharp beaks. The Bannon lounged against the opposite wall, his long cloak sweeping the marble floor, his crimson eyes fixed on Mirachne. "I think they've had enough of your wishes, my lady."

"Oh, wonderful," said Vycorax. "Another one."

Mirachne glared at him. "I suppose you think they'd be better off with one of your bargains, instead?"

"Perhaps," said the Bannon. He gave the prince a wink. "What do you say, my boy? What would you trade me to get rid of that pesky wall of thorns you've got wrapped all around your realm? Rather inconvenient if you want to reestablish trade."

"Excuse me, my *lord*," said Mirachne, turning the title into something more like a curse. "Those thorns are mine. I set them in place when the other realms begged me to protect them from your *pesky* little blight, if you recall."

"There wouldn't have been a blight if you hadn't—"

"Enough!"

Both the Subtle Powers fell silent, staring at Lyrian.

"You're supposed to be better than mortals," he told them angrily. "But you're worse than children arguing over sweets. We don't need you. You've done enough. So just go. Stop interfering in my realm."

The Bannon's lips twitched. He looked more impressed than offended.

Mirachne stared at the prince, her eyes narrowing. Then she fixed a sweet smile on her lips. When she spoke, her voice was as soft as spring lambs. "Dear boy, I only want to help. I'm your godmother, after all. I can make things so much easier for you, if only you'd let me."

"No. Leave."

"But—"

Lyrian snapped his fingers. A twist of glimmering darkness sprouted up into the air. It spun hungrily toward Mirachne. She gave a shriek, ducking aside as it struck the wall behind her. A rose vine abruptly sprouted out of the marble.

"You crimson-eyed fool!" Mirachne snarled at the Bannon. "I cannot believe you actually cursed the boy with such power. And you're just going to *leave* him that way?"

"I made a bargain," said the Bannon. "And besides, the lad seems to have learned to control it."

Mirachne's lip curled. "Very well. I've had more than

enough of this pitiful realm. If you wish to let it fall into blight and ruin, so be it. I am the Lady of Wishes, and my domain is far greater. But I will not forget. The next time you wish, I will be waiting." She looked straight at me as she spoke her final words, holding me with her diamond-bright gaze even as the rest of her dissolved into tiny fragments of light that fled into the night.

I didn't breathe until the last spark was gone.

The Bannon gave the three of us mortals a crooked grin. "Well, then. I think we're done here."

"Wait," said Lyrian. "Tell me. Who made the bargain? The one that set me free?"

The Bannon hesitated, his sly smile almost slipping away. "Your mother. She saw how Mirachne's 'gift' was nothing of the sort. And she called on me to rid you of it."

"And what was her part of the bargain?" asked Lyrian, his brows pulling together sharply. "What did she give you in return? Is—is that why she died?"

"She will not walk this realm again," said the Bannon, almost gently. "But I think she would have been satisfied with the result."

Lyrian's shoulders sagged, but his jaw was firm. He nodded. "I hope so."

"Now," said the Bannon, dusting his hands together, "I really must be going."

"No. Wait," I said, drawing my courage around myself like a cloak. "I want to make one more bargain."

CHAPTER TWENTY-SIX

I *don't like it,"* said Vycorax two days later. We were sitting on the palace grounds, watching as an army of gardeners attempted to subdue one of the blighted topiaries. Every time one of them managed to chop off a bulge, a new one bumped out, like the monster in one of Indigo's stories that grew two new heads every time the hero chopped off one. Abandoning this particular hydra, the gardeners moved on to the yew hedges across the way, which appeared more or less mundane, except that they made rude noises whenever one of their branches was cut.

"You don't have to like it," I said, digging my toes into the grass. "It was my bargain."

She made an expansive gesture with her hands. "You agreed to do an unspecified favor for the Bannon, Fable. The Bannon! The same Bannon who almost got you stuck forever in the middle of that swamp!"

I waved away her concern. "He was just trying to keep us from banishing Lyrian. He wouldn't have left me there forever. I think. Anyway, it's worth it, if he can keep his end of the bargain."

Vycorax stalked back and forth along a nearby bed of creamy lilies, brushing one hand lightly over their heads. She still looked unhappy.

"What are you going to do?" I asked, to change the subject.

"Well, I'm definitely not going back to Fort Blightbane," she said. "If Father thought I was a failure before, he'll certainly see me as one now."

It sounded as if she was trying to make a joke of it, but I could hear the trace of bitterness in her voice.

"You're not a failure," I said sharply.

She arched a brow at me. "Actually, I think a hunter who has the chance to cleanse all the blighted and decides not to is the *literal* definition of failure. But I don't care, Fable. I don't want to be a hunter anymore. I'm not sure I ever did. I just wanted . . ." She swallowed. "Something I can't have. But you know about that too."

I nodded. In the last two days I'd shifted through a hundred different faces. Some were familiar. Most were strange. I'd had noses bulbous as ripe tomatoes and others flat as buttons. Hair of every color I could imagine. Eyebrows thin as threads, or arched into peaks, or fluffy as down. So many faces, and I had no idea if any of them was the one I'd been born with. I would probably never know. But at least now I didn't need to steal them. When one began to fade, I could simply choose another. It wasn't what I'd dreamed of. It wasn't what I'd wished for. But it was enough.

Vycorax drew in a long breath. "I was thinking I could try to sail to the Golden Empire," she said. "My mother had family there. I might be able to find them."

"Oh."

I thought of the vast sea that stood between Thessequa and the far-off empire in the west. If Vycorax went so far, surely she'd be gone for years and years. Maybe forever. It didn't seem right. Vycorax was the one who had stood by me in the face of oblivion. Who had believed that I was real. That I mattered. I couldn't bear to think of never seeing her again.

"But I think maybe I should wait until I'm older," she said. "Maybe then . . . you could come with me? You said you wanted to study the stars, and they have an entire university for that over there."

"Oh." I flushed, feeling a rush like I'd just been spinning in circles. "That would be nice."

"Lyrian said I could stay here for now, though, in the Mirrorwood. There's plenty to do, what with all the blighted creatures and places and people to wrangle. Not to mention all those withered patches we need to keep people from falling into."

"Lyrian thinks he might have a way to fix them," I said. "Or, not fix exactly. He can't bring back what was originally there. But he tried using his twists to fill in the wither in the ballroom and it mostly worked."

Vycorax arched a brow. "Mostly?"

"Well, the withered patches are all gone. Now they're full of honeycomb and a hive of giant bees."

"You see? This is exactly the sort of realm that could use an ex-blighthunter." She was grinning, but there was something more tentative behind it. "Will you come back and visit?"

289

"Of course!" I said. "It's Odessa's birthday in a few months, and I promised Phoula I'd bring her my father's recipe for spicecake. And I want to introduce my sibling Indigo to Dendonderus. They'll either be instant best friends or deadly enemies. And see Elf and Trudi's new inn. But, Vyx, you have to come visit me, too."

Vycorax was quiet, smoothing the hem of her coat. "Are you sure?"

"Of course! My parents will love you. Everyone will. Now that you're not"—I coughed—"trying to kill me."

Vycorax grinned. "It's a deal."

"My father makes the best cheese pie," I told her, my mind unfolding with bright possibilities. "And Indigo will do all their best dramatic recitations, and Sonnet will want you to spar with her, and Thespian will act all dignified and solemn, but don't worry, that's just how he is with anyone who's not family. After a few days he'll probably wake you up at dawn to come see a new lamb."

The dreams thrummed through me, like a song playing in another room that I could almost hear. I wanted desperately to go home. I needed to be there, with the people who had known me forever. To fit the edges of myself back against the old familiar outlines of my life, to see how I had changed. The ache of homesickness was a constant sharp thorn, stabbing at me.

"You miss them," said Vycorax softly. "Why don't you just—"

"No," I said. "I'm not leaving. Not yet."

Because as much as I wanted to walk through that door, to see my siblings and my parents, to feel their love crashing over me, around me, I knew I wouldn't be able to bear it if I returned alone.

Vycorax must have understood, because she didn't say anything more. She only brushed a leaf from her new jacket—a lovely green-blue that reminded me of deep water—and cleared her throat. "Okay. Well. I promised Odessa I'd take charge of Dendonderus for the afternoon. He's almost finished the last verse of his new masterpiece, *The Champion of the Mirrorwood.* Of course, he's the champion." She rolled her eyes, then set off toward the castle.

When she was gone, I let myself sag down, feeling the clanging of the hollow space inside me that only a small gray cat could ever fill. I closed my eyes, trying to remember the soft weight of him. The tickle of whiskers on my cheek. A purr like honey spilling through my chest.

Breath that smelled like something dead and faintly rancid.

Wait.

I opened my eyes. Green slitted eyes stared back at me, utterly unconcerned, utterly calm.

"Moth!" I shrieked, and cuddled him into my arms, not caring one bit that he smelled like rotten fish. He was here. He was real. He was *alive.* The Bannon had done it. He'd kept our bargain.

I was not gone so very long, he said, sounding perplexed. *And I always come back, Fable. It would have been much faster, but the water magic was tricky and the crow man is not so clever as he thinks. But he was clever enough.*

I sent up a silent thanks to the Bannon. He had done his part. My favor still hung over me, but I meant what I'd said to Vyx. I didn't care. I didn't need my true face. I knew who I was. I knew who I loved. That was my life. That was my truth.

"Come on," I told Moth. "Let's go home."

Acknowledgments

This was a challenging book to write for so many reasons, not least of which was the fact that I did the majority of the drafting and revising in the midst of a pandemic. As such, I send endless thanks to the nurses, doctors, scientists, teachers, postal workers, store clerks, and all those who were so essential to keeping our society functioning during that time.

I am grateful, as always, for my fierce agent, Hannah Fergesen, and my brilliant editor, Julia McCarthy, for guiding this book into the world. Many thanks as well to the entire team at Atheneum/Simon & Schuster, in particular Jeannie Ng; Tatyana Rosalia; Shivani Annirood; Karyn Lee, for the beautiful design work; and Sylvia Bi, for the gorgeous jacket art!

I owe so much to the helpful feedback and encouragement of my writer friends, especially R. J. Anderson, Geoff Bottone, Stephanie Burgis, Megan Crewe, Chris Herrmann, Anne Nesbet, and Jenn Reese. Big thanks as well to the communities at the Sandwich Club and the Mighty Pens who cheered me on.

Melissa Caruso was there during one of the hardest parts of the revision process, to help me see my way through with her keen insight into structure, as she has helped me so often in the past.

My parents, Paul and Cynthia, and my brother, David, were my heroes during a particularly difficult time, when I was dealing with a major health concern while also attempting to finish this book. I literally could not have written this without them.

The Mirrorwood is, in many ways, a love letter to the fantasy movies that shaped my imagination when I was a kid in the eighties. So thank you as well to *Labyrinth*, *Legend*, *The NeverEnding Story*, *The Last Unicorn*, and *The Princess Bride*. If my book can bring even a fraction of their magic and wonder to readers, I will be happy.

Last and always, my love and thanks to Bob, who makes me believe in fairy tales.